Happy Birthday
& Merry Christmas,
Grandma Datz,
Love,
The Kampens

love
Song

By the same author:

NOTHING BUT THE BEST: *The Luck of the Jewish Princess*

LESLIE TONNER

St. Martin's Press, New York

Library of Congress Cataloging in Publication Data

Tonner, Leslie.
  Love song.

  I. Title.
PZ4.T6717Lo [PS3570.053]   813'.5'4   78-19397
ISBN 0-312-49948-5

For my mother and father

love
Song

CHAPTER

1

♈

Before I learned to love her, I never knew
how silent my life had been.

Odd, admittedly, since I am in the music business. But I refer to a different kind of silence, a more
profound silence—the quiet that comes from an absence of feeling. Once I came to know Jesse, and the
emptiness was filled, her music never left me.

As I listen to her recording of the Mahler *Kindertotenlieder,* I find I am as moved by her artistry as I am
by her wholeness and her indomitability. When the
record ends, I still hear the sound of her voice. I am
loath to let it go. After all this time, I cannot always
see her face, but I hear her voice night and day.

Life would have remained empty for me had I
not been led first to the young genius of Martin Boyd,
and then later, through Martin, to my beautiful Jesse.
Isn't it strange that Martin, a rather more awful ver-

sion of my youthful, pompous self, should have been the instrument through which I would find my only love?

She is the star of my story; I am what was once called the second male lead, the one who never got the girl. I didn't really get her this time either, but I am content with knowing that she was as much mine as anyone else's. The beauty of it is that she became more herself, even though I was of little or no help to her; she found her soul and her artistry at a time when anyone else might have simply let go.

And now I am quite a different man—at least I like to think I am. The great Nicholas Kogan, the impresario, the name in small type above the artist's. The Kogan of old was an acerbic wit. I wrote my lines well, for they served as good protection. I used to say that those who can, play; those who cannot, organize concert tours. It caused some mirth and, generally, weeded out those of a soppier, more sentimental nature. Often, gushed over by some elderly fan who mistook me for the concert artist, I was asked, "Do you always play such gorgeous Beethoven?" "Never Beethoven," I would reply with a low bow. "Madame, I play the ego."

And so there I was, and would have remained forever, playing my own ego as well as those of my artists—until Jesse Sondergard changed my life. She used to say that I was on the verge of my renaissance, my golden age. But what could I reply when I knew she had entered her darkest time?

Jesse haunts me and I realize she always will. Her music, her voice, her bravery, and how I felt when I was near her; in many ways, that was the most important part of all. The music I keep hearing is a love song, *liebeslied* if you wish—haunting and lovely and quite addictive. I cannot get it out of my head.

ONE

CHAPTER

2

Forty years ago, I was seated at a proper, private dinner amid a boatload of spry old Puritans from New England, watching the host who was watching the valets pour out stingy measures of a very expensive wine.

The host was one of the brilliant Boyds of Boston—benefactors of musicians, concert halls, podiums and parterre boxes. The guests crunched on their squab and commented on the betrayal of the country by the Jew-loving Roosevelt, hoping that Mr. Boyd would notice which side they were on and endow another auditorium. But he was too busy eyeing the wine pourers. With his political views in mind, it would not have surprised me had we been served a Riesling, in honor of our host's well-known admiration for der Führer.

I was present at table due to my association with

the Austrian, Wurtzberg, the premier impresario of our time—inspired, sly and a trifle mad. I had been given the rare privilege of answering his telephones and rejecting hopeful résumés due to Wurtzberg's friendship with my mother. She believed that if I dirtied my hands in the business world I would soon grow tired and return to a life of gentlemanly sloth. In fact, that very evening I was toying with my pudding and with the notion of resuming my career as a Latin scholar at Yale. My meeting with Martin Boyd changed my mind and deterred me from my mother's goal of high-class unemployment.

After the pudding and the ladies had vanished from the ducal dining room, and as the brandy was measured out in careful doses, I heard the sound of a piano.

Mr. Boyd (descended from William Bradford on his maternal side) creased his forehead and gestured at a butler. Soon the playing grew louder—Brahms—and I wondered if a smaller wayward Boyd tucked away upstairs was disobeying a parental invective against listening to records during dinner parties. I excused myself and went to investigate. All-male conclaves are my worst proving grounds; that is why I left Yale.

I pursued the sound of the piano to the top of the stairs and down a lengthy hall filled with family portraits. At a heavy door left conspicuously ajar, I heard the music more clearly. I peered inside. The room was hung with heavy tapestries and opened into a curved bow of windows at the far end. Nestled into the curve was a grand piano—a piano which seemed to have no relation whatsoever to the musical instrument at which men sit and depress keys. It was richly carved and inlaid, decorated in a baroque style out of keeping with the medieval decor of the rest of the room.

The only light in the room was the single bulb in a small enamelled lamp close by the piano. It illuminated the figure of a small child seated at the keyboard, his music lying flat as if he had been afraid to raise the elaborate music stand. His short legs jutted from the bench, one stretched toward the pedal, barely able to depress it.

The playing was quite decent—in fact, as I listened, it seemed indecent. He played with more sensibility than most of my employer's young Juilliard graduates, and far better than any small child should. His playing made me feel resentful and rather anxious, as if my presence might disturb him. But he never looked up to consult his music or, for that matter, to acknowledge me. He played in the lovingly complete, compulsive fashion of all true musicians. Nothing in the world exists for them but the notes, phrases, and passages, and they play until the piece is finished as others would complete a gesture or a sentence. The Brahms Intermezzo was woven to an end; the boy finished because he had to. Then he placed his hands in his lap.

He was an arrogant, horrid little child and because I disliked his father I was glad. I was certain the child was his father's purgatory.

"The bathroom is the other way," the boy said. He never looked at me; he simply paged through his music, glancing up and down the lines, searching for some suitable reflection of mood.

"How long have you been playing?" I asked, a bit in awe of such a small being whose self-possession rivalled that of my aging, brittle-boned mother.

"Fifteen minutes," he said. "Five before my father sent word that I should stop. Five more before you turned up. Go away."

"All right," I said, wondering how old this precocious midget was and why his father wanted him to stop playing and how he had learned to play so truthfully at his age. Well-tutored children often play the way well-tuned automobiles run. Everything is smooth and in gear, well lubricated—but after all, it is only a machine. Genius children instinctively feel the music, and it is that sensibility to which we adults respond. We who listen realize that we will never reach the point of understanding grasped automatically by a mere child. And we are in awe.

"Will you play something else?" I said to the boy.

He screwed up his nose in the first childish expression I had seen cross his haughty little face, and he settled his pudgy body back on the piano bench. "My father," he said, all flat *a's* and Boston Brahmin hauteur, "does not wish to hear me play. He'll be angry. I'm supposed to stop."

"Do you have a teacher?" I asked.

"Of course," he replied, looking at me for the first time. He had blue eyes and a square, pink-tinged face surmounted by a fringe of straw-colored hair. A cowlick stood up in the back—a strange, Huckleberry All-American touch. He could have been Andy Hardy, but Andy Hardy at the Steinway? Andy Hardy plays Brahms?

"I'll say a word to your father. I am," I hesitated, "a manager. I'm interested professionally in good musicians."

"I see," he nodded. "My father forbids it. Mrs. Davis has already asked."

Leora Davis was the wife of a respected music critic who had passed away, leaving, as his legacy, a collection of intelligent writing on musicians and quite a bit of money for music scholarships for the very gifted. It was the first I'd ever heard of anyone so young being offered a Davis. Feeling satisfied that my ear was as discerning as Mrs. Davis's ("Of course you know music, Nicholas," mother had said. "It's about all I can safely say you do know. I've seen to it.") and inwardly thanking my mother for knowing Max Wurtzberg, I persuaded the child to play another piece.

He thoughtfully paged through his book and found a waltz. "My name is Martin Boyd," he said, and then he proceeded to play. His little fingers drew the most aged, mellow tones from the depths of that overcarved piano.

It was then that I decided I would set up a management office of my own and that Martin Boyd would be my first client. A young genius would be just the right beginning for the Kogan enterprise.

"How old are you?" I asked when the last notes had been released into the evening air. I had judged him to be close to ten, perhaps a short and stubby eleven.

"Seven," he replied. "But I shall be eight in March."

Seven years old. Though taken aback, I did not reveal my feelings to Martin. He might have laughed in my face. Strange how he always had this capacity to make people feel as if they were not measuring up to some ancient, legitimate standard of which he was the sole bearer.

"I see," I said. But all I saw was, inevitably, trouble. The boy was so young, and I had a feeling that the elder Boyd would most certainly not be interested in my fledgling offer.

I was right. That night, our first meeting, was also the last time I would see Martin Boyd for fifteen years. I remain one of the few, along with Leora

Davis, who knew that Martin was a musical genius. It was a select circle: Leora, myself, and, of course, Martin.

CHAPTER

3

ᛣᚠ

According to my mother, I ought never to have been drafted. "You've a disability," she said. "You're much too intelligent for the army."

If I was so smart, I have no idea why my early attempts at artistic management failed so miserably. At the siren song of World War II, a legion of undraftable Carusos and Paderewskis came crawling out of the woodwork, and as I sifted through their résumés, I prayed that my own *1-A* status might remain undetected. Of course I was drafted and was forced to leave the agency in the hands of an asthmatic friend who spent his afternoons drinking Manhattans at the Yale Club. I trudged off to war and after the horror of basic training (I had wisely refused to be an officer's candidate, believing that stars and bars made excellent cannon fodder), was assigned to the office of a colonel as typist and general *factotum*. For

11

three years I batted out his love letters on my old Remington and kept track of the radio soap operas. The colonel's lady-love sang detergent commercials on the air, and I was expected to keep my charge abreast of her schedule as tightly as a bomb crew adheres to its flight plan. "Fourteen hundred hours, Sir!" I barked smartly, waking my boss up from his afternoon snooze to turn his attention toward the opening chords of the bright-and-clean ditty she burbled so shamelessly. So passed the war.

Upon returning to civilian life, I discovered that my poor little agency had vanished along with my besotted friend, so I spent the next months living with mother and reestablishing contacts—a euphemism for drinking, going to parties, and sleeping until thirteen hundred hours, er, one p.m. I would awaken crossly to sip my coffee and angrily scan the theater pages, only to see that my former employer, unlike his homeland, had profited mightily from the war and was the most powerful force in the music world.

Only Leora Davis was able to save me from this rut, and she was merely the instrument of my good fortune. She sent Martin Boyd back to me. It took fifteen years and Boston's grandest funeral to bring Martin Boyd to the concert stage. But first, he had to put in an appearance at my shabby professional digs.

He entered my office wildly, like a madman, and stood panting, staring at the empty walls and the metal desk as if he'd never seen anything so frightful. "*Ghast*-ly," he said, rolling his eyes, and I knew instantly who he was and also that I wasn't sorry he was there, though he irritated me at once. His pudgy face was still young, childlike, and would remain so for many years. He wore a black coat that flapped open untidily and a dirty white silk muffler which was fraying at the edges. He appeared to have slept in his clothes. The blond hair had darkened slightly, and a forelock fell over his eyes. Later on, that messy piece of hair would become famous. *Time* magazine would write of its effect on women: "It is Elvis's hips and Sinatra's Adam's apple and James Dean's swagger, falling loose and lank, obscuring his boy's blue eyes." At that moment it looked sloppy, and I wanted to rise and order Martin Boyd off to the barber. But I did not. No one could ever tell Martin what to do because that curious control he possessed as a small child was still with him. It was not merely the Boyd of Boston in his blood; it was the assertiveness and confidence of talent. He knew he was good. In fact, he knew he was great, and although he liked to hear it from you, he didn't need to. Not needing is a great attribute. It is the secret power behind the power. We think we can buy a measure of control with talented people by being sycophants but, in truth, they control us. We need to fawn, but they are complete. So it was with Martin Boyd.

"Kogan," he intoned, "I wouldn't be here but for Mrs. Davis." Ever the schoolboy at dancing class, this polite Boyd. "She has made me promise on the absolute pain of death that I'd see you before I went over to the mad Austrian. She hints that you'll give me the requisite attention. Would that be because there is no one else?" His eyes swept my empty walls.

I allowed his lack of an introduction to pass. He knew I remembered him. I shouldn't have permitted it; the tone was set for all our future dealings. But I was still innocent then. "When someone deserves to have his photo in his manager's office, then perhaps you might wonder who manages whom," I managed to reply. I liked the irritation bubbling up inside. I enjoyed the abrasiveness of the contact. I knew instantly that I would take him on.

He marched around the office as if pacing off his territory. The miserable coat flapped around his heels. "What will you offer me," he said, spinning around to face me, "aside from the standard contract?"

"How about no contract?" I said, just to be different.

His mouth dropped open. "You mean you'd take me on a handshake? That's unheard of, I never dreamed, I never thought—well, if you'd do *that*." He stepped back and assessed me briefly, his blue eyes growing misty and limpid. Morning on the moors—or was it dusk?—when the werewolves come out to play. "Trust you to be perverse. I remember you had the audacity to confront my father with a deal at a dinner party."

"It was what you wanted," I reminded him.

"Yes," he said instantly. "You're quite right there. The old bastard never relented. Not until he dropped dead in his wine cellar. I was allowed lessons, but no more. I could have been a sensation. And now he's dead," he said with some satisfaction. "Died three months ago."

"Did he?" I said, knowing exactly who attended the funeral. The world of music benefactors is fairly select and it is my business to know of all entrances and exits. God knows, musicians are subsidized to within an inch of their lives.

"Do you think Mozart's father would have made him go to Harvard? And join the Hasty Pudding Club?" Martin smiled, all innocence, and twiddled the ends of his scarf. At certain moments, he had the fleeting glow of a Raphael angel. Old Boyd was truly a son of a bitch if he'd been able to resist a child such as this. But old Boyd probably thought musicians were fags or, even worse, immigrants. War in Europe had washed quite a lot of phenomenal talent up on our shores; but it was accented talent—shuffling, Ellis Island poor-soul talent, and certainly not purebred Hasty Pudding material.

"So you want to be Mozart, is that it?" I leaned back in my chair and tried to look prosperous. The chair emitted an awful series of squeaks.

"I've gotten off to a rather shaky start to be the next Mozart," he said. "No great progress in diapers as it was. But I've studied composing and conducting and, though I'm not much at writing music yet, I'm insane about working with an orchestra." He stopped twitching his scarf and rocking on his heels and stood still for a moment. "At first, it was always just the piano. But conducting an orchestra goes so much deeper into the music—you just can't compare it with anything else. . . " His voice drifted off as he stood immobile, transfixed by the image of an orchestra before him, his soft body swaying before it, coaxing forth amazing sounds. "I want it all," he said on his return to earth. "I was prepared to go straight to Wurtzberg, but Mrs. Davis said it's bad for the music world if there's only one game in town. So you and I will form the opposition. I shall be your star."

I hid my own excitement. If, as Leora Davis had said, he was as good at twenty-two as he had been at seven, we were in business. "And what do you see me getting out of this deal?"

"Oh, you'll be famous, too. You shall pick and choose your clients. All I want is your complete loyalty and your attention. I'm fed up with being ignored. My late father was an expert in that field.

Once, when I'd finished playing a Rachmaninoff prelude, he said, 'What a noisy piece of music.' I waited all my childhood for him to die. I scarcely need another father in his place."

But he did need another father, and I was willing to try and fill the role; properly this time, of course. "All right," I gestured toward the only other chair in the room, motioning for him to sit. "We'll take you on. And I will try and find you some sort of booking."

He blushed suddenly, a canned-salmon pink—the sign which I later learned meant heightened ambition rather than embarrassment. "Use Mrs. Davis," he said.

As I had already used her, in a sense, I was delicate enough to shake my head.

"Use her," Martin insisted. "She said to call her. She wouldn't do anything for me until I was represented. That's why I came rushing over here, practically right off the train. Call," he directed, taking the receiver off the hook and holding it toward me. Scrupulous fool that I was, I hesitated. I wanted something of my own achievement out of this, not a client and concert debut presented to me as a gift-wrapped package. Martin jiggled his foot impatiently as I debated the propriety of such an imposition. Eventually I relented and made the call, and so it was from the start that Martin played the tune and I shuffled my feet. I was not able to recover my footing with him for many years. Even then, it took heaven and earth, and Jesse Sondergard and Gabrielle Klee, before I could stand up to him.

Leora Davis arranged a suitable debut at Town Hall, employing her vast network of connections. I contributed the services of my tailor, to whom Martin was sent to be fitted for a proper evening suit. I forgot to tell him to see a barber, but that omission, at least, proved fruitful. The boy wonder dashed off to buy a new pair of shoes, and I sat at my desk wondering if I'd sold my soul to the devil. If indeed I had, at least I could now say I was living. My secondhand life in the shadows had been a debilitating experience. Real life would never prove so exhausting, would it?

CHAPTER

4

Ϙ

Martin refused to call the facility assigned to him backstage his dressing room.

"It's a veritable toilet," he said, brushing the lock of hair from his eyes. I could detect no nervousness in his nonchalant behavior. "This doesn't matter at all, not really. What I'd like is to get my hands on an orchestra. Not necessarily a great orchestra, but a decent orchestra. I'd whip them into shape, turn them around, make them great. Will someone out there hand me my opportunity?"

"Not if you can't wear evening clothes," I said, unbuttoning his jacket and shifting the seams at the shoulders. The material strained as it pulled across his chest. "Have you put on weight since your fitting?"

His eyes shifted slightly. "Uh, there've been a lot of dinners—old friends of my father and all."

"No more *coeur à la crème*," I dictated. "Bad for

your image." Wrong again. Martin's portly cadet girth was as much loved as his lock of hair. The public likes its idols slightly flawed. The humanizing fact of fat drove away some of the shyness experienced by mere folk when they confront great art. To the audience, Martin was a real person; he was huggable.

When he walked onto the stage, the private Martin became public—his mannerisms were carved into public memory. His hair-tossing, his shambling gait, his intensity at the keyboard—all of it captured the imagination. Martin was young and overconfident at the right time. He had arrived.

His program consisted of several small works sprinkled among the larger "prove-yourself" pieces of the pianist's repertoire: Beethoven's "Les Adieux," a Schubert impromptu, several Chopin mazurkas, and the Liszt B Minor. Of all the pieces he tackled—and he played them all exquisitely—the Schubert, I believe, came closest to his true feelings about music. The others were necessary displays, bows to convention by which fledgling artists are judged. But inside the Schubert was a secret door through which Martin Boyd could be glimpsed, a look behind the flushed arrogance into some calmer recess of the soul. Here, perhaps, was the source of that unusual sensitivity which heightened his music.

Audiences then were less volatile than they are today. Still, Martin rated solid applause. By concert's end, his clothes were a mess. He always looked as if he'd slept in them; even the best tailoring fell prey to his restlessness at keyboard or podium. His baby face was stricly composed, however—blank and innocent. *Am I not lovable?* his demeanor begged.

"Hot, cool, hot," he murmured as he wiped his face on a towel and prepared to play an encore. His jacket was soaked through, but he refused to change it, beginning a superstition that persisted throughout his career. He might change his shirt but never the jacket. As he stumbled back toward the stage, he said, "I need this," and lurched out once again. Martin crossed the stage with a drunken, rolling, sailor's gait, as if he were on a ship at sea. His bearing added to the excitement of a Boyd performance, for one often wondered if he would fall off the piano bench before a piece was finished.

"Solid!" he yelled as he crashed through my office door the next morning. "Solid, like a brick wall. Sturdy, well built. They've dug my grave for me." He dumped a sheaf of newspapers atop my desk, which was already piled high with the same editions. He was dressed in the black coat again, along with the dirty scarf. "Like a concrete sidewalk, for God's sake. Whoever told that man he knew anything about music?"

"What did you expect?" I said mildly, picking up his pile of papers and dumping them into my wastebasket. He gave me an open-mouthed stare and then fell to his knees, pawing through the trash to retrieve his clippings.

"You of all people ought to know," he replied huffily. "My manager."

"Oh, come now, I've seen many debuts and yours went very nicely. Not brilliant, not dazzling—they didn't write that either—but whom did you dazzle? And what happened to that stepping-stone to an orchestra? I *had* thought you were biding your time."

He flung himself into a chair and brooded like an insulted peacock, all long-necked indignity. "That son of a bitch—if I'd debuted at twelve, even thirteen, I could have had it all."

"You might have burned your little self out."

"Burned out? Locked in that dismal stone palace, no one listening. Boyds are *expected* to be great. But how would he know? He ignored me. His own son. Not proper to have a musician in the family. Hand out money to them, yes, but wandering minstrels? Pimps and whores? We don't want to be related to one of those, thank you."

"Your father isn't writing your reviews," I remarked, wondering if I were not turning into George Sanders, much to my disgust, playing the bitch to Martin's tortured soul. Ah well, Martin had to contend with an attic full of chain-rattling ghosts. He couldn't erase his father's memory with this triumph because, as he perceived it, there was no triumph.

"My father should rot in hell, a place where his carefully maintained cellar full of wine turns to piss."

"On the strength of this debut," I ignored him, "I can arrange a small concert tour this fall. Denver, San Francisco, several midwestern halls, some of the universities."

"Denver?" He pronounced it as if it were a four-letter word. "*Den*-ver? You are joking. I should go abroad."

"They will have you abroad, you think? On the contrary, you'll have to prove yourself here first."

"I won't go."

"You will, or there is no deal. You cannot skip what you think of as the provinces. You shall learn here, be seasoned here."

"Like a duck for roasting," he mumbled.

"Like a professional. Do you want your orchestra, as you so often remind me? Then you must build a reputation for reliability. No one likes to gamble on a prima donna."

"Stokowski?" he countered.

"Wait and see. Spotlights on his head and hands, but see what orchestra he runs and how long he lasts. You aren't the first firebrand to come down the pike. Just keep working."

I thought I glimpsed some mild anguish in those blue eyes, but I was mistaken. It was only hunger. "I'm going to eat," he announced. "I'm starving. Arrange whatever you think is best. I'm tired of discussing it."

"No more starches," I warned as he shuffled off, but he wasn't listening. So I picked up my coat and followed him down to his late breakfast. At least I could slap his hand when he ordered pancakes. We could not yet afford to buy him a new evening suit every time he decided to stuff himself. After some argument, he settled for two fried eggs and a side order of bacon.

As I watched him eat, I knew what a publicist's delight he would be—the young, eager, careless genius—the rich boy with a taste for hashed brown potatoes (which I hadn't let him order). "Ketchup," he choked. I passed him the bottle and watched him drown his eggs in a red sea. The sooner he went on tour the faster he would emerge in interviews as an eccentric, but charming, subject. "Eat up," I said, patting his shoulder and shoving away the bread basket. He'd get his orchestra, I was sure. And I? I would become my own man. To hell with George Sanders waiting in the wings.

CHAPTER

5

♈

Martin travelled the concert circuit alone. Alone, that is, until I had to fly out and slap his hand again. This time, however, it was not ordering pancakes that caused the fuss.

Martin was playing the spoiled brat. He rejected assigned hotel rooms, sent back his meals, failed to turn up for dinners in his honor and, at one airport, handed a bouquet of flowers back to its silver-haired presenter with the immortal words, "I'm allergic." At one stop, he halted his performance between movements of a Mozart sonata for five minutes, waiting for a woman to stop jangling her charm bracelet. And as he waited, and the audience waited, his reputation as a difficult performer grew and was embellished with half-truths and outright lies. I think he was enjoying himself. All of the impossible traits he loathed in his father he cultivated in himself. An *artiste?* Ha. He was a Boyd, through and through.

The minute I arrived at his hotel room in Chicago, I told him so. "You are exactly like your father. You've picked a fine time to flaunt your exquisite breeding."

He ignored me and sipped his mineral water. The hotel manager had been obliged to order Martin's special brand, the only one he claimed did him any good. The delicate Boyd digestive tract not at work, no doubt.

"You shall have a very short career if you keep this up," I told him. "I wouldn't want such a little prig performing in my theater."

He slurped his water and shrugged. I would have loved to punch him in the nose, but as he was my meal ticket, I turned around and stared out the window at Lake Michigan. Large bodies of dark water give me claustrophobia, as if I were on the bottom of a mine shaft, and I shivered at the sight. But I preferred it to the sight of Martin's ill-tempered face. "I only hope," I said to the window glass, "that you'll get yours someday."

"That's not highly likely," I heard him say. I turned and watched him gulp down his water and then yank off his bathrobe, revealing none too clean underwear beneath. "I shall try and take your advice to heart," he said as he walked to his pigskin suitcase and extracted a shirt from the bottom of a rumpled pile. "I feel that I can change my attitude a tiny bit, if necessary. After all, you did fly all the way out here to scold me."

"Wurtzberg would never have put up with you," I said.

"But he doesn't have to," Martin smiled as he buttoned his shirt. "You do."

I didn't bother to stay for his performance. I felt I'd already seen enough.

Martin calmed down enough to complete the tour, and I was able to get him a slot at Tanglewood, which appeased him, as well as a festival in Bath, England (his postcard from the Pump Room read, "Now this water really does the trick!"). I added several promising musicians to my roster on the strength of managing Boyd; perhaps they only thought I was a glutton for punishment. In music circles, I was no threat to Wurtzberg. But the sight of *Kogan* alongside that wonderful word *Presents* no longer looked so strange to me.

One afternoon, in fact, I did receive a call from my arch-rival. "It's *impossible*," he began, "simply not to be dreamed of that I should not have in my stable someone available right away. It's a great opportunity for your young Boyd, perhaps, who seems to be working very hard but not running with the ball, as they say in your country."

"I don't say," I replied, failing to understand what he was talking about.

"Great opportunity, some very influential people to be assembled. She will sing for them tonight, very intimate—a favor for me, they all think. The great man. She is ravishing. I may sign her. But the accompanist is ill, suddenly. I want Boyd."

"Forget it," I said. "He won't do it."

"But you must know who is to be there. The best people, unheard of for a newcomer. Even Steiner might come. Just to hear her."

"Who," I said, "is she?"

"Jesse Sondergard."

"Never heard of her."

Of course I had. The music world was buzzing with news of the young mezzo with the gorgeous voice and, even more unusual, the gorgeous face and shape to match. Jesse Sondergard had come out of the cow pastures of Wisconsin (though perhaps not literally, her father was an obscure music professor at the university), to study with the best of the blue-chip coaches (Karl Preiss in Chicago, Annabelle Liebling in New York); and then on to the *de rigueur* testing abroad—first Germany, then a *Nozze di Figaro* in Paris that had knocked the audience flat. Suspicious of any and all *wunderkinder*, I had dismissed most of the information as unfounded speculation. It wasn't until I heard a recording that I was the slightest bit interested, and even then I had no intention of signing on any *girl* singers. I would leave them to Wurtzberg, who had, as I knew only too well, quite an eye for the young ladies.

"She was the Cherubino in *Figaro* that brought down Paris. I call your bluff," insisted Wurtzberg.

"Would I bluff you, friend and former employer?" I protested.

"Hah!" Wurtzberg exclaimed. "Still, it would be very good for Boyd, and my nice singer would have someone who knows how to play properly. I see your young man has ambition to conduct. The right people to see the versatility of the boy, a word here, a word there—in the proper setting, of course."

"He'll never do it," I said, wondering how I would talk Martin into it.

"Mention Steiner," Wurtzberg urged. Steiner was a real draw, the most powerful music force in the city. If there were ever a chance for Martin to conduct a great orchestra like the New York Philharmonic, ever a glimmer of a prayer, Steiner could arrange it.

"I'll call you back," I told him. Then, after taking my pulse, I telephoned Martin. He was scheduled to fly to Mexico City that evening.

"I don't accompany," he said.

"But this is different. You'll meet important people informally, at home, a private gathering. You have a chance to overcome your reputation, correct a few of those past errors."

"My father knew loads of people like that. They don't know a thing about music."

I did not say a word. I knew that he was close to saying yes. He was dying for a chance to conduct.

"I'm getting old," he said suddenly. "I'll be twenty-five soon."

"You'll do it?"

"I dislike lieder."

"It's the Schubert. You play Schubert so beautifully. They say she has talent."

"The hell with her," he said. "I don't care about her."

"Do it."

"This is the first and last favor I'll ever do for you," Martin said. "What about Mexico City?"

"You can leave in the morning. I'll make all the arrangements. You're doing this for yourself," I added piously.

"Nope," he said. "For myself, I would replace the singer, not be her second fiddle. This is a one-shot deal."

CHAPTER

6

༃

Martin had seen enough black tie dinners throughout his childhood to have come to associate them with snobbery, vacant conversation, empty-headed politeness, and expensive jewelry. Ladies fearlessly took out their diamonds and wore them at their ears, on their necks, and piled over their elbow-length white gloves. It took a certain courage not to display everything one owned, and few had reason to be so bold.

Standing alone in the doorway of the fine, long room made ready for a musical offering, Martin tugged at his lapels and tried to overcome his customary uneasiness with such affairs. He felt that his suit did not fit correctly. Kogan's tailor had urged him to keep to his diet, but he found so little consolation while touring that he had continued to gorge himself on room-service meals. He never refused the foil-covered baked potatoes or the cottony rolls and butter. He gave his jacket another tug and then moved in among the *Louis Quinze* chairs to see to his piano.

The room was painted a pale apricot, the white moldings accentuated with gold trim. The chair frames were gilt, as were the three-pronged sconces protruding from the walls alongside the marble mantles. Landscapes of Constable cows and hay carts were interspersed with portraits of solemn children at whose feet lay sour-faced spaniels like fur-covered offerings of appeasement.

He struck a chord which echoed through the empty room. He frowned. The piano was far too brilliant. He would have to adjust his playing. He hoped the girl singer had the sense not to compete with his instrument. The notion that the human voice was the finest interpreter of music was anathema to him. Singers were so smug, but they rarely sang *a capella*. He sniffed, then played scales up and down the keyboard. She needs me, he reminded himself. Then he glanced up and saw a woman smiling at him in amusement.

"Here." She held out a pile of music. "You'll be needing this tonight. It's awfully short notice."

He did not take the music. He barely heard her voice—hushed, resonant, the diction impeccably clear. He thought she was the most imposingly lovely person he had ever seen. Taller than he, swathed in a Grecian toga-like dress, her hair piled atop her head, she was a goddess, stepped down off a painted urn. Ordinarily, Martin dismissed women as weak, anemic creatures, less than fully alive. But this one was not of the same species. And she aroused in him the purest terror.

"You are Mr. Boyd, are you not?" she asked

pleasantly. Her eyebrows arched theatrically over dark eyes. She used stage makeup to heighten her features with a ghostly luminosity—white powder over her eyelids and beneath her eyes, with no gash of color to distract from the stark effect of dark hair and white skin.

He struck an emphatic minor chord on the piano. "Yes," he replied angrily. "I am he." He always showed his temper when he was threatened or afraid. It was an old trick he'd used with his father, and now he hoped it would drive this girl away as well. Obviously, any fool could see that she was the singer. In a few minutes he would have to sit down at the piano (my God, how she would tower over him then) and play songs of love and loss, while her Amazonian lungs drowned out his accompaniment.

"Sorry to have intruded—I realize you must want to practice. I'm Jesse Sondergard, as you may have gathered from my state of nerves. I'm scared silly," she confided in a low voice. He was wary and suspicious; would she lull him with her beautifully-timbred voice before moving in for the kill?

He kept a nervous eye on her as he backed away from the piano. "I've played this cycle before," he said. "I don't need practice."

"Is that so," she replied, opening her eyes in mock amazement. Martin, alarmed, did not know where to look. He settled for staring at his feet.

Jesse tossed the pile of music atop the piano and dusted off her hands. Then she asked him, "How do I look?"

She's making a fool of me, he said to his feet, but he heard himself reply. "Fine, just fine."

"There is one thing. Can you do my clasp in back?"

His head shot up. She had turned and presented him with her back, and swirling layers of some soft fabric through which gleamed the metal of a zipper. "It's up top," she directed, placing both hands lightly on her neck, fingers pointing toward the nape. He reached up hesitantly, conscious that his own fingers were stone cold, and brushed against a strand of hair that had fallen from its pin. He drew his hands back. "Please?" she whispered.

He hesitated in confusion. Amid the wisps of hair he saw a tiny hook. His hands shook as he reached for it. He smelled her perfume and the scent of her hair—a different, fresher odor, as if he were outdoors. He made a sudden brave movement, and attached the clasp. Her hand shot up and patted the hair that had fallen on the nape of her neck. "Oh, dear," she said. "I must fix myself." And she was gone.

Suddenly the room was invaded with people; noisy, chattering, laughing people. The dinner was over, and guests drifted into the room in twos and threes. Several men held the long ends of after dinner cigars. Others steered their wives in by a gloved elbow. Ladies were tiaraed, dressed in expensive, flounced evening clothes which showed bare shoulders to an advantage. The hostess, Mrs. Lanier, glided in proudly alongside Jesse Sondergard. Jesse smiled beautifully, and Martin, watching her smile, wanted to move up and smell her hair again.

"The spider and the fly, eh?" a voice said in his ear.

Martin kept his eyes on Jesse. "Kogan, she's tremendous."

"You are no sylph yourself, dear boy."

"That isn't what I meant."

"Lord knows, she's as big as that ballerina,

what's her name—the Indian. This one looks like the end of the Copa line, though."

"She does not," Martin said. "She is stately."

"Martin is smitten," Kogan said delightedly. "I do declare. *Stately.* Like Blenheim? Women like that are to be avoided. She'll devour you at one sitting."

"What do you know about women?" Martin replied. He watched the crowd around Jesse grow larger. She was smiling, nodding her head, but not speaking, saving her voice for the performance.

"Ah hah," Kogan said. "And you, with all those anemic Radcliffe bluestockings? Your Boston Brahmin debutantes, with their bowlegs from riding and their scarred shins from field hockey? Surely that specimen there is a woman. I haven't seen a bosom like that in years! But I warn you, she'll smother you to death in it."

"Nicky, such distaste, really. It makes me want to see exactly what it is you're warning me off."

"Leave her to the Austrian," Kogan said, brushing off the shoulders of Martin's suit with the flat of his hand.

"Stop grooming me," Martin said impatiently.

Mrs. Lanier had arranged the seating cold-bloodedly, giving the best places to the most important patrons. Steiner, the promised draw, had not shown up yet. But his wife was there, wearing one important jewel, a huge emerald. She sat beside an empty chair, awaiting her husband. Wurtzberg was present, leaning on his cane and chatting with the host, Edward Lanier, who was somewhat deaf (an endearing trait in a music patron). The room quieted as Mrs. Lanier took her seat. Martin felt Kogan give him a shove. "Get up there," Kogan hissed. "You're on."

Jesse approached the piano, her dress flowing from her straight shoulders. She assumed a sedate pose by the curve of the piano and nodded gently as Martin sat down on the bench. He lifted his hands, she gave him a wink (a *wink*, he realized with amazement as he began to play) and, when the song started, her voice flowed out—rich, lush, powerful, threatening to escape the bounds of her art. Jesse trod on dangerous ground when she sang; critics would later call this her only flaw. "Experience will bring the sureness of control for which her big voice begs, but audiences defy seasoning and adore occasional lapses of artistic stricture. Miss Sondergard, like a high wire artist working without a net, smiles down benignly, seemingly unaware of the danger. She holds the promise of greatness like a parasol, extended in one hand."

That night, Martin was completely aware of what she wanted. He understood her phrasing and breathing almost instinctively. They were together. The song cycle had never seemed so short to him. As always, he concentrated on the piano, on the notes he was to play. But he experienced a loss of identity new to him. Though he disliked the feeling, he found it also exhilirating and in a way as charming and terrifying as Jesse herself.

The small audience, which by now included Steiner, applauded genteelly, white gloves muffling the handclaps of the ladies. A crowd formed around the piano. There was praise for both singer and accompanist. "Marvelous, wonderful, simply divine," breathed the guests. Jesse turned toward Martin, her face flushed, perspiration gleaming on her forehead. He moved toward her, bent over and lifted her hand to kiss. Several of the women let out an audible sigh at his gesture, "*Ahhh.*" Martin straightened up, then bent toward Jesse's ear. "Very nice," he whispered, "but you forgot something. This is lieder, not *Aida*. You can't do a Verdi aria in a tearoom. It simply doesn't work."

He slipped from her side and left the room, confused, and furious with himself for having played so well. As he walked down the long corridor toward the stairs, he heard footsteps moving up swiftly behind him. He turned around.

"You bastard," Jesse said. And she lifted her arm and slapped him across the face, hard. Then, with her dress sweeping in a long train behind her, she turned and retreated regally, back to the room full of guests.

Kogan emerged from the salon and walked over to Martin and peered at his face. "What is the sound of one hand slapping?" he said. "You're going to have quite a bruise from that one. Come along, little boy. I've some delicious news. Steiner is interested in your future."

Five months later, Jesse Sondergard was signed to a contract with the Metropolitan Opera. Martin, under the guidance of Nicholas Kogan and with help from Rudolph Steiner, accepted an offer for the upcoming opera season. He was to conduct four performances of *Der Rosenkavalier*.

CHAPTER

7

☙

"Who the hell does he think he is? Arturo Toscanini?" the oboist said to the second flute.

"He's a conceited bastard. Is that so new?" the flutist said, flexing his fingers automatically.

The oboist mouthed a reed. "*Naw*. But is it my imagination, or are they breeding them younger? He looks like a friend of my kid's."

A bassoonist tapped the oboist on the shoulder. "He thinks he's the second coming of Lenny Bernstein."

"My gracious, no," said the flutist. "Spare us."

"Bernstein?" the oboist said, wiping his reed carefully. "Maybe. But he's the new heir apparent. Steiner's protégé. He's a Boyd of Boston. He went to *Hahvahd*."

"Do tell," said the bassoonist, who had never been to college at all.

Martin Boyd stood on the podium, wearing crumpled khaki pants and a fraying tennis sweater. "Gentlemen," he said, world-weary and patient. He tried not to show his delight with himself. He knew how sensitive orchestras were toward a conductor's mood. They could make his life miserable. He had never spent enough time with one orchestra to allow them the luxury of knowing him. But this was his third orchestra rehearsal for *Rosenkavalier*, and the New York musicians were a tough lot. Steiner had warned him. "Those bastards won't let you have an inch if you coddle them. Crack down on them right away."

Martin pulled up his chest and sucked in his stomach. He had been trying, unsuccessfully, to diet. "We'll start at number six. Cellos and basses remember, no grace notes on the last two. Let's make it flow, gentlemen." He raised his arms. The orchestra played half a page. "No, no—more of a diminuendo in the woodwinds there; please mark."

The oboist pulled a pencil from behind his ear. "Saints preserve us," he remarked. "He thinks we're the Philharmonic."

The first flute glanced at his watch. "My kid's playing basketball at three. Think I'll make it?"

"No way," said the second flute. "We'll be into overtime before the middle of the first act."

Martin felt the orchestra resist his efforts and he pushed even harder, continuing his abrupt interruptions. "If you don't get it right we'll stay all day. The singers are going to sing *with* us, not over us."

"That's what he thinks," the concertmaster said to himself. Then he raised his violin and tried to banish all unprofessional thoughts. He'd have to take this kid aside and teach him how to talk to an orchestra. Most of the musicians were hardened veterans of the opera season and did not need anyone to lecture them on what was expected in the music department. *Rosenkavalier* was a particularly trying opera because it was so long and there were no breaks for recitative; it was a sheer wall of sound to ascend. The concertmaster, fifty-five years old and still moonlighting with private lessons in order to support his family, sighed as he waited for Martin Boyd to finish his lecture. *He thinks we are a lot of schoolboys.* Then he shrugged. *Ah, whatever the conductor wants;* and he turned to frown at the woodwinds, who were chatting rather loudly.

By the end of official rehearsal time, the orchestra had reached the Italian singer's aria, and Martin was exhausted. "We'll call it a day," he said, wondering how they would ever perform in a week's time. "Thank you, gentlemen."

As the musicians noisily packed up, the concertmaster approached the podium. "It will all go well," he said.

Martin Boyd glared at the man, who held his ground bravely. "I'm sure I don't need to tell you that it is very undisciplined and unprofessional, to say the least, for musicians to chat during rehearsal time."

"I will try and see that it does not happen again," he said stiffly. "But Mr. Boyd," he hesitated.

"Yes?"

"I would like to suggest that perhaps a quickened pace might prevent such occurrences. You see, the men—"

"I conduct the way I see fit. You may do as you please in my absence. But I expect this group to live up to my standards. Is that clear?"

"Thank you very much, sir," the councertmaster said with a formal bow.

Martin, left alone in the orchestra pit, moodily

turned the pages of his dog-eared score and wondered how he would survive the certain debacle of the first performance. He could see the reviews. "Martin Boyd, boy wonder, made a complete ass of himself attempting to conduct at the Metropolitan Opera last evening. The audience responded by throwing the paper napkins from their intermission drinks." He scratched his neck and shuddered. Perfection; he wanted absolute perfection from these musicians. Had anyone ever demanded that before? He poked unhappily at his thick score, which was filled with margin notes, comments, handwritten directions. The pages were a mess, but Martin, accustomed to the chaos, began to read through the score once again, adding even more scratches with a ball-point pen.

"And so they meet again," a woman's voice said, "destiny having flung them together like the star-crossed Verdian lovers—the gold curtain descends as Milton Cross describes the costumes and the soprano's chesty bows."

Martin, standing at the podium with his arms raised before his invisible orchestra, knew at once that Jesse Sondergard had caught him behaving like an ass. He lowered his arms and, as coldly as he could, turned to her with a withering stare. She stood at stage left, dressed in an open-necked shirt and a wide, heavy cotton overskirt that looked bulky and unmanageable. She grabbed the sides of her skirt and hiked it up. Martin stared. Was she disrobing for him right on the stage? The skirt lifted to reveal heavy men's cavalry boots pulled on over a pair of riding breeches. Jesse yanked at her skirt and tried to arrange it more comfortably on her hips. Even with the layers of thick clothing she was an elegant figure.

She stomped across the stage, counting aloud. "Step, step, one and two—no, that's not it; ball of the foot, *hard*, one, two, three." She moved from side to side, trying to perfect the walk of a young man dressed in women's clothing.

As Martin watched her, he felt a distinct pleasure at her presence. Much of his anger at the memory of their past meeting had faded. He even thought of a pleasantry. "You're getting the hang of it," he called to her.

"Oh?" she said, still strutting about.

"Just try and forget yourself a bit more. I think a man in a dress with boots on would exaggerate what he thinks is female, but if he's weighted down in his feet, he'll lapse and slip up now and then. It could be a nice comic touch."

She stopped her pacing and stared down at him. "Why the sudden interest in my stage business?"

She looked quite beautiful to him, pale and nervous up on that bare stage. He recalled the lieder concert and the slap. "Look," he began. "Awfully sorry about that business when you sang. I guess all that touring had me a bit off. You were quite good, really."

"No I wasn't," she said. "I was almost as bad as you said. I think I'm not really ready to do justice to that Schubert. I overreached."

"But you got your contract here," he said, suddenly aware of his dirty clothes and uncombed hair. When had he showered last? He couldn't remember.

"I need to work. My biggest problem is my self-indulgence. I need discipline so desperately, but I can be such a lump about that!"

"Are you rehearsing now?"

"Just this business with the costume. I'm doing it

on my own. I have two hours before we work on the next act. I have to be careful about the time. I was almost late yesterday."

"Almost late?"

"In the words of our director, who caters to the Marschallin as if she were paralyzed."

He had another idea. Brilliant thoughts seemed to fly spontaneously into his head. "Would you like to go out for a cup of coffee?"

She glanced down at her costume. "Only if I go as is. Don't you think I look perfectly stunning?"

They sat across from each other in a coffeeshop booth, Jesse still in her costume, Martin embarrassed to be seen with someone so ridiculously attired and so beautiful. He noticed the way other men looked at her. Covetously. They wanted her. *But she is with me,* Martin realized. *I'm the one with the girl they're all looking at; she's with me!*

Jesse pushed the pile of change and the empty plates to one side. "So," she said, plopping her elbows on the table. "Tell me your life story in one sentence."

"One?" he said.

"It's my acid test. If you run over, you lose."

He thought for a moment. A sentence popped into his head. He spoke it. "My father died, and I started my career."

"Isn't that odd? That's precisely what happened to me. Except it was both parents. I'm an orphan."

"Sad," he said, thinking of his mother still living in the big house, occupying only two rooms, ever mindful of the old man's stingy rules about wasting heat and electricity.

"But I ended up going abroad," Jesse went on. "If I hadn't gone to Germany, I'd never have had a career at all. I was terribly sheltered. I grew up in a big small town."

"Did you like Germany?"

The waitress threw down two menus and scooped up the pile of change. Jesse grabbed one and began reading it.

"I'm dying for pancakes and bacon, but I can't do it. Do you think a cheeseburger is just as fattening?"

"You're asking me?" Martin said incredulously.

"Well, it doesn't seem to matter as much if a man is a little fat. Oh, I've wounded you. Poor thing, I'd have never known you were vain about your appearance."

"You're making a fool of me again."

"Again? Was there a first time?"

"We'll both have Bartlett pear and cottage cheese salad," he pronounced.

"Very masterful of you. I like a man who takes over. Doesn't that sound awful, though?"

They ordered roast beef sandwiches.

"Have you been to Germany?" she asked.

"I studied there one summer. I was a struggling student on a small allowance, so I drove a cab for a while, ferrying around American tourists. One time a couple asked me what there was to do, and I told them about a concert that evening. They asked me what was being played and I said Beethoven's Fifth. "Oh,' this fellow said. 'We've heard that one already.' "

She laughed; a deep laugh, unembarrassed. Martin saw several heads turn their way. He leaned over toward her, pretending he was going to say something intimate, the way he'd seen men behave in Paris cafés. "How was your time abroad?"

"It changed my life," she said, her face growing

sober and thoughtful. "I was always such a baby; I'd led a very sheltered life. Then all at once, over there, I was plunged into the most shocking destruction, incredible desolation. It opened up my world. It made me a true artist, a real musician, for the first time. And I almost didn't get to go at all. After my parents died—it was such a stupid death, a hit and run driver—I was taken in by my father's friends, the Ruddingers. Incredibly kind, wonderful people. They live here, in the city. I'd been living with them while I studied with Annabelle Liebling. They became my second parents.

"At any rate, they're Jewish, and they'd always opposed my father on the issue of my going abroad. He wanted me to study in Germany. After the accident, I suppose they felt they ought to fulfill his wish and so they sent me abroad. They paid for everything. I think they were afraid I'd be corrupted in some way, spoiled by a horrible place. But instead it was the first time I'd really felt alive, even with all those ruins around me."

"It sounds grim," Martin observed, feeling ill at ease.

Jesse sensed his discomfort. "Oh, don't listen to me." She waved a hand in the air. "I make it sound so gray when it was really quite marvelous in its own way. I met wonderful people—serious music students, devoted, sensitive teachers. I learned so much. I grew up. That was where I met my first boyfriend."

"Who was he?" Martin asked, feeling jealous.

"A rich, lazy boy who had all the talent and intelligence one could bear in another person but who did nothing with it. He had been sent on an unbelievable sort of grand tour. He went wherever he liked, at will. He stayed in Germany a bit longer than he'd planned."

The waitress put down their sandwiches. "That'll be all?" she said.

"Maybe," Jesse replied. "I don't know how strict I'm going to be today."

The waitress stared as if she thought Jesse was one of those city lunatics who babbles on buses and totes garbage around in shopping bags.

"He was running away," Jesse continued, taking a huge bite of her sandwich and chewing rapturously. "Pass the Russian. Thanks. He was married."

"Married?"

"Where have you been all these years? Are you sure you're not from Madison, too?"

"Boston."

"I know. I looked you up."

"Where?"

"Never mind. I thought you wanted to hear about me. . . . He had left law school and was drifting around. I don't know where the wife was. Tucked away somewhere in the states, I suppose, but he never said. He wore a wedding ring. I met him through some rich people who came to the opera. They'd been told to keep an eye on him. They all trouped backstage one night. It was *Zauberflöte*; I'd sung the Third Lady. He said he loathed everything to do with music; I think because his parents had been very involved—season tickets, endowments, all that. He had slept his way through every great performance of the last two decades: Flagstad, Melchior, Gigli, Lehmann. The idiot had been exposed to everything I'd missed. But that was part of the attraction. It's masochism, watching someone denigrate the thing you love most. He would buy me valuable old recordings, the rarest of the rare, and then toss them around as if they were cheap popular music. We didn't last too long. He enjoyed hurting me. It was even better than sleeping through *Tristan*." She finished her sandwich. "My, that was good. Want to share another?"

He waved his hand at the waitress, who ignored him.

Jesse laughed. "You have a very commanding presence, maestro. Now tell me about your life and loves."

"There's nothing to tell."

"Come now—all those girls who sneak into dressing rooms and offer themselves to Art."

"And Art gets all the girls. Martin Boyd doesn't."

"But you're so cute," she said with a straight face.

"I loathe that word." He waved his arm at the waitress.

"You are," she insisted. "You'll see, they'll soon find out. Hasn't anyone ever told you?"

"Nope. My manager says I'm impossible."

"That man Kogan," she said. "I don't think he likes me very much."

"Why do you say that?"

"He doesn't like women. I can tell."

"He's not that way."

"I don't mean carnally. I don't care about his tastes. I just think he doesn't like women in the abstract, as an idea."

Martin said, "I'm going to give that waitress one more chance. If she doesn't get over here, no tip."

"How about not paying?" Jesse said.

He waved frantically. "Okay, that's it, she's ignoring me on purpose."

"Let's go," said Jesse. She grabbed his hand and they ran out of the restaurant.

They were still holding hands when they reached

the opposite corner. Jesse was laughing. "Hey Boyd," she puffed. "I have news for you. The world isn't designed especially to thwart you."

"So?"

"Loosen up. You can't make lovely music with a tight ass."

"You have a very foul mouth."

"No," she said. "It's your imagination. It's a hungry mouth." She pulled him toward a delicatessen. "Can we go in there and have just one teeny weeny sandwich? On a roll this time? Please?"

"You're very easy to please," he said.

"No I'm not." She pushed open the glass door. "Just easy to feed."

CHAPTER

8

♈

For both Martin and Jesse the courtship was strange—frightening, yet exhilarating. Each believed that no one had ever really listened before. They met whenever they happened to be in New York provided their schedules coincided, which was not all that frequent. They spent most of their time together talking, especially after Martin revealed his affinity for drinking in bars. Long hours passed while Jesse nursed a drink or two and Martin downed several, and they spread out the contents of their lives atop the tiny cocktail tables, examining each part meticulously. Jesse also enjoyed eating the free bar food. She devoured bowls of mixed nuts, picking out the almonds first and then the cashews, saving the meaty Brazil nuts for Martin. Their favorite meeting place had the mixed nuts, but when that bar was crowded they ventured north to a theatrical restaurant with a long, curved, mahogany bar that served potato chips. The potato chips were a nice change from the mixed nuts and, after the pretheater crowd had bolted their dinners and raced out to make the curtain, Martin and Jesse had the place virtually to themselves.

"Don't you think it's strange that we spend all our time drinking in bars?" Jesse said as they perched on the high padded stools, watching the bartender rinse highball glasses. It was false spring outside, an extraordinarily warm, muggy day for March, and they were celebrating with gin and tonics.

"Have you got an alternative?" Martin asked, tearing up a matchbook cover neatly and stacking the pieces into a star-shaped design.

"*Mmmmm,*" Jesse replied, spearing a piece of lime with her plastic stirrer.

"What?"

"I'm not telling. It isn't appropriate."

"Okay."

"Aren't you going to ask me what it is? Won't you beg me to reveal my secret?"

"Nope."

"You are the most infuriatingly self-contained individual I've ever known!"

"Practice, Jess. Living with my father taught me the tactics. It was a war of nerves, and if I withdrew, I generally won. But it was usually a Pyrrhic victory."

"Stop using your Harvard education and talk sense."

"You're far more worldly than I am. You ought to give yourself more credit. I was brought up with blinders on. No one had a more insular childhood than a baby Boyd." He waved at the bartender and pointed to his empty glass with a gesture worthy of a conductor.

"Impossible," Jesse protested. "Madison, Wisconsin is an overgrown small town with a university that teaches dairy science and agriculture to a lot of people who aspire to be farmers. My parents shielded me from everything and everyone, even the nicest of my father's music students. They didn't want me to be corrupted. I was a lump of clay, a big cow of a girl with no experience and no depth. When my father discovered I had a voice and that I loved to sing, he was devastated. It was as if I wanted to be a burlesque queen. He saw me as his one hope, his true star pupil, the next great female pianist. Singers were less than top grade in his eyes. And my first voice teacher was just as unworldly. Sanford Donnelly thought that I might have a chance to sing in the chorus of the Chicago Lyric Opera. To him, Chicago was the end."

"Donnelly—was he your teacher?"

"Yes, my first for voice." She smiled prettily and glanced down at her drink. "He was very young, in his twenties then, I suppose, though that seemed old to me. He was terribly in love with his own voice. I was his great discovery. I would pay him back for being stuck in Madison. So he sent me to study with his teacher in Chicago. It was the greatest thing he could have done for me."

"Better than kissing you?"

"I was sweet sixteen—and then seventeen and eighteen—and had never been kissed. I was so busy shuttling back and forth to my lessons in Chicago that I never saw any friends my own age. When I was eighteen, my father sent me to New York. Poor Papa. It was the hardest thing he ever did. When I first started voice lessons, he came to me and asked if I really wanted to sing more than play the piano. I couldn't answer. Saying yes to him was out of the question; it would have hurt him too much. I let him decide. I was a competent pianist, not great— nowhere near as good as you—but my talent gave him all sorts of notions. I'd never thought about a real career in music. I just thought I'd end up playing the organ in a church somewhere, raising a lot of kids, and running a little music group on the side— madrigal singers, that sort of thing, maybe an annual Bach cantata. But my father knew. He took my face in his hands and told me that if I was to be great, I would have to go abroad. *Eat their food,* he said, *breathe their air, learn the language properly, study with the best people.* Of course, it was wartime. There was no question of going anywhere overseas. But he said I could go to study in New York, to prepare. He knew enough to be certain that I didn't belong in the midwest."

"He sounds incredibly kind."

"Oh yes. But everyone's been so kind. I've been lucky that way. Didn't you like the Ruddingers? Aren't they wonderful?"

"Did I meet them?"

"Of course you did. After the opening of *Rosenkavalier,* they came backstage to see me and I brought them into your dressing room."

"You know what a zoo that can be. Yeah, I guess I remember them. Old people, right?"

"Martin, you're so mean. They're very important to me."

"I know, I know. I liked them a lot. Really. They're very protective of you."

"I have no one else. I wish Madame Liebling was still teaching. She was a real tyrant, but I needed that kind of discipline in my life. My parents had indulged me, and then the Ruddingers. She stood up to me.

She accused me of memorizing notes and phrases, of not finding the feeling under the music. She was right. She said I was malleable, that I'd always listened to other people but that I had to make decisions for myself. *Go to Germany,* she told me. And then my parents died, and the Ruddingers stepped in. I wonder if I would have become anything at all if they'd lived."

Martin swallowed his gin solemnly and stared straight ahead into the mirror facing the bar. He turned his head to one side and examined his profile. "My father had a massive coronary. *Poof,* he was gone. I thought there was a God then, and that He was the sort of being who answered prayers very literally and very directly."

"Do you like to pretend that you don't care?" Jesse said. She put her hand on his arm. "That's not what you're like. I think I know you better than that."

"I care for music," he said stonily.

"We both do. But you've got to admit there's a lot more tied into that package than simply appreciating the classics. You want to master it because it means mastery over your self, over your life. Self-determination, right? And I want to be great because it's the only way I know to express how I feel about myself. It's my coming out as a person."

"You'll be great," he said briskly. "Even Kogan admits that."

"Your manager doesn't seem to be the sort to toss off compliments. I suppose I should be flattered."

"Very flattered. You're right. He and I have been in this thing from the start and I must say I find him the biggest puzzle I've ever tried to decipher. You can be around him for months and never learn a thing. He plays his hand very close, Kogan does."

"He doesn't seem that odd; just a bit stiff, I'd say."

"The understatement of the year. But he's good for me."

"Not too unlike your father, I suppose."

Martin turned and stared at her, his expression shocked, much like a priest's when he overhears a horribly irreverent comment from a loyal parishioner. "Not in the slightest."

"But you had said—"

"Let's get out of here," he said abruptly.

"If you like. Don't be angry—I didn't mean anything so dreadful."

Martin signaled for the bill. He left a wad of cash, hardly bothering to count the difference, and said "Keep the change" magnanimously to the bartender.

"Where was it you wanted to go before?" Martin said as they stood on the sidewalk. The streets were still crowded with nighttime people who meandered past lighted store windows and looked in, waiting for something to happen so they might have cause to stop.

"I was going to suggest a hotel," Jesse said in a quiet voice.

"My hotel?" Martin blurted out, his voice shooting up an octave.

Jesse started to laugh. "Silly boy. I wouldn't dream of compromising your situation."

"Jesse, you can't mean," he began, and swallowed hard, stuffing his hands into his pockets and hunching his shoulders.

"But I do mean. Don't you think we know each other well enough?"

"Sure—sure I do. But a place to go? Suppose they ask us for a license, suppose they look for a wedding ring, or luggage?"

"Come on, we'll take you home," she said maternally.

"No, no wait. Where did you want to go?"

"The Plaza."

"Out of the question."

"You're a nervous wreck. What's the matter? Haven't you ever done this before?"

"No," he said defiantly.

"Follow me," Jesse said, and they began to walk. They moved together, arm in arm, and she set the pace down the street. After ten blocks of silent walking, Jesse stopped and pointed to a building diagonally across the street. "That one looks promising." It was a slightly run-down, once respectable hotel. "Just remember to sign in as Mr. and Mrs., otherwise they'll know something's fishy for sure."

"How do you know all this?" he asked curiously.

"Haven't you ever read a novel, or been to the movies?" she replied with amusement. "God, I thought I was provincial!" She shook her head in amazement, and he was struck anew by how beautiful she was.

The desk clerk peered at them suspiciously as Martin held the pen to his mouth and chewed the top. Finally he wrote something down. The clerk turned the register around and said, "Fine, Mr. Joyce. And do you have any identification for that address?"

Panic swept over Martin's face as he turned toward Jesse. She shrugged and glanced away, then walked over to the newsstand and began leafing through a fashion magazine. Martin shifted from one foot to the other as he patted his pockets. His face grew redder and redder, and finally he burst out, "Gadzooks! It appears that I've been robbed. Help! Stop thief! They've taken my wallet!"

"Mr. Joyce, good heavens, right here? I'll call the police." The clerk picked up the phone.

"Come, Daphne," Martin said dramatically as he grabbed Jesse's hand and drew her out behind him, almost crushing her foot in the revolving door.

Spilling onto the sidewalk, he continued his getaway for three blocks crosstown and several more uptown for good measure. They finally stopped, panting and perspiring, in front of a jewelry store with small, porthole-sized windows.

"This is too much for me," Jesse said as she limped up exhaustedly. "Quite a workout. Well, that about takes care of this evening, doesn't it?"

Martin, collapsed against the front door of the jewelry shop, loosened his tie, and gasped for air.

"You were so funny in that hotel," she said, starting to laugh. "I think I'll never be able to keep a straight face remembering the sight of your frisking yourself for your wallet. What did you sign on that register.

"James Joyce," he gasped.

She began to laugh again, and Martin pulled her close and kissed her. Then he leaned his head on her shoulder and said, "I think I'm having a heart attack."

"Nonsense." She shoved him away. He peered through the porthole window and saw the jewelry glittering on the black velvet.

"C'mere," he said to Jesse, and when she did he pointed to a row of bracelets and necklaces set with rubies. "You like those? They're my favorite stone. Someday—"

"I know. You'll buy me everything in this window."

"Let's get married."

"What? You're out of your mind."

"I want to," he insisted. "I don't want to go to some hotel with you and be sleazy and cheap. I want to get married."

"You're crazy." She pushed away from him and began to walk down the street.

"Hey, Jesse, come back. Jesse, what's the matter with you?"

"I don't want to get married," she called over her shoulder.

"Why not?"

"I want to be a great singer, the great Jesse Sondergard in recital!"

"You can still be that, too." He began to run after her, at a slow trot, calling her name. "Jesse—Jesse, please say yes. I'll take you to Europe."

"When? You haven't got the time," she called back. "And neither do I."

"Then we'll make the time. We'll be together."

"We will not. We'll never see each other. And I have to think of my career."

"You'll have your goddamned career!" Martin exploded.

She stopped walking. "That's just what I mean. It's not goddamned at all. I intend to be great, and no one is going to stand in my way, or tell me that it's not what I intend to do. I won't bury myself in a marriage."

"Jesse, I love you very much. I want you to be happy. If you want a career, you can continue just as you've been doing. I won't interfere. I just don't want to share you with anyone else."

"There is no one else," she said impatiently.

"If you don't marry him, I'm calling the cops!" Martin and Jesse looked straight up. Three stories above their heads, a man was leaning out of a window. "Enough, already," the man said. Jesse laughed her wonderful, throaty, singer's laugh as Martin tried to apologize, but the man cut them short. "Is it yes?" he asked. Jesse hesitated, then looked up at him and said, "Okay, fella."

"Good," he replied. "Now I can get back to sleep."

And so, on Sixty-first Street and Madison Avenue, they were engaged.

CHAPTER

9

꾼

When Martin announced to me that he was going to marry Jesse Sondergard, I was reduced to a state of apoplexy. "My mother always warned me. She said I'd be wiser to organize blind nuns tatting lace than to herd around insufferable ingrates like you. But don't come running back and say I didn't warn you. I don't care how big you think you are, she'll try and be bigger."

"Kogan, listen—I haven't been working well. I'm not concentrating."

"See? She has you confused—precisely what I'm talking about." I yanked at my desk drawers, searching for nothing in particular inside their well-organized depths.

Martin picked a piece of lint from the sleeve of his cashmere coat and examined it as a fortune-teller might a tea leaf. In six months of courtship, he had lost twelve pounds and acquired a wardrobe from Brooks Brothers. His face had decorated the cover of Opera News with the tag line, "A Young Conductor to Watch."

"Two careers in one family," I prophesied darkly. "No good."

He pouted.

"Can you stand the competition? And what sort of a makeshift marriage will you two globetrotters have?"

"I want to do this, Nicky."

"Don't call me that," I said, insulted that my excellent advice was being spurned.

"I don't need your written permission, or even your blessing. I want your approval because you're my friend," Martin pleaded.

"Do as you wish." He was such a child, a little boy dressed in grownup's clothes. I could not imagine him married, least of all to that Valkyrie who would wear him thin and exhaust him totally.

"You don't like her, Kogan. You never liked her. Why not? Because she's Wurtzberg's discovery? Because she's a woman?"

"Whatever gave you such preposterous notions? I simply find her excessive. Too much makeup, too much hair, too much voice. She towers over you. In ten years she'll look like your mother."

"She's marvelous. She's going to be a great star."

"What if she's greater than you?" I said. "What if she becomes the powerful one? John the Baptist ended up as the entrée, my boy."

He pulled at the brim of his felt hat. "Impossible. We're in different areas. We have no intention of becoming the Lunt and Fontanne of the music business. Our careers shall be entirely separate. She's a woman, after all. . . And should we decide to have a family. . . " He shrugged, and his elegant cashmere coat slipped off his shoulders to the floor.

"Martin, is there another reason for marrying? Is there some, ah, pressing condition which you are not mentioning to me, your oldest friend?"

He picked up his coat and dusted it off. The expression on his face told me he was still a virgin. Will wonders never cease? I had been positive she'd woven a spell of consummated sex over my boy. Now I realized that it was unconsummated sex which had him reeling. She was smarter than I thought.

"We must discuss business," Martin said huffily.

"You'd better not cancel," I warned. "They're screaming in the sticks for the boy wonder. Hot stuff, to say the least."

"I want you to represent us both."

"Absolutely not," I said immediately. "Never. Case closed."

"We've been together from the beginning. And I needn't remind you that I can go anywhere I choose. But my loyalty has always been to you. We must share the same manager; our schedules have to be coordinated. It's the only way we'll have any time together. I'm sure when Wurtzberg hears the news he'll make me an excellent offer. He'll scream a lot if he thinks he'll lose Jesse, and surely that will get you reams of publicity. They'll hear your name a lot more in this town if you manage us both."

I did not want to manage Jesse Sondergard. Her excesses made me shudder. She fell into the same category as Rococo ceilings, Liberace, Viennese pastry, and the music of Franz Lehar. Excesses, florid excesses. I like things done to a turn. A three-minute egg should be a three-minute egg; no more, no less. I cannot handle anything that tips my sensibility too far in one direction.

"When you get to know her, you'll love her," Martin promised, as if I had already agreed.

"I doubt that," I said.

"Kogan, for heaven's sake, can't you bend a little? Sometimes I think you're going to crack in half. Won't you ever mellow?"

"I shall not discuss this any further," I said, wounded by his accusations. "Haven't you a plane to catch?" I reminded him.

"Oh my gosh," he puffed out his cheeks. Grabbing his coat and slinging it over his shoulder, he leaned across my desk. "Would you please send her a dozen roses? No, make it two dozen. She's staying with the Steiners." He beamed and ran out of the office, leaving behind a pair of expensive Italian leather gloves. I picked them up. They were brand-new, still slightly stiff but beginning to get more supple. Jesse Sondergard trapped herself quite an exotic species—*hominus virginis,* the last one over the age of twenty-one left in these parts. Of course, my own status doesn't count. I had refrained for lack of taste in the whole business, remaining comfortably neuter, by choice.

I called my florist and ordered an austere, waxy potted lily for Jesse Sondergard, a direct reference to any number of pre-Renaissance annunciation altarpieces. I enclosed my card, trusting that she would get the message.

CHAPTER

10

℈

The setback caused by the Boyd-Sondergard
nuptials, to which no one was invited because the
idiots eloped to Venice, caused me to do something I
hadn't done for a long time. I went to see my mother.
She was quite close to the end, though I didn't know
it at the time; it seemed as if she might last forever. I
had always kept in close touch by telephone, but of
late I could never seem to face her in person. She'd
wanted me to be, above all else, a gentleman; and she
believed my profession made me as trashy as a white
slaver.

But of all my circle of acquaintances, no one
would understand my objections to the marriage as
well as mother. I went to her for something she had
withheld throughout my childhood—succor and
sustenance. She wasn't much of a mother in that respect. I hoped that ripe old age had softened her.

Her little bird eyes peered up at me over her half-frames. "Mein Gott," she said, "it's my son." She craned her neck and leaned toward me. "You are Nicholas, are you not?" she asked ironically. I came by my own wit quite honestly, you see, through the genes.

"Hello, darling," I said, knowing in an instant why I'd avoided seeing her during the past months. She could be such a trial.

"Has the business failed yet?" she said mildly as she rang the small silver bell for Ellen, the maid.

"No, dear. It's doing quite well."

"I see they're bringing that foreign dance company here next year. Some cultural exchange nonsense or other."

Right to the point, Mother was, right on target. Importing the Soviet dancers was Wurtzberg's great coup for the coming season.

I stared at her, noticing the way her hands lay tidily and gracefully in her lap. Every inch a lady, as always. Since I'd last seen her, the violet eyes seemed weaker, more myopic; her gray hair a bit more lifeless, still tucked into a proper *chignon*. A lace handkerchief protruded from the sleeve of her ubiquitous cashmere cardigan. She adored cashmere, she adored cardigans, and she owned dozens in exactly the same style, all with little mother-of-pearl buttons. She seemed more frail, but her voice, sharp and crackling, belied her appearance. Mother always criticized ladies who sounded like truck drivers, but she was never quite aware of her own vocal power. Often, when we attended opera performances during my childhood, her comments on the soprano's poor pitch seemed to echo through the hall. Or was that just my child's imagination?

"You didn't use the tickets I sent you," I scolded her for her failure to appear at a recent sold-out concert by one of the masters.

"Why? Why should a tottering old woman drag herself out to see a tottering old man strike the keys on a piano for two hours, then bow like a feeble old fool and shuffle off stage?"

"He'll be gone soon," I remarked. "One of the true greats."

"I'll be joining him then," she said matter of factly. "Ah, here she is at long last. Ellen, do bring us a tea tray, if you will. Some toast with a bit of that plum preserve from England—and lemon for the dear boy." She made an acid face, as she always did at my taste for lemon in tea. She affected the habits of the English at teatime, based on what she read in her favorite ladies' novels—and she maintained that they would never hear of lemon slices in the *right* British homes. But she had Ellen slice the lemon paper-thin, with a special knife, and it became part of her ritual when I was present. Stiff-spined though my mother was (as I am, too; it's another trait that runs in the family), she could be flexible at odd moments. She wouldn't dream of making a guest in her house feel uncomfortable, even under the most trying of circumstances. I had once watched when she saw someone snuff out a cigarette on a Meissen plate in our house. Mother had bitten her lip, but she went on smiling, saying nothing.

"Are you making a living?" she asked, offering up her usual question about my affairs, followed by a bored little shrug. It was her way of showing interest in my work and, ordinarily, it was as far as we went in that department. I would answer yes, and she would proceed to tell me who had died recently, and who had been cut out of the will (wills loom large in her thinking; she drove our lawyer stark raving mad with all of her own daily changes). If she ever noticed my concert programs—and she did read the culture pages, after the obituaries—she never chose to discuss the details of my work with me. I had disgraced her by not becoming a gentleman of leisure. As she often reminded me, she could have supported me in style. Ah Lord, what a mother.

"As a matter of fact," I said this time, altering my reply, "I am doing rather well."

"Oh?" her narrow, pencilled brows shot up at this deviation from our customary ritual of polite question and monosyllabic answer. "Good for you," she said after a pause.

She poured the tea into her thin china cups, carefully filling them to precisely half-level, even though I, for one, don't take milk. I could see the little ticker in her head going like mad, registering my last reply. I recalled a similar expression the day I announced that I was leaving college. Before I'd said a word about my intentions, her brain was racing ahead to sort out all of her objections, as if cleaning out a dresser drawer stuffed with mementos. She was a master cleaner, one of the greats. Her household, like her head, contained no excess, no wastage, no clutter that takes up precious space. Only the essentials, the things of most import, were permitted to occupy room.

"So it isn't money you need," she said finally, after sipping her tea and blotting her mouth lightly with her lace-edged napkin. She spooned a dab of preserves onto a triangle of crustless toast. I sensed that she was stalling for time. For once, she wasn't sure what I wanted. I felt a distinct sense of triumph.

I had caught my mother off guard. Then shame swept over me, as if I had spied on her dressing in her bedroom. She was my mother, after all.

"Dear, I want your advice concerning Martin Boyd."

"My advice? Yes, your young protégé, that brash child from Boston. I knew his father. He was not a very kind man as I recall. His wife, I think she was a Hopkins, was tormented by his extreme tightness with regard to matters of finance. They say he left most of it to cultural organizations. She was a very pretty girl in the old days. Sargent painted her when she was a child. Or was that her sister? My, I must inquire." She picked up a small, gold pencil and wrote a note on a pad. She carefully wrote down anything she might not remember, and then called one or another of her friends to do what she called "research." Anyone else might have called it gossip, but not my mother.

"There is a complication," I explained. "You see, he has just eloped with a singer."

"Really?" she said, and by the expression on her face, I could see that she thought I meant singer as a euphemism for some disreputable occupation.

"Opera singer," I hastily corrected. "I don't know if you've read about her—she made quite a smash this season in *Rosenkavalier*."

"Sophie?" my mother asked.

"No, a mezzo."

"Ah, the pants role. And she was good, you say?"

"The critics were quite impressed."

"But what did you think, dear boy?" She had always asked me what I thought, through all those years of concerts and operas during my youth.

"She'll be better when she performs more. She has a tendency to let her voice loose. It's a big voice, and she's a big girl. Sometimes the effect is a bit overwhelming."

"I think I may have seen her photograph, perhaps in that oversized magazine. But in black and white one can hardly tell."

"He wants me to represent her."

"Doesn't she have her own person to arrange her affairs?"

"Yes," I said. "But Boyd insists that I handle them both."

"Then do so," she replied. "Is that what you wanted to ask me?"

"I suppose I'm not sure that I want to get involved with her—with both of them," I added quickly. "I think the marriage is a hideous mistake, and if I take her on I'll get too involved. It's going to be one of those messy affairs."

"And if you don't take her on?" Mother asked, biting into her toast with a delicate crunch.

"He'll go over to her manager, he says."

"Let him. Why should you have to do anything you don't feel comfortable doing? There must be some reason you can't support this boy's choice, if you think it's so wrong. Is she a person of background?"

"Her parents are dead. She's from a college town in Wisconsin, I believe."

"Does she lack manners?"

"No, it's more her excessiveness. She rocks the boat when she steps in."

"Dear, she sounds like an elephant."

"No, no—in fact she's lost quite a bit of weight recently. She's very tall, but she has charm for someone that size."

My mother shook her head. "I've always said you were not cut out for a certain kind of woman."

"What kind is that? I never heard you say anything of the sort."

"I used to say it a great deal, though I suppose you never paid much attention. Some men are simply not made to be ladies' men. You are one of them. I always knew you would fare better without a wife. And I was right." She set down her teacup triumphantly, and smiled.

I shifted in my chair, distinctly uncomfortable and becoming quite angry. "Well, who could I have possibly brought home to mother? You would never have approved."

"Didn't I try and take a liking to that silly girl you had such a crush on, even though she used chemicals on her hair?"

"I didn't have a crush. I was simply given her name by a friend."

"You were smitten. I don't think I've ever seen you quite so taken with a woman since. She had no class. But I was prepared to try and do something with her if you wanted me to accept the inevitable. But, as I say, some men are not cut out—"

"Yes, mother, I heard you the first time."

"Oh dear—have I stepped on toes? I'm dreadfully sorry. Nicholas, you must understand one thing. I never meant to be cruel. You know how I loathe cruel people—Lord knows your father excepted, rest his soul. But you must admit, I've never insisted that you marry, have I? I've never said a word. And now I'm very old."

"Not very, mother."

"Very, Nicholas. And while I can still say this, I'm going to tell you again that you will never be happy unless you accept the fact that you are, like me, meant to be alone."

"Mother," I said patiently, "you are not alone. You had father, and me."

"Your father was the equivalent of living alone. He was never around. Yes, you have been present, to be sure, but for just a few years. Most of my time has been spent here, with my favorite things around me, with my friends, and with my sanity. You are like me in that respect. Maybe if there had been a very special girl—someone extraordinary, with taste and charm and the right background—perhaps then there might have been a match. But I never found her." She focused her gaze on me. "This singer disturbs you because she is everything you have been brought up to dislike in women. How can Martin Boyd, who is, after all, from a good family, find her attractive?"

"He is a child; that's why I'm so worried."

"Perhaps you ought to keep watch over him. You have some sense of responsibility in this business, have you not? If the match is poor, then it will pass, and she will drop out of your life and go on her way. There really isn't any need to be afraid of her, my dear. She doesn't pose that much of a threat. Class tells, Nicholas. It shows in the end."

I supposed then that mother was right and that the union was to be a transient affair. Martin and Jesse had eloped to Italy, as far from those of us who objected virulently as they could get and still be someplace with charm. I would have to make the most of their marriage—help to capitalize on the publicity, and arrange their schedules so that they might not have too much time together. After all, she did have talent. I wasn't being forced to sign on someone inept. I would have to accept Martin's actions and proceed carefully from that point. I suppose I faced a Hobson's choice, but there you are. Life had never seemed to offer me too many soul-stirring crises.

I left my mother's apartment then, and never saw her again. She died several weeks later. The apartment was sold and I kept a few of her best things, including the fragile tea service we had used that afternoon. I pensioned Ellen off, as my mother's will directed, and bought a great many tax-free bonds with my inheritance. I wondered if my mother's predictions for me would come true. As it happened, for the first and last time in her life, she was wrong. But as my luck would have it, she wasn't there when I could tell her so.

CHAPTER

11

༄

"I don't remember Venice being so cold this time of year," Martin said to Jesse as they left their tiny *pensione* to search for a place to have dinner. "It's damn chilly." His tone was hurt, as if the weather had offended him personally.

"It was warmer when you were here before?" Jesse asked him, trying to hide her amusement at his outfit, which consisted of heavy pants, two floppy sweaters stuffed under his jacket, a woolen scarf wrapped around his neck and ears, and a knit cap pulled over his head.

"Warmer, maybe, but not better," he said. "I was traveling *en famille*. Those were not the best of times. I trailed around behind them while they did the guidebooks from page one to the end, from the grandest canals to the lowliest little latrines. My father believed that tourism had to hurt in order to be beneficial, so we walked until we dropped from exhaustion. I never paid too much attention to what was going on. Thank God it was warm then, because I never brought along a sweater. You see, our next stop was in Switzerland, and I always got a sweater there; it was one of the few allowable purchases. You bought a sweater in the Alps. Anything else was considered a waste of money. This place is marvelous when the sun comes out."

"I realize it's quite an unusual city, but the sun doesn't ordinarily shine at night," Jesse remarked.

"Brother, is it freezing. Look, my hands aren't even working right."

"We'll get you some dinner. Does it all look like this?" They were walking down a narrow street, much like the street of a toy town, the shops small and shuttered, the pavement flagstones damp and glistening where the rain stood in puddles. "It's lovely and eerie all at once."

"It's damned ridiculous that our honeymoon has to coincide with whatever passes for their monsoon season," Martin fumed, wrapping his scarf more tightly around his neck. "My throat feels scratchy already."

"I'm the one who's supposed to be worrying about her throat," Jesse said airily, pausing in front of a small, lighted restaurant and peering at the posted menu.

"You don't want that place," Martin said.

"Why not? It looks pleasant enough, and I'm starving."

"Look, they have a translated menu, just for tourists. We want some place with real local color. Leave it to me."

Jesse shrugged and followed Martin as he wound

around through the labyrinthine streets, turning sharp corners, crossing open plazas and then curved stone bridges, making his way further and further into what should have been the heart of the city but which seemed, to Jesse, to be an area as deserted as the one they'd just left. She had a natural sense of direction, but the combination of the dark and the unfamiliar architecture—which made it impossible to use certain monuments or buildings as landmarks—left her feeling confused and unsteady. She had no idea where they were.

"This looks just right." Martin stopped in front of a small *trattoria* and rubbed his hands together as he waited for Jesse to catch up. Jesse, who was uncomfortably sweaty from the long walk, felt even more uncomfortable as she stared into the place. There were simple wooden tables and benches, no tablecloths, a fat proprietor, and what seemed to be several progeny, also fat, rushing about planting silverware and plates haphazardly atop tables.

"If you say so," Jesse agreed warily.

It took them four hours to eat, not entirely due to the charming local custom of lingering over meals. The service was relaxed to the point of nonexistence, and Martin discovered that no one in the place spoke English. He cleared his throat and tried working off the menu. The appetizer plate, including *tonno* and *uova sode*, turned out to be tuna and hard boiled eggs. He could not convey his desire for butter; the proprietor's children gamely fetched all sorts of seasonings, cheeses, even a bottle of ketchup, but no butter. Martin kept shrugging and staring around at the other patrons, who nodded and smiled back amiably as they continued their chatter, moving their hands as they spoke. Jesse pronounced the acid house wine "delicious," and Martin was glad that at least *vino* was one word he hadn't forgotten. Dessert, when it finally arrived, was a bowl of bruised fruit.

"We'll go out somewhere," Martin proposed, counting out his lire several times and calculating the dollar exchange again and again.

"Does it matter how much that dinner would have cost in New York?" Jesse asked.

"Of course it does," Martin said crossly. "The rate of exchange is a very important figure."

"Why?"

"Because then you know what the real value of your money is."

"But you're paying in their money."

"I know, but I bought *their* money with *my* money. Look at this cash, isn't it silly? All those colored pictures, like some banana republic."

They wandered the streets for more than an hour, trying to find their way back to the hotel. "I'm getting really cold," Martin complained, as they emerged from their sixth or seventh *cul-de-sac*, past what seemed to be the hundredth shuttered-down street of small shops. "Want some coffee?"

"That would be nice," Jesse said, and after some searching they found a small place which had counters filled with cheap candy and a small luncheonette-style bar at one end. One patron was sipping what looked like hot chocolate with whipped cream on top. Martin pointed with excitement. "That looks good. Let's get some, okay?"

They stepped up to the counter. Martin's impatient requests for *chocolatte* confused the proprietress, who produced a glass of chocolate milk, several chocolate bars, and a bottle of chocolate syrup. Martin was feverishly blowing imaginary steam from an imaginary cup when the inspiration dawned on him, and he pointed to the customer whose enticing drink had drawn them to the restaurant initially.

"Sì, sì," said the woman nodding and smiling, "Cioccolato," and in a whisk she'd produced a cup of steaming hot chocolate.

"See?" Martin said. "Nothing to it." He repeated his order, pointing to Jesse, and another cup came from behind the counter.

"Very good," Jesse said. "Now how about that whipped cream?"

"Watch this," said Martin. He turned confidently to the proprietress.

"Signora, mit Schlag."

Jesse burst out laughing. "Does this look like Vienna? Does she look Austrian, or am I missing something?"

The woman shrugged.

"Crema," Martin tried. A small pot of cream was produced. "I see," Martin said, and he made a fast stirring gesture with his hand over the pot of cream.

The woman nodded vigorously, and she disappeared for a moment, then returned with a small plate of ice cream. "Eccolo," she said happily. "Gelato."

"No, no," Martin pointed at the top of his hot chocolate. "Ici, dammit, parlez-vous français? No? What's the word for milk, latte? No, no," he said as she brought out a glass of milk, and the woman nodded again as if to indicate that she understood, but what was his problem? Martin collapsed against the snack bar. "I give up. The Venetian White Castle and I can't even get one of their famous hamburgers."

"Poor Martin," Jesse said sympathetically, sipping her hot chocolate.

"Don't you know any Italian?" he asked her.

"Wait a minute, you're the opera star. Why aren't you doing the ordering?"

"My darling, you're in charge. You love to run the show. Why should I deny you that privilege?"

"For Christ's sake, Jesse, at least you could have helped me out."

"I only know Verdi, not conversational Italian. You want me to order a patricide? How about a trip to a convent?"

"Surely someone in one of those outmoded costume dramas drinks a cup of hot chocolate. Think, girl."

"Hmmmm. I think the Marschallin has some for breakfast, and Octavian is with her. Let's see—" Jesse began to hum some music.

"Well?"

"No good. It's in German. We tried that already."

"I'm being thwarted by forces beyond my control," Martin wailed, and he sipped his cup of chocolate. His face instantly changed from an expression of resignation to one of shocked surprise. He swallowed hard and then accused Jesse, "Why didn't you tell me there wasn't any sugar in it?"

"Do you want to stay here all night while you make that request understood?"

"Aw, what do you think I am? *Dolce, Signora, dolce.*"

The woman brought him a slice of *zuppa inglese.*

Back at their hotel, Jesse read aloud from the guidebook. "Venice has 400 bridges. Do you think we crossed them all tonight?"

"Nearly," Martin said, flexing his feet in their wooly socks.

"I think I'm going to be very ill."

"What's the matter? Too much exercise?"

"Martin, does this sound like what we ordered for dinner? *Calamaretti?*" she asked expressively. Then she stuck out her tongue.

"I don't know. Is that what it was called?"

"I hope not."

"What is it? We had fish, that much I know."

"A fish has fins and gills and swims straight ahead. What do you call the thing with lots of arms that kind of slinks along sideways?"

"Good Lord, Jess. Did we eat that?"

"Squid," she cried. "Romantic Venice, *mit Schlag* and tentacles, through rain and wind and hail." She flopped on the sagging bed and buried her face in the pillows.

"Jesse?" Martin walked over to the bed and put his hand gently on her hair. "Are you crying? I'm sorry it's not turning out too well. Please don't cry."

She lifted her face from the pillows. "I'm not crying; I'm laughing. This is absolutely the funniest twenty-four hours I've ever experienced."

Immensely relieved, Martin flung himself down on the bed and began to make a list. "We'll make it all up—we've still got a day. We can go to the Lido, we can see the Doges' Palace, and have proper hot chocolate at the most expensive café on San Marco Square; and then a surprise stop, and the *Accademia*—you want to see the Titians, don't you?"

"What's the surprise?"

"Oh, just something to remember Venice."

"I'll remember Venice, all right. Martin, sometimes when things don't go exactly as planned they're more memorable than when everything is absolutely perfect. Don't you agree?"

"Not when I'm conducting."

"I don't mean work, though Lord knows who can forget disasters. But what I mean is, life shouldn't be perfect. It should have lumps and bumps, like this adorable mattress of ours. Do you know I love you because you don't speak Italian?"

"If my father had traveled decently and hadn't cut every damn corner, I'd know what to do a bit better. Next time, the *Danieli*. That's what we should have done."

"Are we so rich?"

"Maybe we should act like we are. It's better for the soul. If we'd made our reservations in advance, we wouldn't have been stuck in a hole like this."

"Darling, it's only because of that Italian dental convention that we couldn't get into that nice place on the little canal."

"This is no way to start a marriage," Martin fumed. "They didn't even know who I was."

"Do you want to do everything the way other people do? I thought you hated things for tourists. Besides, our time together is precious. You go to London, I go to San Francisco; you go to New York, I go to Dallas, and so on. It's Venice or nothing."

"No, my love," Martin bent over her and touched her face. "Venice and something."

"What?"

"Tomorrow."

"I certainly hope it isn't squid with whipped cream." Jesse said solemnly.

The surprise was a trip to a jewelry shop on San Marco Square, and a bracelet of handworked gold set with rubies. "Oh, the exquisite thing!" Jesse said when she saw it. Martin handed her the box. "It's yours, my love."

"I can't take it; it's too much. The wedding ring was enough."

"Take it," he urged. "I want you to have it, to remember."

"I've never owned anything this *real* before." She held the bracelet in her hand and watched the stones glint in the sunlight that streamed through the shop windows. "How did you find anything so beautiful?"

"For a beautiful lady, madame," the jeweler said with a small bow.

"Ah *hah*," Jesse pronounced, fastening the clasp of the bracelet on her wrist. "Speaka da English, I see."

The proprietor pointed to a sign: *We Take American Express.*

"Well, you can't expect me to go bargaining in little dark alleyways, can you?" Martin asked. "Happy Venice, Jesse. Happy marriage."

"Just married?" the jeweler said as they embraced, and he counted his piles of lire.

"Sì," Martin said, "and if you don't mind, how does one say 'hot chocolate with whipped cream'?"

TWO

CHAPTER

12

♈

After their elopement to Venice, Jesse
Sondergard Boyd rarely saw her husband. The three
days they spent in that city were the longest stretch of
time they would share for many months. They entered into an era Jesse called their "false marriage," a
heady time for Martin, who loved the illicit quality of
their hotel rendezvous, but one which left Jesse with
a sad feeling of impermanence.

Martin loved hotels. Once married, he took great
delight in pretending that he was having an affair. He
loved to sign registers with false names; his particular
favorite was Mr. and Mrs. George Sand, but he also
favored the surnames Barber, Bloch, and Britten. Desk
clerks always got the names wrong. "Anything we
can do for you, Mr. Sands," they would say, and
Martin would give Jesse a conspiratorial wink and
solemnly reply, "Certainly." He loved the small

cardboard "Do Not Disturb" signs which swung from the door handles of their rooms, and he amassed a collection of the cutest specimens—cherubs and snoring, gray-bearded Rip Van Winkles. Clean sheets, fresh towels in a multitude of sizes, and paper-wrapped glasses were as fascinating to him as artifacts of an archeological dig. They were emblems of another world, the transient life, in which he could assume whatever role he chose. In romantically-lit, Old World style hotels, he was the gentleman with *savoir-faire* who ordered twelve-year-old Scotch from room service and then complained about the lack of sufficient ice. In brightly-lit, modern rooms he was all prim efficiency, checking the cleanliness of the basins and tubs, ordering complete balanced breakfasts with freshly-squeezed orange juice. If they chose the hotel which accomodated other prominent musicians, he would call ahead to request a suite complete with baby grand. Then he would be the *maestro*, wearing dark glasses, his trench coat over his shoulders, a copy of the *Wall Street Journal* outside his door each morning.

Jesse observed all of this with some amusement, aware that if she took it seriously she might begin to cry. Martin was too much in love with the disarray of their lives, their comings and goings and almost accidental collisions. She suspected that Nicholas Kogan arranged their bookings with an eye to keeping them apart, but if she tried to discuss her suspicions with Martin, he bridled at her criticism of the man he called "my one true friend."

Once she spoke up bravely and asked Martin why they couldn't have more time together, why Kogan couldn't be instructed to handle their tours differently. She hated the way she sounded, like a jealous, possessive nag.

"Jess, he's doing us a big favor by handling us both," Martin replied patiently. "Just keep that in mind when you get annoyed."

"But darling, we're making him a great deal of money."

"He has money of his own. He doesn't do this for financial reasons."

"Then why does he do it?" she asked. "It can't be pleasure. He always looks so sour."

Martin ignored her. He stood in front of the full-length mirror in their hotel bedroom, clad only in his underwear, waving his baton in the air. "Shall I grow a mustache?" he asked her. "Would that make me look older?"

"No, I'll grow one," Jesse said, but Martin made no comment. He wasn't listening to her. "Martin," she persisted, "why does he dislike me?"

Martin sighed. "So we're back to that one again. Jesse, no one dislikes you. Didn't Hoffberg write 'it's impossible not to like Miss Sondergard'?"

"Your manager doesn't like me one bit."

Martin waved his baton and smiled at his image. "He's your manager too. He likes you enough to get you *La Scala* in '63. You want your ex-Nazi back?"

"He's not a Nazi. He discovered me."

"How about a beard?" Martin asked.

"You're impossible," Jesse sulked. "I want a home of our own."

"Now don't be unreasonable, darling. We don't need one right now. We aren't in one place for more than five minutes at a time."

"But I don't like staying with the Ruddingers any more. When you're not in the city I feel I have to go back there, and I'm much too old to play the obedient child. I'm a married woman. Besides, they feed me too much. They think I'm too skinny to sing opera. And of course you wouldn't deign to stay at the Ruddingers; so when you're here, we go to hotels. I hate hotels."

"I like hotels," Martin said, striding over to the desk and leafing through one of his music scores. "They make me feel clean and well cared for. I'm not the neatest individual in the world."

"You needn't point out your failings to me," Jesse said dryly. "I do live with you, in a manner of speaking. Martin, we need our own home."

"When we have more time together, we'll see. We're building our careers now, and that means traveling. Surely you realize *that*," he added prissily.

"But what if we performed together? We could do one tour as husband and wife," Jesse began to get excited. "Why not? Everyone wants to know about the great musical marriage. It would be ideal."

"I'm not an accompanist," Martin said flatly.

"But conducting an orchestra—surely you wouldn't feel you were accompanying. You appear with guest artists all the time. Why not me?"

"It won't do, Jesse. Now drop it."

"I won't until you give me a good reason why not," she insisted stubbornly. Suddenly she didn't want to tour with Martin—she didn't even want to be with him. He was infuriating. But she wasn't going to allow him to refuse so easily.

"It isn't fitting," he said finally, through gritted teeth.

"Bull."

"I don't want to. That should be enough."

"Did Kogan tell you not to?"

"If you want to think that's the answer, fine. You think it."

She rose up from the bed and escaped into the bathroom, closing the door firmly and turning the lock. Then she sat on the toilet lid. There was no way to change anything unless one of them spoke to Kogan, or unless they got an apartment. She was convinced that their own apartment would turn Martin into a kind of homing pigeon, a sure nester who would want to spend more time with her in their own place. It would make them feel more married, more of a couple, and less a convenience between performances. Illicit-style hotel encounters held no charm for her; she had been brought up in a house, and now she wanted one of her own. The next time she raised the issue she would make certain that Martin wasn't in one of his queer, insular, *me-only* moods. And, if necessary, she would speak to Kogan herself; even though Kogan didn't like her and wanted no part of her career or her person.

Several months later, in early spring, they decided to spend a free afternoon together on a picnic in Central Park. For once they believed they were lucky with the weather. It was warm, but not unpleasantly so; and, since it was still early in the season, many of the local insects had not yet made their appearance. Jesse had ordered a fancy lunch from a French restaurant. It came packed in a wicker hamper with a checked cloth, wine glasses, cutlery, and china. "Fancy-*shmancy*," Martin said, yanking out the long loaf of bread and tearing off a chunk.

"Hold it." Jesse rapped his hand with a sausage. "Wait till I get it all unpacked." There were olives, little pickles, cold chicken with a lemon glaze, bread, quiche, an eggplant salad, three kinds of cheese, and ripe pears. The wine was white and chilled; Martin drank most of the bottle. Jesse carefully sipped at her single glassful and waited for her husband to mellow.

They lay back on the cloth and stared at the sky.

"Are you properly pickled yet?" Jesse asked.

"Am I what? Let's go back to the hotel," he suggested suddenly.

"Why? It's so pleasant here."

"The ground is lumpy."

"Like our *pensione* bed in Venice."

"That was awful, wasn't it."

"Let's stay a little longer. We never seem to get outside much. It's always rehearsals, performances, cocktails, dinners—ugh!"

"Comes with the package," Martin said.

"When we have our own home, I'll never give such boring parties."

"You will. It's inevitable."

"I'll have my own place?"

"You'll give boring parties."

"I really want a home so badly," she said, trying to sound light and amusing.

"Why?"

"Martin, how can you be so insensitive? Since my parents died, I've always lived in other people's houses—a permanent guest. If it weren't for the kindness of the Ruddingers, I'd have had no place to go."

"Vell, I vouldn't vant you should feel you have no home."

"Goon," she said, punching him in the side. He fell back on the blanket and covered his face with his hands.

"Don't hit me in the nose—please—anywhere but the nose!"

"Why are you so unkind about them? I think it's

because you're a total snob, a Boston snoot. I suppose it's very convenient you married an orphan. I'd hate to have seen what you would have said about Professor and Mrs. Klaus Sondergard."

"Now that's unfair, Jess, and you know it."

"You're the one who's unfair," she said in exasperation. She lay back on the blanket, furious at his unkindness. He couldn't appreciate her position. The Ruddingers were almost parents to her, and she owed everything to them. Perhaps if Martin understood that better. . . She turned toward him and touched his arm.

"Martin," she began.

"Mmmmmm?" he murmured, licking his lips, his eyes half-closed. He looked comfortable and content. "I'm listening."

"It's nothing," she replied. She watched the clouds gathering overhead and wondered if it would rain. Whenever they were together, it seemed to rain. She remembered that in Germany, where the skies should have been dark and gloomy, there was sunshine everywhere, birds twittering, flowers growing up amid the ruins.

"When I was in Cologne," she said aloud, "I met a young conductor, a boy from Baltimore." She knew that Martin always displayed high interest in her former loves.

As if on cue, he raised his head and stared at her. "What? Yet another figure from the past?"

"This was different, not like the others."

"Why—he wasn't married?"

"As a matter of fact, he wasn't. But it was another kind of romance. Michael introduced me to lieder. I'd been studying opera all along, learning all these arias which meant very little to me, and he brought me songs by Richard Strauss. Strauss was still alive then. Imagine! Michael helped me. We studied the words and music together, and he got me to see that songs can express any number of emotions in a small but extremely potent way. He taught me that it can be the same even in grand opera, which I had found so intimidating. He made me aware of how to make a song *live*, that there can be a whole universe in one song. We'd sit in this haunted old run-down café just around the corner from streets of pure rubble, nothing but bricks, boards, and holes in the ground. But it didn't matter—we were in another world."

"Hah," Martin grunted. "Some other world. Look at what they'd done over there."

"But the boy was Jewish. He knew, and he was still there. I told him how the Ruddingers felt, that they held everyone responsible; not just Hitler, but Wagner, Strauss, even Schubert and Bach. So he took me to Dachau, to show me what had happened. He said everything would have to be absorbed, that this terrible tragedy would have to be part of our lives, part of the music we were making. That's when I realized that the Ruddingers were wrong to want to keep me away.

"I saw everything there; most of the evidence hadn't been moved. There were piles of shoes— terrible, huge mountains of them in all different sizes. We walked in the sun in a big open field where the grass and wild flowers had begun to grow back, and Michael told me about the camp orchestras that were forced to play. Suddenly, this mixed-up picture came into my mind of Mr. Ruddinger, one of the only Jewish people I had known, sitting at a piano in that open field, playing my father's favorite Beethoven.

The music was so beautiful; I thought I'd never heard
anything so exquisite before. I wondered if it would
be possible to sing that way. The pain and death
made me want to sing. Isn't that mad? Isn't that the
strangest thing you ever heard?"

"Mighty peculiar," said Martin in a strange, light
tone of voice.

"Are you making fun of me?" Jesse drew away
from him, shocked at his reaction.

"Well, you've got to admit those crazy visions
don't have a hell of a lot to do with being an artist.
Either you have it or you don't, and then you study
like mad and work until you drop; and then maybe,
just maybe, you get a fraction of what you want."

"But I'm not speaking of that side of it. I'm talking about what you feel when you create music, when
you *make* music."

"What you feel? What I feel is that the music better sound right or I'll break the orchestra's arms."

"How is it that you take your problems with your
tightwad father incredibly seriously, that your studi-
ous little cloistered childhood is now legend, sac-
rosanct, while the things that happened to me are just
peculiar?" Furious at his indifference, Jesse began to
stuff plates and food back into the hamper. She
forced the lid down and the wicker cracked.

"Are we going?" Martin said ironically.

"You never change, do you? The world should
come to your door, make a local stop just for you,
then turn into an express for everyone else."

"Aw, Jess, cut it out. Of course I respect what
you say."

"The hell you do."

"I do, really. I believe you."

"It isn't a matter of belief," she insisted frantically. "It's a matter of the person closest to you, the one person who's supposed to care about important things—"

"But I do care; I care about your career. You know I think you're terrific. It's just that when it comes to music, well, there's just so much romanticizing you can do about it and then the real parts take over—the studying, the learning, the practice."

"Forget it," Jesse said wearily. "Forget I ever mentioned anything."

"Why are you so angry?" Martin asked innocently.

"From now on, if I care to do anything, I'll do it myself. Let's go. It's clouding over; I think it's going to rain."

"I'm sorry if you thought I wasn't listening," said Martin as they folded up the cloth.

"I broke the hamper."

"It doesn't matter. Look, what would you like to do? Want to eat at that Italian place?"

"I want us to have a home, Martin. I want us to have a life together."

"Jesus, we got married, didn't we?"

"Yes, we're married."

"And do I hand you that *music is my mistress* garbage? Do I? Come on, tell me the truth. Are you smiling, just a little? Are you pretending you're still mad? Oh, look at that, audiences—a little smile is just sneaking through."

"Okay, big shot. Take me to dinner tonight."

"Sure thing. And if you want a place so much, we'll just have to start looking for one."

"We will?" Jesse dropped the hamper and threw

her arms around Martin. "Oh, that's marvelous! I'll buy all the papers tonight. We can read the ads after dinner. Believe me, you won't regret this decision for a minute."

"I may not regret it, but you might if we don't hire a cleaning lady," he said as he peeled himself from Jesse's grasp and picked up the hamper.

"I'm sorry you'll miss your hotels. Maybe we can steal some towels and ashtrays to decorate—make you feel right at home."

"Jesse," Martin wailed. "I forgot. We're supposed to meet Kogan for dinner tonight."

"Are you sure?"

"How could we forget? He's got those new contracts for me, too. Why didn't you remember?"

"I won't go. I'm not in the mood for our manager just now," Jesse said quietly. "I'll just stay home and read the apartment ads."

"Jess, I'm sorry. Why don't you come?"

"I can't abide your snide remarks, the pair of you, when we have one of our evenings out."

"We always go to great places."

"Yes, and he never eats. He makes me feel like a stevedore for ordering a full dinner."

"Look, this apartment thing can be your project, if you like. I'll give you *carte blanche*. Whatever you come up with is okay with me. And if you want to skip tonight, that's okay. I'll get back as soon as I can," Martin said, looking relieved.

"Sure, Martin."

"Come on. If we hurry we can get a taxi. I've got to call Kogan, and shave and shower and change. Jesse, leave all that garbage. Let someone else pick it up!"

And with that, the sky opened up and the rain

poured down, soaking the scraps of bread, the napkins, and the paper wrappings which were strewn
about on the ground. Jesse stared sadly at the mess,
then shrugged her shoulders and slowly followed her
husband down the hill toward the rain-slicked road
where the yellow cabs stood, waiting for the traffic
light to turn green.

CHAPTER

13

As Martin's fame and following grew, Jesse saw a good deal more of Nicholas Kogan than she might have wished. At times Kogan was more body-guard than manager, standing at the dressing room door and keeping out undesirables. Sometimes Jesse thought he might bar her entry as well, but he merely gave her an icy stare and allowed her to pass without comment.

Martin's devotees now included many women who openly invited him out for drinks, dinner, or to private parties at their apartments. They were well-dressed women—women in fashionable new clothes, evening gowns with long white gloves, smart black suits, and ropes of pearls gleaming expensively. Jesse always noticed their shoes, which looked as if they had never been worn. She wondered if they wore each pair of shoes only once, and might have asked one of them if she'd had the opportunity. As it was, she retreated to a corner of the room and waited until someone recognized her, causing a flutter of embarrassment among the women (but not much) as someone pointed out the conductor's wife. The moment of recognition was sometimes Jesse's sole amusement, for she found these evenings incredibly tedious.

Sometimes there were post-concert suppers in one of the popular restaurants, usually an unpretentious ethnic place with mismatched silverware and delicious food. Kogan would call ahead and arrange for a long table in the back, to which the critics, courtesans, and patrons would repair after the dressing room niceties had concluded. Jesse was remanded to Kogan's care on these nights. They would sit together at the foot of the table, he picking at his food and she trying to make polite small talk.

"I think I've finally found us an apartment," Jesse told Kogan at the supper following Martin's appearance as guest conductor with the Boston Symphony at Carnegie Hall.

"Indeed?" Kogan said, his face not changing one bit.

"I think even you might approve. It's got a grand view of the park, it's not terribly expensive, and we can each have our own room for practicing."

"Twin pianos, eh?" Kogan parried, making a great show of slicing his veal, but not eating a bite. His eyes were on the other end of the table, where Martin courted two female admirers, both great patrons of his home-town symphony and both in a position to boost Martin's career should the orchestra decide a new conductor was in order.

"I think it will make a great difference for all of us when we have a proper place to live," Jesse said pointedly. "Martin hasn't had a real home in years. And frankly, I couldn't care less if I never see another hotel in my life."

"There will always be hotels in your stars, dear Jesse, as long as you desire an international career."

"That's different. Engagements always come to an end."

"So do marriages," Kogan observed icily.

Jesse took a long drink of Scotch to dull the pain of his remark, then took a deep breath and said, "Why is it you dislike me so much?"

"I?" he said, toying with the veal as if he were tormenting a small creature before stabbing it to death. "I dislike no one in particular."

"I believe you don't like me at all," she continued bravely. "If it weren't for Martin, you'd have nothing to do with me."

"That may well be, but it does not affect our relationship. We are tied together in a firm knot of business ventures."

"Come off your horse, Kogan; get it out once and for all. Come on." She waved her empty glass at the waiter and indicated she wanted more.

Kogan watched her over his plate of untouched food. "Do you find it necessary to seduce everyone? Let's just say that I am somewhat immune to your varied charms."

She put down her empty glass and looked him straight in the eye. "Kogan, I think you stink."

"Don't be childish," he said prissily.

The waiter put down a fresh Scotch. Jesse gulped most of it hurriedly and patted at her mouth with her napkin. Her stomach burned and her head began to spin. She was angry and, quite possibly, very drunk. "I think I'm going to be sick," she said quietly.

"Then let us pray it's the liquor and not the honesty," Kogan said as he helped her to her feet. "Let's get you outside."

He nodded and murmured greetings along the length of the table as he steered her toward the front of the restaurant. They moved quickly past Martin, who didn't seem to notice their exit. Kogan led her past the empty bar, out the door, and up the short flight of steps. He released her with a light push, as if she were a trained bird about to embark on a lengthy homing journey. She almost stumbled, but caught herself and took in deep gulps of night air, throwing her arms up over her head. "My mother always said to raise your arms when you feel sick. Or is that for hiccups?" She then hiccuped quite loudly, and laughed. "I guess it causes hiccups."

"Feeling better, I see," Kogan observed. "We'll go back now."

"No, wait." Jesse touched his sleeve. She could see that he wanted to withdraw his arm instantly. She took her hand away. "You can tell me now."

"You're not the sort of person to cringe from the truth, are you?" he said, examining her closely. "I will say that for you. Still, I don't believe there's any love lost on your side either."

"We have to live with each other." She stared back boldly at him. He was a hard one, a hard person. But she wasn't afraid of him. Many things, but not afraid. "You're a hard man, Kogan. But Martin needs you. He needs me, too. We're the only ones who can save him from becoming a total ass. You don't have to comment on that if you don't want to. I know how loyal you are to him, as he is to you. I guess that someday I'd like someone to be as loyal toward me."

Kogan stared at her with calculating, assessing eyes. "I will say this for you. I think you face facts more realistically than he does. You're tougher than you think, Jesse Sondergard. Shall we strike a bargain? I will be truthful with you if you will be with me. We don't have to like each other but at least we can arrange to have some good faith between us."

"It's a deal," she said, extending her hand. He hesitated, then took it. His palm was warm and dry, very comforting, somehow; but he withdrew his hand quickly. Her skin felt alive where he had touched her. "Once in a while you can hold my head when I drink too much," she joked.

"I trust not too often," he said. "Shall we return to the banquet?"

"You go. I want to stay out in the air a bit more."

"As you wish," he shrugged. Was she imagining it or did he look at her more kindly? She watched him as he walked back into the restaurant. Never a button undone or a hair out of place. Fancy being so set, so utterly complete. *The poor man,* she decided. *Here I am trying to make him into my good friend when he wants no part of such a relationship.* She grabbed the rail by the restaurant's entrance and swung herself up to perch on the top bar. But he was such a smart man. Was she, as he had observed, trying to seduce everyone? Seduce was such an unkind word. It implied so many nasty things. And she was a married woman. Very married, in spite of Martin's traveling and her schedule and those women in the dressing room. She certainly didn't want to seduce Kogan. But she did want to be his friend. She needed a friend. "I have no real friends," she said aloud, testing the sound of it.

How true. Her parents, Sanford Donnelly, Madame Liebling, Michael the young conductor, her rich, married suitor—they were all far away, or dead. The only people she had left were the Ruddingers; and Martin's cool disdain had made meetings with them awkward. With Martin back in town so much, she had avoided seeing them lately. What a fool she'd been to lock out the only friends she had in the world! She would call them right away and make a date. Excited and eager, she ran back into the restaurant, but noted with dismay that it was one A. M. The call would have to wait until morning. Still, she felt a sense of triumph. She did have someone after all; she wasn't so alone. And she'd see them, with or without Martin's approval.

"Arnold, Arnold," Mrs. Ruddinger called excitedly as Jesse waited on the phone. "It's Jesse! Oh my dear, I'm so glad to hear from you. We weren't sure where to send a letter and we didn't want to disturb you now. You must be so busy."

"I should have called much sooner, really. I apologize."

"Don't be silly. We see how busy the pair of you are. Won't you come here for dinner?"

"No, I can't. I have only the afternoon free. I'm flying to London quite early in the morning."

"London—my goodness! Did you hear, Arnold? We're so proud of you. How happy you must be. Come, we'll all go out for lunch together."

"Martin's sleeping now. He had a performance last night; I'm not sure if he'll come," Jesse explained, quite certain that he wouldn't want to come.

Mrs. Ruddinger mentioned a small restaurant near their apartment building, and asked if Jesse would mind if they went to a nearby museum after lunch. "Just for a short visit. The show will soon

close, and we get out so rarely these days. Arnold is
so anxious to see it, but he doesn't want to go without me."

"Is anything wrong?"

"Nothing, my dear; nothing's wrong."

"Of course we'll go—we'll do whatever you like.
Just being with you is all I want."

"And bring your nice husband, if he is free."

Martin was not being particularly nice at all. "I
want to sleep," he growled at Jesse. "They're your
friends. You go."

"They just happen to be my only friends, as a
matter of fact. Look, you can skip the lunch part. Just
meet us at the museum, please?"

He groaned and stuck his head under a pillow.

Mr. Ruddinger walked a bit more shakily with his
cane. Mrs. Ruddinger had grown plumper, and she
had unusual high color in her cheeks. But otherwise
they seemed much the same as when Jesse had seen
them last.

They were dressed in their best out-on-the-town
finery. Mrs. Ruddinger wore her little fur piece with
the head and claws still dangling, and a hat with a little veil. Mr. Ruddinger, dapper as always, was in a
light suit and a straw hat. A fresh handkerchief was
tucked into his jacket pocket and he smelled of his
favorite after shave lotion. Jesse remembered dressing
for dinner in their house, the meals served on silver
trays and each course accompanied by a different
wine. She had grown huge during the time she lived
with them, plump and content, and Mr. Ruddinger
had approved. "Now you look like singer," he'd said.

Greeting her warmly, he looked her up and
down. "Lost weight," he pronounced. "That gentleman friend not feeding you right?"

"Idiot, he's her husband," Mrs. Ruddinger said sharply.

"Oh yes, yes." They linked arms and walked down the street, a Ruddinger on either side of Jesse. She was a head taller than both and felt like an anchor, keeping their frail forms from blowing away in the gusty wind. Mr. Ruddinger gripped his hat. "This is some day," he exulted.

They took Jesse to their favorite restaurant, a Hungarian place that served substantial, steamy meals of thick meats, cabbage, dark bread, and thoroughly cooked vegetables. Jesse ordered a salad, and Mr. Ruddinger wrinkled his nose at her. "Singers need the weight; pushes out the voice better. Eat for your strength."

"Arnold, shush. We want to know all about the career, the marriage, the husband. Tell us, please."

Jesse tried to talk, but she was bombarded by a constant stream of questions. What had she been appearing in recently? What would she sing in London? Was that the same famous conductor they knew, working on her opera? Where would she and Martin live? Were they going to settle in the city? Jesse told them about the apartment she'd found and the Ruddingers approved of the location. "I know the building; Central Park West—it's a good neighborhood," Mrs. Ruddinger nodded.

"But watch the side streets," Mr. Ruddinger cautioned, shaking his head as he ate his sweet and sour cabbage. "Nogoodniks all around."

"You two are my only family," Jesse said suddenly.

"Ah," Mrs. Ruddinger clapped her hands with delight. "We're so glad to see you. Don't be such a stranger to us."

The waiters, who knew the Ruddingers quite well, hovered close and brought more dishes and baskets of bread. Jesse ate a good deal more than she wanted, to please Mr. Ruddinger, and Mrs. Ruddinger's face grew even redder as she ate her favorite roast duck. They continued to talk over the strudel and coffee until Mr. Ruddinger peered at his watch and informed them that it was time to take in the museum.

"Whew, I need this exercise," Mrs. Ruddinger said as they strolled out of the restaurant.

"Too hot for furs, I told her," Mr. Ruddinger said to Jesse. "You'll be quite interested to see this show," he gestured with his cane as they approached the entrance.

The placard outside the museum read, *Inspired by the Holocaust: Paintings and Sculpture.* Jesse hesitated slightly, then moved up the steps. The Ruddingers moved eagerly; their faces bore an expression of anticipatory remorse. They wanted to be reminded; they wanted no reason to forget. They waited solemnly in line to pay admission, not saying a word.

The first objects in the show were simple stone monuments, stark and geometric, tragic only in their association with the theme of the exhibit. They were, like all modern war memorials, anonymous and cool.

The other rooms contained more graphic statements—canvases lit with fire, ringed with barbed wire, alive with reaching hands. Mrs. Ruddinger said something in Yiddish. Jesse stood silently between her friends, forcing herself to study the paintings. Most were too emotional to be great works of art. Perhaps with time, with more detachment, there could be greatness. Jesse recalled Martin's criticism of her singing, and Kogan's remark about her seducing everyone. She knew she was too emotional in her art as well. The Ruddingers had once mentioned that the Nazis forbade the Jews to play Aryan music: Beethoven, Schubert, Bach. Music unplayed—how much more potent that idea was than all of the music she had ever heard.

The three of them moved toward a doorway marked by an arrow. They parted a blackout curtain to enter a dank, unlit room. As their eyes grew accustomed to the darkness, they hobbled across a broken stone floor. There was a low concrete step in one corner on which rested a small metal ball. The room was cold and the brick floor was cracked, showing dirt beneath. Jesse closed her eyes, chilled to the bone. The room was an evocation of a death camp, perhaps from a child's-eye view. The floor underfoot, the blackness, the terrible unreality closed in on her, and she clenched her fists tightly. Where was Martin? Why did he leave her alone so much? The children had gone to slaughter alone, many without their mothers or sisters and brothers. She could never have done that, could never have faced anything so hideous all by herself. Everyone was so much braver than she!

The Ruddingers moved haltingly toward what seemed to be an exit, but it turned out instead to be a false passageway with a sheet of copper-colored metal hung at the end. Mrs. Ruddinger gasped and they backed into the brightly lit gallery once more. Jesse smiled with relief, then she saw that Mrs. Ruddinger's face was crimson. The woman was gasping for air.

"Eva," Mr. Ruddinger called as his wife collapsed on the floor. Someone screamed, and the ladies on the guided tour crowded around curiously as Mr. Ruddinger knelt clumsily and bent over his wife.

Jesse was paralyzed with terror. A museum guard pushed the crowd back. "Air," he called, "give her air." Jesse ordered herself not to faint. The museum guard elevated Mrs. Ruddinger's head and tried to give her a paper cup of water. Someone fanned her with a museum brochure. Mr. Ruddinger mechanically patted his wife's hand. "Eva, Eva," he said over and over.

After what seemed like a long time, two attendants in white arrived and took Mrs. Ruddinger away on a stretcher. Jesse followed Mr. Ruddinger out the front door. The museum steps were crowded with onlookers. Jesse saw Martin at the edge of the crowd and called to him, but he didn't hear her. She helped Mr. Ruddinger climb into the back of the ambulance. "Shall I come?" she said, but the attendants pushed her away and closed the back door. Then they took off, the siren resuming its interrupted wail, moving down the street and through the traffic.

Martin shifted through the lingering crowd and moved up to Jesse. "Pardon, pardon," she heard him repeat. "Hi," he said. "Where are they?"

"You were right," she said.

"What?"

"You and Kogan. You're both right. Now there isn't anyone left."

"Jesse, what's going on? That ambulance—that thing that was here—was that them?" he said in astonishment.

She nodded. "The wife."

"Is she dead?" he asked in hushed tones.

She shrugged lifelessly. "You're all I have left now." She moved toward him but did not touch him.

He put his arm around her. "There, there," he said mechanically. "There, there."

CHAPTER

14

ℜ

The cover of *Photoplay Magazine:*
WHO IS MARTIN BOYD'S SECRET SWEETHEART?
Details Inside.

New swoon-conductor-star Martin Boyd shown leaving New York's *21 Club* after dining with starlet Gerrie
Belle. Mr. Boyd's wife, a well-known opera star, was
in Europe at the time.

"What is this shit?" Jesse said as she threw the
magazine aside.
"You know what trash they print; it doesn't mean
a thing," Martin said.
"Kogan, what is he doing behind my back?" Jesse
asked, thus neatly drawing me into their latest argument. Ever since they'd moved into their new apartment, they'd been doing their own *Private Lives* bit.

"Leave him out of this." Martin retrieved the magazine and stared at the photograph. "At least they spelled my name right. Say—her chest looks enormous! They must have airbrushed in at least three inches."

"Marvelous publicity right before you're going to the White House to play at Jackie's posh little party. Those Catholics really love a little adultery," Jesse hit back.

"I was never at 21 with her. They took the picture outside the stage door. Look, there's the alley wall right off the exit. She came backstage to tell me how much she liked my Beethoven."

"Everyone loves your Beethoven; we all know that," Jesse remarked.

After three years of marriage, their mechanical fighting was all they seemed to share. That, and their new, enormous apartment. The hotel living, with its chambermaids, room service, and impermanence had been exchanged for the security (and dullness) of Home. They were two disorganized people trying to create order out of incredible chaos. Their famous *His* and *Hers* music rooms (pictured in *Life* Magazine) were in reality littered with coffee cups, unopened mail, and stacks of newspapers. Publicly, Martin continued to play the peacock, but their home went more with his old black coat than with his stylish new fur.

Home didn't seem to be where his heart was, either. Swarms of women were constantly at his side. I never knew if he was flitting from bed to bed; I never asked and he never told me. Martin was a late bloomer, the boy who discovered his charm several beats after his contemporaries, and he quickly made up for lost time. Then, too, the number of women seemed to increase in direct correlation to the growing momentum of his wife's career. When Jesse triumphed, Martin gathered his female followers more closely to his side as if they could provide some sort of bulwark for his pride; living proof of his potency and desirability, a fence of caryatids to keep out the demons of envy. There was plenty of professional jealousy, just as I had predicted.

I gathered up the contracts I had brought for them to sign. "Fight on your own time, darlings. I'm going."

"No," Martin insisted.

"Stay, Kogan. You're on his side. He needs moral support." Jesse stood with her back to us, staring out at the park. Her body was perfectly still; she always had control over herself. I had never seen her cry, not even when she was told that the Ruddingers had died, one soon after the other. She was quite a stoic, this girl.

There wasn't much satisfaction for me in seeing my dire predictions for their marriage come true. Ah, if the *Life* subscribers could see them now! I clapped my hands and called them to attention. "Cease these current maneuvers, for we must lay out '64 and '65 immediately, or we don't work."

Martin sullenly turned a silk cushion in his hands. Jesse remained glued to her window. "Good. Jesse, I'll go over yours first." She listened, as usual, without comment.

Frankly, though I was still not comfortable around Jesse, I was as loyal to her career as I was to Martin's. I never tried to convince her of that, however, for I knew she would merely shrug her shoulders. We kept a good distance from each other.

Martin was just the opposite. He yelled and punched pillows and flung himself about, protesting concert halls, program suggestions, and accomodations. He wanted splashy tours on a schedule that would have placed him thousands of miles away from his next appearance. "I can do it," he insisted. "I've kept to tough schedules before."

"I daresay we've seen some of the results," I said, as close to criticizing him as I dared. "The boy wonder is less the boy. No one expects you to have those prodigious energies anymore. You won't be much of a wonder if you're exhausted."

"They do expect me to be invincible," he gestured wildly at the pile of magazines on the floor. "It's all in there; it's part of my image."

"Your image doesn't hold your baton, dear boy."

He fussed a great deal, but finally accepted a revised version of my original plan.

"By the way," I drew a letter from my briefcase, "this arrived yesterday. I wouldn't bother you with it, except Wurtzberg called me on the same matter proposing a possible joint appearance. I told him I'd ask you."

"What's this about?" Martin creased his brow. He loved playing business tycoon, though his judgment on most practical matters was poor.

"He's interested in a little girl, a prodigy who is rumored to play the piano like a shrunken Rubinstein. I hate that sort of thing. There's something so freakish about adults accompanying children. I'm not sure you should do it."

"Let me see," Martin waved his hand.

"It's not the best idea." Children and dogs are notorious scene-stealers.

He grabbed the letter and put on his reading glasses. "Gabrielle Klee? Someone told me she was good."

"Just think about it." I knew it would soon be buried in the piles of mail and clippings in *his* music room. "Goodbye Jesse," I called. She lifted a languid hand and waved backward at me.

"I'll call tomorrow," I said automatically, but neither one was listening.

I slammed their apartment door shut and took a deep breath. I'd take blind nuns tatting lace any day. The Boyds were playing their third-rate Noel Coward and I, as usual, was their favorite audience. Next time I must remember the foil-wrapped mints and the opera glasses.

CHAPTER

15

♈

I cannot say when I noticed there was something wrong with Jesse; so it came as a surprise to me when she asked me for my doctor's name. I had stopped by to see Martin, but she was in the apartment alone. As I looked at her after she made her request, she suddenly seemed drawn and pale. Without her customary theatrical makeup, her skin had an unfamiliar waxy quality. The discovery startled me.

"I get so tired," she rubbed her eyes. "All this traveling."

"Shall I trim down the schedule a bit?" Her appearance was alarming, and I accused myself of hideous neglect. I had taken a girl as healthy as a horse and worn her down. Shame on me. "We can eliminate one of those benefits. I'm sure we'll become known as 'those bastards who don't want to save the children,' but I'd rather we not sacrifice your health."

"No, it's just something dumb—anemia, something silly."

"Call Dr. Nininger. And go fix yourself something to eat."

I should have known there was trouble when she said she wasn't hungry. Ordinarily she even finished the food on my plate.

"When is Martin going away? Isn't it soon? I lost the schedule." Her voice drifted off.

"Tomorrow," I replied. "He's going to Scotland." Martin hadn't said a word to me about Jesse's health. A fine pair of egotists she had watching over her!

I heard nothing more of her condition for a week. Then Jesse's accompanist, Eric Oldfield, collared me at a dinner party.

"What have you done to my girl," he said accusingly. "She's run ragged."

"I've sent her to my physician," I said.

"We know it's not Martin," he remarked coyly.

I was disgusted, as I usually am, by people who shoehorn sex into every conversation. I turned my attention toward the platter of stuffed mushrooms which had been shoved between us.

"You ought to take better care of her," he said sharply. "She's looking rather peaked."

Peaked is a word that conjures up barn-raisings in the wilderness. But it also aroused my concern, and I decided that my telephone calls were not sufficient. I would go around to see for myself just how peaked she was.

She came to the door very slowly. I stood in the hall peering about, counting the painted *belles dames* curtsying across the apartment hall wallpaper in flocked splendor. It was ugly and it depressed me, as cheap imitations always do. When the apartment door opened, I saw that Jesse was wearing a robe. "Excuse me," I backed away. "You were resting."

"Please," she said, holding the door wide for me, and the sound of her word hung in the air. She rarely asked anything of me. "I'd like it if you came in."

The air in the apartment was musty and dry. I went to a window and raised the shade. "Why are you locked in your tower, Rapunzel? It's such a lovely day. Would you care to go for a walk?"

I noticed that she dragged her steps slightly. Her face looked a bit less tired, though. Perhaps rest was all she needed.

"I'm feeling better. I know I don't look it dressed in this old thing, but the infection is clearing up."

"What infection?"

"Didn't I tell you? Your doctor sent me to another doctor, a specialist who said I have a bug in my bladder and gave me pills to take. He said it could make anyone very tired. But I am feeling better," she insisted.

As she spoke, I glanced around the living room and saw no sign of activity: no television drawn up to a comfortable chair, no books or magazines lying open; merely a half-filled coffee mug and the bottle of pills atop the coffee table. "What have you been doing, locked in here all day?"

"Working. Going over scores. I like to study the whole opera." She giggled. "Jon Danzig was furious with me when we did *Nozze* in Chicago. He said I knew his part better than he did. And do you know what? He was right."

"But my very own dear, don't you do anything that isn't musical? Don't you ever read a book, or watch one of those intolerable family comedy shows on TV, or see a play?"

"I'm not interested."

"Well, we'll see how interested we can make you. Put on something nice and we'll take a stroll."

She hesitated.

"We will not mention music or bookings or operas. This is strictly entertainment. Call it a short vacation, if you like."

"Don't let them see," she said. "Once they find out you're a sucker for charity cases, you'll have to buy shoelaces and pencils at every corner."

"Or lace from nuns," I added.

"What nuns?" she said as she walked toward the bedroom. Her gait was better, even sprightly. She seemed much like the old Jesse. I was quite relieved. "I always thought they used little orphan girls," she said. "Like me."

"You," I called out as she closed the door, "do not fit the description."

"I'm an orphan," came the muffled reply.

"That may be," I said, helping myself to a glass of sherry. "But you are certainly no little girl."

The people on Fifth Avenue stared at Jesse as we walked by. At first I thought it was recognition, for she made quite a figure with her Russian-style fur hat and boots. In fact, the hat was genuinely Russian, the gift of a Soviet diplomat who had attended one of her concerts in London.

But as we passed more people, I saw that it was her magnetism, the force of her presence which drew glances. Surely I would never have given her a second look, for I am immune to passing fancies. But she was an exotic, exciting figure.

I marched her into Doubleday's and proceeded to load her arms with books—handsome, oversized art books, biographies, best sellers. "What are you doing?" she said as a clerk scrambled to grab the overflow slipping from her grasp.

"Getting you an education." I ran my hand across the shelf. "Of course you've never read *Lolita*. It might be just the thing. And here, take Philip Roth. Do you know any Jews beside Bernstein? Katherine Anne Porter, no; Iris Murdoch, yes. Where do you hide literature which is more than fifteen minutes old?" I asked the manager.

"We carry the Modern Library editions," the gentleman said.

"'Tis better than nothing," I pulled Jesse by the arm. "Here—Tolstoy, Thackeray, James. These are books about very interesting women—in fact, the only kind I can abide. They are larger than life, but safe— safe on the printed page."

"And they can't get to you," Jesse said, blowing the fur out of her eyes.

"Precisely."

"Kogan, that's very sad."

"No it isn't. Some do not," I replied. But she was not yet a reader.

We ate lunch in Schrafft's.

Jesse didn't want to go in. "Martin says Schrafft's is decadent and geriatric."

"What? That's a *non sequitur*."

"It is?"

"Jesse, you are an ignoramus. They have marvelous cheese-bread and wood panelling on the walls. You shall try their chocolate sundae."

I lectured her as we ate our skinny sandwiches. "Someday they won't be here anymore, and then you'd have been sorry you didn't come. You're used to your husband's taste in pastrami, all those delicatessens with the sauerkraut sitting in communal metal bowls. *Ugh.*"

Jesse spooned up her sundae eagerly and, as I watched her, I realized that I was enjoying my afternoon. I had not planned to like it; my time with Jesse was merely a gesture. But I was actually having fun. Had I taken a sheltered orphan beneath my wing? Was I really Daddy Warbucks?

I bought Edith Piaf records for her at the French bookstore, and snatched two fat pretzels from the price-gouging vendor opposite Saks. "I'll bet you want to run to Schirmer's, like a homing pigeon. But I won't let you." I pulled her off toward Times Square and we spent two hours playing *Pokereno* at a machine in a penny arcade. "Some penny arcade," I said as I fished out more silver for another game.

"Can we do the fortune teller?" Jesse asked.

"I had no idea you were familiar with this place."

"They had one like it in Chicago. Doesn't she look like a stuffed corpse? Or a mummy, without the dirty bandages? The first time I saw her I was terrified. I thought it was a real person trapped inside."

The figure behind the glass in the booth began to bend from side to side and turn its green cheeks coyly into a witchy grin. The hands flipped over cards— one, two, three, back and forth—until a fortune slipped through the slot in the front. The figure stopped with a clutching jerk.

"You first," Jesse said, peeking at the piece of cardboard.

You are secretly loved, it read.

She stifled a laugh, then said, "Pardon me," with false solicitude.

"It's my mother's former maid. She loves me because I send her pension checks on time."

"Don't you always suspect they stack the deck? These machines would go out of business if they started giving bad news."

The waxen lady twitched stiffly and went into her dealing routine. Soon another card slipped through the slot. Jesse reached for it. I saw that her hand was shaking slightly. I had no idea why she was so nervous over a silly game.

"Jesse," I tried to warn her. But warn her from what? From a phony fortune-telling machine that sat in a filthy storefront side show?

The card fluttered to the ground. "Let's go," she said instantly.

"Are you all right?"

"I'm very tired. Can we get out of here?"

"I'll get a taxi." I picked up the pile of packages and guided her out the door. I wondered briefly what had been on the card, but in my concern for her sudden fatigue I let the matter drop. When the cab arrived at her apartment building, the doorman helped her out and took the packages. "Please don't come up," she said. "I'm going to take my pill and lie down. Thank you for the gifts." She smiled at me. "You're a very nice man once you take the broom out of your ass."

She followed the doorman into the lobby.

I went home and immediately telephoned Martin on the trans-Atlantic line. The connection was terrible, filled with static. "There's something wrong with Jesse," I yelled.

"What?"

"Your wife, Jesse, dammit. I want you to fly home for a few days."

"How is Jesse?" he called as if from the bottom of a well.

"She's a nervous wreck, and if you don't catch the first plane out of there we're finished."

"Yes, Nicholas," he said meekly.

I wondered, then, if he really loved her at all.

CHAPTER

16

༉

Martin's sudden appearance seemed to help Jesse. Before he returned to Scotland, she gave what critics called the performance of her career. It was not, however, without its cost. In her dressing room during the intermission I could see how exhausted she really was.

Martin, aware of her success, was unsettled and nervous. He paced from one corner of the room to the other. Her triumph unnerved him far more than her exhaustion.

I stood behind her as she sat at her dressing table, reapplying dabs of pancake makeup to the shadows beneath her eyes. In the bright light her pallor took on a greenish tinge.

"Can't you tell Oldfield to slow down a little and not race toward the crescendo?" Martin carped.

I placed my hand on Jesse's shoulder. Her skin

was ice cold. A muscle jumped nervously beneath my touch. "He's doing fine, Martin. I thought he was splendid," she replied.

"I quite agree," I put in, unasked.

"I rather think I'm more qualified to discuss tempi," Martin answered touchily.

"Oh Martin," Jesse said wearily. "Can't you just shove it tonight?"

"I'll tell you one thing, Kogan—pulling me away from rehearsals at this time wasn't funny. I'm beginning to think you want me to fail, both of you," Martin whined.

"I hope you didn't come back just to quarrel with me," Jesse cried.

"Do you dare to make a scene in the middle of her concert?" I demanded.

"She's a wreck, Kogan. You should never have allowed her to perform. Look at her!" He pointed at Jesse's trembling image in the dressing table mirror.

"I think she looks lovely. And I think you should go get a drink. Why don't you do that before I hit you over the head with a bottle?"

He slammed the dressing room door as he left. Jesse bent her head in defeat. "It's my fault. He wants me to see a psychiatrist. He says it's all in my head. I should quit my career, take a long sabbatical, find out why I'm in love with my father."

"He said that?" Martin's stupidity never ceased to amaze me. "He's the right one to talk about fathers. He's afraid of you—afraid you'll surpass him. And if you keep it up tonight, you just might. Do you feel strong enough?"

She nodded hesitantly, then with more assurance. "He'd be surprised how much the pain helps me."

"You're in pain?" I was mortified. What kind of manager was I?

"Not so much physically—I'm sure that's only nerves—but his anger, his selfishness. He keeps reminding me that he's only here because of my condition. And because I've nothing to show for my troubles but a bottle of pills, he thinks I've made it all up to distract him."

She peered at her face in the mirror and applied a new streak of rouge above her cheekbones. Blending it in with expert fingers, she said, "I'd been feeling so worn out, and suddenly, when he started in with one of his tantrums, I knew that if I had to leave him, I could. I'm proving something to myself tonight."

I felt a flutter of anxiety. If she left Martin, surely he'd insist that I drop her as a client. I wanted to keep Jesse but I owed my career to Martin's loyalty. And despi, > his fits and starts of temper, he was my most produ tive client. Their breakup would be a resounding crisis I simply had to avert.

"Wouldn't divorce be too dramatic a solution? You know how Martin is working himself to death over this festival. He's too involved."

"You're right, Kogan. But that son of a bitch thinks there's only room for one person on a stage, and he's got to learn he's wrong." She pulled a brush through her hair with a jerk. "Sometimes I hate him so."

"You love him, don't you," I said, feeling infernally sorry that she did.

"Yes. I do. But whatever I do hurts me. Martin is invulnerable. As long as he can work, we could all collapse tomorrow and he'd never notice."

"I think you're wrong," I said as she stood up and smoothed down her dress.

"Wait and see," she said, my lovely Cassandra. "You shall see."

"All of this must be behind you," I whispered as we stood in the wings.

"No." She pressed my arm with limp fingers. "All of this shall be out there, now." She pointed toward the piano. Then the lights in the hall went down and the stage lights came up as Jesse walked out followed by Eric Oldfield. She nodded briefly at the applause and glanced, for an instant, at me. She was afraid—of Martin, of the audience, and for herself. But she turned back bravely toward the music as she would toward a friend. I suppose that for a musician, music is the only true friend. That night she embraced it and sang beautifully. She had never been better.

The music poured into the hall where, back behind the standees, Martin Boyd paced like a caged animal, tormented by the notion that his wife would become more famous than he; while she, up on the stage, alone with her words and music, sang Schumann.

O könnt ich die Liebe sargen hinzu!
Auf dem Grabe der Liebe wächst Blümlein der Ruh,
Da blüht es hervor, da pflückt man es ab,
Doch mir blüht's nur, wenn ich selber im Grab.

"If I could only bury my love here," she sang. "On love's grave, the flower of peace blooms and is picked. But I'll be in my own grave before it blooms."

CHAPTER

17

♈

Jesse's worst problem was her vision. No
one, not even sharp-eyed Kogan, knew how bad it
was. Each time she studied a score or read a book,
the printed lines separated into two parts and drifted
before her eyes. An eye doctor diagnosed eyestrain
and prescribed reading glasses, which made her head
ache even more because she was forced to peer
through an added layer of obstruction. Her voice
coach suspected something, probably that Jesse was
having a nervous breakdown. She was not unlike the
model of the prima donna—nervous, high-strung,
and edgy.

Since her triumphant lieder recital she had many
new offers to sing, but she told Kogan to be selective.
She wanted free time—time for her disorders to pass,
time to think about her marriage. Sometimes she
wished she had filed for divorce; other times she

wanted Martin. She loved him; she loved his talent, his eccentricities, even his ego. The other women scarcely mattered. Jesse believed that she would prevail—she, who endured pain so well. She would carry on.

Virginia, her dresser, often remarked how patient Jesse was with all the fuss made over her husband. Virginia read all of the Hollywood magazines; she could even recognize blind items. She sewed, and clucked her tongue over everyone's indiscretions. She altered hems and seams and said, "Oh *my*," as she read about Martin appearing on Ed Sullivan, Martin taking a model to dinner at Le Pavillon. "You bear your burdens as the Lord meant us to shoulder our woes," she told Jesse. "He will reward you." There were tears in her eyes as she helped Jesse into Donna Elvira's flowing dress and cloak.

Jesse spent a great deal of time in her apartment resting, wondering how much of the gossip was true. If it was, why hadn't she fought back? Wasn't it in her nature to try and fight for what she wanted? She remembered how docile she had been as a child, how malleable. She had not exerted her will at all. It was a complete accident that she had ever achieved her career. She thought of Sanford Donnelly, the baritone from Chicago, and wondered if he'd ever gotten his spot with the Lyric Opera. Perhaps he should have been the one with the great career, and she should have remained the vastly appreciative amateur who sang in the church choir and tuned in the Met radio broadcasts on Saturday afternoon.

The letter she was using as a bookmark slid to the floor and she bent over to retrieve it. She groped around and found it slightly to the right of where she saw it. Her vision was slipping again. She read the return address with difficulty, then slipped out the handwritten page to look it over once again. The writing was loopy and schoolgirlish. "I am twelve years old," it read, "and my name is Gabrielle Klee." Such a brazen child—writing to her as Martin Boyd's wife, asking for help in securing an audition with the great conductor. Such nerve, such terrible audacity for so young a child. The little girl was perhaps the only person in the world who might imagine that Mrs. Boyd had any influence with Mr. Boyd.

She held the letter in her hand, and thought about children. Perhaps the time for feminine wiles had arrived. If she wanted to keep the marriage together, why not have children of their own? A child—yes, a child might save the marriage. She was sick of just Martin and Jesse. The notion of extending herself toward another tiny being was delicious indeed.

"What are you doing?" Martin asked as he came into the living room. He saw the letter in her hand. "Is the mail in yet?"

She put on her reading glasses and stared at the envelope again. "This came for me last week. Actually, it concerns you. Shall I read it?"

"No. Here, give it to me." She handed it over without comment.

He started to laugh as he read it.

"What's so funny?" Jesse asked indignantly. "I think it takes a hell of a nerve."

He looked at her as if he thought her remark was very peculiar, then said, "I think it's very cute."

"Cute!" Jesse fumed. "And on the basis of that, you'll see the little girl? This child who writes to me at home?"

"Don't you think it exceedingly clever of her? Come on, Jess. Someone fed her the line."

"Didn't she write once before? Wasn't there something else?"

"Maybe it was Kogan. That child prodigy Wurtzberg had wanted me to hear," Martin said.

"You'd better have your audition soon if you want the child part to apply. Only a couple of years to puberty, my dear, unless she's an early bloomer. Then you're sunk."

"Did you develop early, darling?" Martin murmured. He stroked her hair. Should she mention the baby? "Martin, I—" she began.

Their maid came in and announced Mr. Kogan.

"Hello, Martin. Jesse, can you perform? Are you up to it?" He was quite excited.

"I'm not sure if I can do a whole evening."

"Just a song or two. It's for a gala, just been announced for next week, to raise funds for the Landmarks Preservation people. Carnegie Hall, all the best names to appear. All soloists, otherwise you'd have been asked, Martin. But the list is divine: Stern, Rubinstein, Tucker—the crème de la crème. And they want Jesse."

"I could do the Brahms, or the Strauss. . . what dress should I wear? Shall I buy a new one? I must call my coach right away—oh, and Eric!"

"That was a fast recovery," Martin remarked, seemingly pleased for her.

Kogan went off to the telephone, and Martin gave Jesse a hug. "This is quite something. I'm very proud of you."

"Are you really?" The day, which had begun so badly, was turning out wonderfully well.

"Was there something you wanted to ask me?" he said. "Just a few minutes ago?"

"Was there?" she said absently. "Let's go inside

and you'll help me pick the music so Kogan can tell the program people. You're so smart about that. I want something that makes an impact, you know? So they'll remember me."

"Don't worry," Martin said. "They'll remember."

CHAPTER

18

⚘

The quality of an audience, the intensity of its listening experience, affects every performer. Artists may claim they do not notice, but a restless crowd is painful. Martin Boyd claimed that conducting, with its enforced rear-face, was the easiest way to bear offensive audiences; but he was just as aware now of clanking charm bracelets as he had been in his days as a soloist.

Jesse, extremely nervous and jumpy, dressed for her Carnegie Hall gala borne aloft in a realm of muffled noises and a dull, soothing roar not unlike the sound of the ocean. She felt lightheaded with excitement as she stepped into her evening gown. The room spun as she put one foot, then the other, into the skirt. She had spent a great deal of money on the dress; it was a pale, apricot-colored chiffon with a high neck and plunging back. Virginia had helped her pin up her hair. She had borrowed diamond earrings and wore her one good piece of jewelry, the ruby bracelet from Venice. Jesse, who hated superstitions, had lately referred to it as her lucky bracelet. *I shall sing ruby tonight,* she decided, as she turned the bracelet on her wrist and watched the stones gleam. She held her wrist against the dress. The stones clashed with the delicate chiffon but she didn't care. She needed all her luck.

"May I enter?" she heard Kogan call.

"Yes, come in," she called back, and Virginia opened the door. Kogan stepped in bearing an enormous bouquet of red roses. Jesse squealed in excitement and ran to sniff the flowers. She pulled a rose toward her and sank her finger into a thorn.

"Ouch. Dammit."

"*Tsk,* Sleeping Beauty gets the spindle straight to the index finger. Hurry up and finish your 'Rose Adagio'; I'm allergic to these damn things." His eyes were watery and bloodshot.

"You and Martin," she said. "But I adore them. Where is he?"

"Banned from your presence. He'll be conducting from his aisle seat, so I'll not tell you where we'll be sitting. Try not to look for him, he'll distract you."

"I feel as if I'm caught in a barrel, or under water. Sometimes things sound so far away. I hope I'm not getting the flu." Jesse's hands moved to her throat and she swallowed experimentally.

"You singers are such terrible hypochondriacs." Kogan dabbed at his eyes with a handkerchief. "All is in working order, I trust." He picked up a pile of telegrams and began riffling through them.

"There's the nicest one from Wurtzberg," Jesse said as she arranged the flowers in a vase.

"On a night of nights," Kogan read aloud, "it is the little girl from Wisconsin who will win their hearts." He smiled. "I've not the same facility for Western Unionese but my sentiments are much the same. My dear, you should apply a bit more rouge; that pale color is very draining."

"I've already done my makeup," she rushed over to stare in the mirror. "Maybe you're right—I do look awfully pale." She threw a towel over her shoulders and stuck her fingers in the rouge pot. "Stern and Istomin are playing the Cesar Franck Sonata. It was one of my father's favorites; he used to play it with his friend. My father used to say that the music he loved was his soul. He said that once—about a Beethoven sonata—but when I think of him I hear him saying it all the time, as if they were the only words he ever spoke. Actually, he never did say much. He was a quiet sort."

"You're sorry he isn't here."

"He'd have loved the Franck. But no, he really wanted me to be a pianist. He never thought the voice was a great achievement. It seemed too easy to him."

"He was like Martin in that respect," Kogan commented quietly.

"Yes, that's true," Jess admitted. "Just like Martin. But they were as unalike as can be—earth and air. Sondergards and Boyds don't mix well."

Kogan made a fumbling gesture with the telegram he held, then he placed it on her dressing table.

"Do you think it's a mistake to do the Brahms first? Rather a slow start." Jesse stared at him brightly.

"It's fine. I must be going, I want to watch from

the audience. You don't mind, seeing as it's only two songs?"

"Kogan, you old goat, you don't have to wait in the wings for me. Go enjoy the program. It's more high-class company than you'll ever see me with. Lord, do you remember that Michigan opera group? My God, the lead was seventy, if he was a day, a geriatric Don Giovanni. And the Dona Anna thought she was singing Donizetti. I kept whispering '*Gion-vanni, Giovanni*—you've got your *Dons* mixed up.' She'd trill away, the idiot. How did you ever find such a booking?"

"Come, come; Elvira is one of your favorites. 'Oh, Kogan,' you said to me, 'I'll sing it *anywhere*.' Well, my child, you did."

"And now this." She turned back toward the mirror. Her mouth trembled.

"You shall be as glorious and charming as ever," Kogan said to her; but his voice leaped out at her in spurts. She heard only *glor* and *char*, then she turned her head the other way and caught *as ever*. She smiled broadly at him and then asked Virginia to leave her alone for the few minutes until her call.

She closed her eyes and took a deep breath. On opening them, there she was in the mirror again. Why did these dressing rooms have so many mirrors? She was a stuffed pig in a chiffon gown, a ruby bracelet on its hoof. She shook her head to try and empty her ear of the dull roar. Had she gotten water in it when she showered? But hadn't she taken a bath, not a shower? She reached for her music, then hesitated, for she didn't have her glasses handy. Where had she put them? "I'm losing my mind," she said aloud, and as she stood up to look for her purse a wave of dizziness swept over her and she sat down, startled. She put her hand over her heart, which was thudding frantically. *Calm, calm down,* she murmured to herself and the queasy feeling began to subside, drawing back like a wave from the shore, leaving her exposed, panting, wet with perspiration. *What the hell is happening to me?* She took a breath and sang an *A.* She heard it clearly. Satisfied that the mysterious trouble had passed, she tried to stand up again. This time she rose easily. "Thanks," she said, and she hitched up her dress and yanked down her slip, then checked to see that it did not hang out. No need to show up onstage trailing lingerie.

There was a knock and a call, "Fifteen minutes." She walked over to smell her roses, this time bending her head and burying her face in the blooms. There must have been at least three dozen. A pity to be allergic to such beautiful things. Their smell was intoxicating but heady, excessive, verging on the cheap, like the perfume sold in dime stores. She removed one rose from the bouquet with careful fingers and held it between the thorns on the stem. She sniffed it, pleased by its individuality. Then she placed it between her teeth and clicked her fingers. Carmen. Her Carmen had received good, but not great, reviews. Someone had written that she had not seemed confident in the role of seductress. "A more seducible Carmen there has never been on stage. One wanted to race right up there and ravish her on the spot. But seductive is a different matter. She is beautiful and the voice is there, the handling of the big arias impressive, but she must get more conviction into her acting. Miss Sondergard must learn an actress's tricks of deception before she will be exactly right for the role. She is too honest for the part. Carmen is, after all, a hooker. Get some larceny in your role, I would tell her, then come back and do the *Habanera* for me and we shall see."

She dropped the rose. How stupid it was to be so nervous. This was a tiny performance, and she didn't need larceny to sing Brahms and Schubert.

"Two minutes," the voice and knock came again.

She appraised herself in the mirror for the last time. She decided her hair was wonderful piled up on her head, but the dress looked limp. She would have to add some drama to her entrance in order to give the costume some life. She turned around and glanced over her shoulder to check the back of the dress, and as she did she bumped into the small table with the vase of roses. The vase toppled to the floor with a crash. She lifted the hem of her dress and stared at the puddle of water on the floor and the tangle of rose stems and broken flowers that lay at her feet. Someone opened the door and the stage manager's head poked in. "Are you all right, Miss Sondergard? You're next." He saw the mess on the floor and called for the janitor.

Jesse lifted her skirt and stepped over the foliage. She noticed a card on the floor, soaked with water, the ink beginning to run into black splotches. She bent over and tried to see it. *Martin*, the card seemed to read. Roses from Martin. Bad luck, it was bad luck to break the vase. "I'm sorry," she said to the man with the mop and bucket who stood waiting as she made her way through her dressing room door. "I apologize for making a mess."

He was a Negro. His face was impassive. He stared at the flowers on the floor and did not acknowledge her words. The flowers probably cost more than he earned in a week, or a month. The stage manager took her arm and led her into the wings. "How much does he earn?" she whispered to him, but he was feverishly directing the stagehands to give Van Cliburn another curtain call, and he didn't answer either.

Can anyone hear me? Jesse wondered as she awaited her cue.

The minute she walked onstage she knew that Martin had been wrong about audiences. Even with her back to the house she would have felt the intensity of their concentration piercing her like the arrows in Martin's treasured painting of St. Sebastian.

Eric Oldfield took his place at the piano and she turned toward him. He nodded slightly and struck the first chord. The sound seemed to come from far away. She heard it better from the left. A small dart of panic pierced her as she began to sing. Her voice poured out over the audience. She sang sweetly and cautiously, afraid of singing too loudly and not hearing herself properly. Someone in the audience remarked that she sang as if she might shatter.

For Jesse, the experience was pure terror. She couldn't hear the piano properly. The notes came into focus only when the music was loud, but the pianissimo was lost to her. She reined in her voice. *How ironic, for a singer to lose her hearing!* Then she remembered the ballerina LeClercq, who had polio, and she knew that nothing in life is too tragic. Anything is possible, especially the worst of things. Bravely she continued, unaware of the powerful effect she was creating. When she finished, the audience roared and several people leaped to their feet. She ducked her head gratefully, thinking that she could not go on. What had she done to deserve such an ovation? She clung to the edge of the piano and waited for the applause to subside. Then, as the sound grew less intense, she strained to hear the opening notes of the Schubert.

Jesse sensed the restlessness of the audience before she heard their voices. Her eyes flew about the hall, beyond the glare of the lights, and she saw people leaning toward one another, gesturing, staring back at her. She looked around, waiting for the piano to begin. She hoped Eric was not waiting for the audience to settle down, as Martin often did. It was embarrassing, the worst side of egotism. Finally, after what seemed a long time, she turned to look at Eric Oldfield, afraid he was ill, or that he had forgotten the chosen song. As she turned to see, she did not hear any notes but she saw his hands on the keyboard, his fingers slowly depressing the keys. And his eyes were on her. He stared at her with an expression of the profoundest pity, and she could see that very soon he would begin to cry.

CHAPTER

19

Ꮗ

Martin clutched my arm. "Kogan," he groaned, "she can't hear. My God, Kogan." He rose and hurried up the aisle.

I sat in my seat, anguished and ashamed that I had not been waiting in the wings. Why was it the one time someone needed me I was down among the Philistines?

I watched as Eric Oldfield escorted Jesse from the stage. She walked like a queen, nodding her head nobly as he guided her to the wings. The audience regained its composure and burst into applause that was like the aftershock of an earthquake. How they love tragedy. They cheer for disfigurement, old age and death. Where are they when the young, hopeful, healthy ones need them? If Jesse had sung only one clinker, they would have fed her to the lions. But as a reward for the spectacle of her breakdown, they were swooning with delight.

I left my seat and went back to the stage door. A large crowd had gathered by Jesse's dressing room. Eric Oldfield was there, sobbing openly, and Jesse's dresser Virginia was working her fingers as if counting the beads on an invisible rosary. "Let me pass, please," I said, my voice unnaturally high. I ducked through the throng of stagehands and visitors and turned the knob of the door. It was locked. From the direction of the stage I could hear the sound of a cello, unaccompanied, playing one of Bach's suites—a mournful, sobbing melody. "It's Nicholas," I said loudly, and the latch on the door clicked open. I closed the door behind me on the sound of the muted cello and Virginia's "Hail Mary, full of grace."

Martin's face was ashen—for once, he looked his age. His fingers locked on my wrist, his nails digging into my skin. "Is this her nerves too?" he said loudly. He behaved as if she were stone deaf. Jesse, seated on a low couch, said, "I can hear you, it's just on one side. I forgot to turn my head back toward the piano, that's all. Kogan, I made a complete fool of myself up there, didn't I?"

"You're no fool," I said, prying open Martin's grip and watching Jesse shift nervously in her seat, twitching her leg and yanking at her dress as if it were a protective cloak that would magically ward off evil. For the rest of my life I will hate that color, that burnished gold melting into orange and pink, the bastard mixture of hues that reminds me of that night.

"Do you hear this?" I clapped my hands behind her head. She nodded.

"Do you think this is *Dark Victory*, doctor? Are you the suave, romantic, brain specialist who'll diagnose me in a twinkling?" Jesse laughed, a bitter, sour sound that hung in the air.

"Do you want to see a doctor?" Martin asked, keeping a good distance from his wife as if what she had was contagious. "I'll get you the best doctor in the city, in the world, whatever you want."

"You sound like a movie," Jesse said. Then she stood, shakily, and faced her husband. "I wasn't making anything up. This is real."

"I know," he said, burying his face in his hands. He lifted his head for a moment and said, "Kogan, cancel all my appearances. Tell them it's urgent, personal business, and cannot be avoided."

"I don't want you doing that," Jesse said crossly. "It's bad enough one of us will be out of commission. Besides, once this thing in my ear clears up I'll be back on the road and then where will you be?"

"I'll help, Martin. I'll see that she gets rest and sees the right doctor." We all wanted to believe it was nerves. The vapors. Neurotic fixations. Anything but a serious, physical ailment.

Martin gave in easily, relieved that his tour could proceed. He was looking forward to his Mahler programs with the Philharmonic. "Just see that it's the best care possible, no matter what the cost."

"No matter what the cost," I repeated into the telephone the next day. My physician Nininger (what had the idiot missed when I sent her there in the first place? Was this all his fault?) recommended an ear, nose and throat man affiliated with three hospitals. I arranged to bring Jesse to his office that afternoon for a special appointment to be squeezed into his busy schedule. I was able to arrange it only after I discovered the doctor loved opera. He was delighted to have a star in his waiting room.

The offices were enormous, stark, sleek, and uninviting. Jesse placed herself delicately in one of the uncomfortable leather chairs while I settled onto a backless ottoman. A well-dressed matron sat across from us, superintending a small boy who wiggled uncontrollably and vented his childish rage on the supply of waiting room magazines. After shredding several, he tipped over three ashtrays and uprooted a philodendron. His guardian (an aunt or grandmother—she was too old to have mothered so small an offspring) waved a bony finger and said "No," at which the child chuckled and continued his dirty work. Finally the matron rose. I thought she would apologize to us, but she approached Jesse. "Pardon me, but aren't you the opera singer?"

"No," Jesse said. "You must have me confused with someone else."

"Oh, but I'm quite sure. You see, I am a subscriber. I'd swear you were she."

Jesse shook her head.

The woman gave her a sharp look which said *I know you're lying*, but she didn't press any further. She said "No" to the boy, who was dissecting an old cigar butt, and sat down in her chair, nodding smartly at me as if she were aware that I was privy to the truth.

"Your public," I leaned over and whispered to Jesse.

"Pathetic, isn't it?" she said. And she was silent until her appointment came.

Dr. Leopold had black hairs protruding from both his ears and nose, which made me wonder if he were furry-throated as well. I told him the story of the concert. Jesse said only one thing. "They think I'm going insane."

"I do not," I put in staunchly. "Doctor, you must realize she's under a tremendous strain."

The doctor, pleased as punch with his celebrity patient, politely showed me out of the office. "We must examine her now. Perhaps you wouldn't mind waiting outside?" he said with a smile.

By now, the waiting room had filled with assorted patients, bandaged on a variety of outer extremities, or else hawking and sputtering post-nasally. A nauseating specialty, I decided; all sinuses and fluid-filled cavities. But the harmless nature of these ills gave me confidence that Jesse's problems were minor. I had prepared my speech of good cheer when the receptionist signaled me back into the office.

Jesse was curled limply in the same armchair and Dr. Leopold was at his desk as if he'd never moved. "Sit down," he said, waving a gold pen at me. Jesse would not look at me at all.

"I want Miss Sond—I mean, Mrs. Boyd, admitted to the hospital immediately. I'd like her to undergo some tests. I'm not certain if there is anything we need be concerned about but I want to make sure. Think of this as a precautionary measure."

"But the hospital?" I protested, having a dread of the places myself.

"Merely a convenience. She'll need a complete workup and it will save a great deal of time."

Jesse stared at her hands.

"What do you think might be wrong with her?"

He twitched a furry nostril and sniffed. Did he have his own leaky sinuses? A discomforting thought—physician heal thyself and all that. "We'll know when the tests are completed. That's what they're for. She is having trouble with the right ear. It may be associated with the eighth cranial nerve, and that is why we need further tests." He wrote something on a slip of paper. "My girl will call the hospital and give you the forms to fill out. Have Mrs. Boyd taken there immediately."

"Yes." Suddenly I wanted to get Jesse out of that room, out of that office, into the air outside. She was folded up in her chair, her face blank and as abstracted as if she had been hypnotized.

"Don't worry," the doctor said as if finally noticing Jesse's mood. "We'll come up with a diagnosis as soon as possible and get you right back up on the stage. Quite a little star we have here. I'll be at your next concert." He stuck out a hand to me. "Goodbye."

As I walked over to Jesse, he said, "See that Mr. Boyd is there tomorrow as well. We might like to talk to him."

"What the hell do you think is wrong," Jesse suddenly said, stirring from her stupor.

"I wouldn't want to make a hasty diagnosis," the doctor said, backing off.

"She can take it," I said. "She's a trouper."

"I'm sure she is," he said.

"Then tell us," I said harshly, wondering if he'd refuse again. They always hold all the goddamn cards, these doctors.

"Perhaps a nerve disorder," he said anxiously. "Or a neuromuscular condition. We must do these tests."

"How bad is all that?" Jesse asked pleadingly. "At the worst, will I lose my hearing in one ear? What about the other?" He stared at her like a woodchuck startled in his hole; then he ducked, and allowed the buckshot to fly over his head.

"We'll see," he said, ushering the pair of us out.

"If only they'd tell us the worst things first," Jesse said as she shrugged into her raincoat. She had recovered from her stupor in the doctor's office. She spoke loudly; all of the patients in the waiting room stared at her. She stuck her tongue out at them. "Dr. Leopold's house of horrors," she announced as she marched to the door. I was left to follow in her wake, past the horrified stares of all those miscellaneous sufferers.

It was a relief to enter the elevator. "Where to?" Jesse said as I pushed the button for the lobby. Canned music poured into the car from an overhead speaker; one of my least favorite songs, "You'll Never Walk Alone." The Living Strings sawed their arms off as I stared helplessly at Jesse, furious at the notion that it was I who had to put her into a hospital. Where was her husband? Why was I involved with her at such a terrible moment? She needed someone who cared deeply and I, of course, was incapable of caring for anyone. I stared at her face as she, distracted, studied the numbers of the floors as they lit up and flashed by. I could be of no help to her. She was so beautiful, with a scarf over her hair, her face bare of makeup. Could I ever come to care for her? I shook off my feelings. She was lovely—of that I was certain—but no one should ever guess what I was thinking. No one must ever know that I was attracted to her right then, another man's wife, my client. It was shameless and, considering her illness, quite indecent.

She moved slowly beside me as we crossed the lobby, passing a row of floor-to-ceiling mirrors which lined the entryway. I stole a glance at us in the mirrors. I looked so lean, burned-out, while she, for all her troubles, had an aura of tender ripeness as if she were entering her fullest season.

"Kogan," she said out on the sidewalk, "I'll go

home alone now. Got to pack some things, you know," she swallowed and made a face.

"You're braver than I am," I said admiringly.

She stuck out her hand for a cab. "I know," she said. A taxi screeched to a halt. "Just remember that I loathe pecans, gladioli, potted azaleas, and get-well cards illustrated with Hummel figures. That should cover it." She got into the cab and stuck her head out the window. "See you in two hours, in the lobby, or whatever they call it at the hospital. *Anteroom.* Does that sound medical? Anyway, bring lots of change. They always charge a fortune for calls from the room, like a hotel. Do you think it's going to hurt?"

"No, of course not." I was positive all of it would.

"It's in the stars," she called out as the cab pulled away. "The situation is grave."

Later on, waiting by the admissions desk as droves of geriatric patients checked in, I realized that what Jesse had shouted at me was the fortune from the gypsy's printed card in the penny arcade. I cursed myself, fearing I had brought this down on Jesse's head through my confused, hidden passion for her. The curse of the confounded, moody Dane—except on this occasion read "hospital" for "nunnery."

20

When Martin found out about Jesse's illness, he experienced a mixture of anger, terror, relief—and shame. After all, she was the one lying in the hospital bed exhausted from all the tests, unaware of the seriousness of her condition.

Martin had been conducting an orchestra rehearsal, sweating and tense, going over Mahler's Fifth line by line. The orchestra sat dumbly, stupefied by his thorough analysis. "This is like kindergarten," one of the trumpets announced. They had not played a note in two hours. Martin was explaining what he thought Mahler's intention had been in writing great leaps for the horns.

"Thank God we're not doing Schoenberg," the trumpet player went on. "We'd be here all night." He looked at his watch. "Did they say this was sold out?"

The horn player to his left nodded. "Don't you feel like one of those Negro kids from Harlem they schlep in for the children's concerts?"

"Now, this passage," Martin said loudly, slapping his baton on his score.

"Are we actually going to play a note?" the first trumpet said. He was a gray-haired union organizer, a cynical veteran who drove hard bargains during contract negotiations. He wondered if next time they could include a clause stipulating that lectures on music be given only during overtime, at the higher pay scale. Ordinarily, Mahler's Fifth was a favorite of his, rich and full of wonderful passages for the brass section.

"Did you hear the guy's wife got sick last week? Couldn't finish a performance," the second trumpet said.

"She's that gorgeous doll—the opera singer, right?"

"Yeah. What did she ever see in him? He probably explains everything to her when they're screwing." The horns laughed at his remark.

Martin's face contorted with anguish. He was not communicating his vision of this work to the orchestra. He wanted it military, precise: fascist storm troopers assembling beneath a darkening sky, armies massing as if preparing for an attack, swooping lunges followed by measured marches. He rapped his baton and called for order.

Then he saw Kogan enter the room, standing by the rear door and jiggling an umbrella nervously. All at once he remembered Jesse, and that he had been due at the hospital that morning. He stopped the rehearsal and announced a break.

Kogan approached him slowly, his face fatigued.

"Hello," Martin said as he gathered his score up. "We'll get over there right now. I'll have at least a couple of hours with her."

"Just a moment, Martin," Kogan said ominously.

The sound of Mahler's trumpets of doom burst fleetingly through Martin's head, just as he wanted to hear them when he conducted. He opened his score quickly to locate the passage and pulled out a pencil. Kogan cleared his throat and said, "It's bad, my boy."

Martin continued to hear the music and he scribbled down his notations. Through the shimmering brass he heard the melody soar, exactly as it should sound. Come this afternoon, that was how the orchestra would play it. He always felt he had to know exactly what his music was about before he could give it breath and life with the orchestra.

"How she is waiting to get out," Kogan continued sadly. "You must be careful when you tell her that it means she'll need treatment. She won't take it well. She must never know everything." He jiggled his umbrella impatiently as Martin continued to stare at his score.

"What exactly are you saying?" Martin said finally, raising his head.

"It's her career—her life. She may never be able to perform again."

"Her hearing?"

"Oh, Martin," Kogan said in exasperation. "Eventually she could die." The word hung briefly and ominously over their heads.

"From what? Has she got cancer?"

"She has multiple sclerosis. It's her nerves and muscles. She'll have it forever. There are remissions, but no one knows if they'll occur, or for how long. Soon she may not be able to walk. Her legs are getting weaker. The symptoms always seem to look like other diseases; that's why the doctors weren't sure. But she has it, Martin, and she doesn't know it."

"Why not?" he said. "Shouldn't someone have told her? The doctors?"

"I forbade them, that bunch of vultures. She doesn't need their little patient morale speech. She needs someone she loves. She needs you."

"Oh no, I couldn't—really," he said as if declining to play the piano at a social gathering. He felt curiously detached from the conversation. *My wife is ill;* he tested the sound. And then he thought that he would be on his own again, just as before. Before Jesse.

"Is she going to die?" he asked meekly.

"Not now, not right away. Patients can go on for years, apparently, depending on how severely they are affected. They get very weak, it seems; susceptible to germs, pneumonia, that sort of thing. Dreadful disease, horrible," Kogan shuddered.

"My wife is ill," Martin said aloud.

"We must get to the hospital right away," Kogan directed.

"I can't face her. I haven't been much of a husband. How can I tell her this?"

"You must," Kogan said urgently.

"I'll get her the best people, someone to take care of her, a nurse. I'll do extra bookings, I'll keep her in real style."

"She'll need you. She hasn't got anyone else."

Martin saw one of the musicians pass by the back door. "You," he called out. "Rehearsal this afternoon is cancelled. Tell them." He waved the man away. "I'll work twice as hard," he said. "I'll need the money."

All the way to the hospital the Mahler crashed and thundered in his brain. Kogan sat by his side, picking nervously at the handle of his umbrella. *Poor old Kogan,* Martin thought. *He's really grown fond of her.*

When Martin entered his wife's room and saw her lying in bed, he thought she was already totally paralyzed. He almost backed out and closed the door. But she turned her head and saw him. "Hi, kid," he said.

She sat up and threw her legs over the edge of the bed. "I'm so glad you're here. The food is abysmal. Can you run out and get me a shrimp salad sandwich on rye and a vanilla malted? I'm dying for something real. They only cook with styrofoam in this kitchen."

Martin glanced at Kogan, nodding his head as if to say, *Sick? She's not sick.*

"You look wonderful," he told her.

"Do I?" She put her hands to her hair. "I have an awful headache from the spinal tap. Look at you— you're shaking, just at my mentioning it. You're a worse coward than I am."

Kogan edged toward the door. "I'll get the sandwich."

"Dammit," Martin hollered. "You stay right here!"

"What's wrong?" Jesse said immediately. "What's the matter?" She looked from Martin to Kogan and back to Martin again. "You know. They told you something."

"*Shhh,*" Martin soothed. "Nothing."

"Of course they did. And if you think I don't know it's bad you're out of your mind. I can smell it. They all come walking in here together and take a stroll around me as if I were a park. The young ones move in behind the big shots and play guessing games with my chart. And written all over their faces in great big electric letters is one word. *Sick. Boy is she ever sick.* They wouldn't waste their precious time otherwise."

"Please don't get excited," Martin pleaded.

"You'd be excited if they stuck a needle as big as a fencing sword into your spine while you were wide awake and your head blew up with pain. Oh, it's bad and I don't need the chicken-shit pair of you hovering around to tell me so." She tore angrily at her face, raking her cheeks with her fingers. She grabbed the button to summon the nurse and pressed it down again and again. "Get out of that corner, Kogan. Stop cowering."

A nurse came to the door. "Uh-huh?" she said.

"When is that doctor due back, the big one who looks like a polar bear?"

The nurse looked puzzled.

"Gray, big, six feet tall. The one they were all following around this morning."

"You mean Dr. Speno?"

"Yes, that's the one. Is he here? Can't you page him?"

"Ah'll try."

"Now, we'll just let the big shot tell me what ails me." Jesse folded her arms and sat back against the pillows.

"You have multiple sclerosis." It was Kogan who spoke, finally.

"Thank you," Jesse said. "Good of you to tell me. Now it's your turn, Martin. Let's hear all the gory details. It sounds like a real winner."

She was being too brave, and it terrified Martin. Goddamn Kogan, why did he have to tell her anything? Martin would have felt safer with a doctor present—a doctor with a hypodermic needle full of some soothing medicine. Perhaps they all could have kept it a secret. "You get remissions," he told her, trying to sound comforting. "They give you things to help you when you're feeling sick."

"Cortisone drugs," Kogan put in, tapping his umbrella on the floor.

"Oh, God," Jesse said.

Martin desperately wanted to flee the room, with its dying flower arrangements and its stacks of unopened, shiny new magazines.

The nurse returned. "Dr. Speno's in a meetin'."

"Get him here," Jesse insisted. "Now."

"Ah can't promise anything," the nurse warned.

"You just get him here this minute," Jesse yelled. "And show these two gentlemen out, out, out!" She picked up her water jug and hurled it at Martin, then threw a jar of macadamia nuts at Kogan. "Get out," she cried. "I can't stand looking at either of you. It's my life; it's my disease." She threw the moisture lotion, the plastic cups, and the telephone, which fell to the floor with a loud jangling of bells. Martin grabbed Kogan's arm. "She's crazy," he said, wide-eyed with fear. Then they opened the door and bolted through while the nurse stood by, her arms folded across her chest, murmuring, "Y'all may never get this cleaned up, way they work around here."

CHAPTER

21

"How good he is to you," Nurse Norris said for the thousandth time in her five-month tenure. "Such a lovely man."

Jesse sulked in bed, ignoring the tweety voice. She loathed Nurse Norris with a passion. Martin, however, was charmed by the woman's adulation of him and refused to fire her. "She's competent, she gets things done and, most important, she watches out for you. Remember how important that is. You don't want someone lazy around."

Nurse Norris was anything but lazy. She was a thin, angular woman who wore harlequin glasses and ancient cardigan sweaters fastened with a metal clip over a white uniform. She adored her new client's celebrity status but, according to her own assessment, deserved such a prestigious slot after serving many important people well. She forever discussed her past clients, referring to them by their illnesses. "Now, my stroke," she would say as she shook down the thermometer, "he was a real gentleman. He insisted on the finest linen handkerchiefs, hand-rolled, hand-embroidered. And the sheets—have I told you about the sheets? Hand-made as well. But no one was fussier than my amputation. She ordered shoes that cost over a hundred dollars a pair but, of course, she wore only one. She used to say to me, 'Norris, a foot's a foot whether there's a pair of them or not.' She gave all the lefts to charity, though I can't say who might have used them."

"Shut up, Norris," Jesse said.

Nurse Norris arranged the flowers Martin always sent. Today there were white roses. Jesse hoped Norris would stick herself. She did not; she wore rubber gloves. The sight of the gloves made Jesse ill. They reminded her of the indignities of her hospital stays.

"We'll get some air today," Nurse Norris announced, propping up the card at the pedestal of the vase.

"No we won't," Jesse said, aware that of course they would go because Norris was Adolph Hitler in whites and she controlled the perambulations of the wheelchair with an iron hand.

Nurse Norris placed her hands playfully on her bony hips. She pursed her mouth and said, "I'll choose your dress." No-nonsense Norris. Jesse believed that the rashes on her body came from contact with Norris's sharp little fingers.

"You're being just as nasty as my heart failure," Norris said. "Are we going to sit here in this dungeon? We need our light and air. And besides," she added nastily, "you're not so sick anymore."

Jesse wanted to hit her. Norris was right; the

drugs had helped and though Jesse felt as puffed up as a toad, the weakness was better. Jesse had decided that she would soon walk again, and she looked forward to the day when she would rise from her bed and strangle Norris with her bare hands.

She hated going out. She hated her wheelchair, hated being confined to it, hated being rolled about like a children's toy. Nurse Norris pushed her around at a ladylike gait and when they hit a curb, Norris would say, "Bumpety-ump;" and if they went down an incline on a path in the park, Norris would say, "Whee!" Jesse's jaw would lock tight and Norris would bend over and say, "All right, Miss Snapping-Turtle Face?"

Someday, Jesse knew, Norris would speak of her as "my multiple sclerosis," and she could even predict some of what Norris would repeat to her future clientele. *How awful my m.s. was—sulky, sullen. . . But what a charming husband—famous, you know—sent flowers, worked his fingers to the bone to keep that ingrate in luxury.* Norris believed what she saw; there were no deeper levels of understanding for her. What was there was the whole, true picture. She was highly literal. When Martin had showed Norris his painting of St. Sebastian, she'd crossed herself and counted the arrows. "Not quite right," she'd said. "They all take liberties, you know."

Martin had laughed, but Jesse wondered how long he could have put up with her. Norris daily, Norris nightly and, of course, Norris and Sugar. Sugar was Norris's parakeet. Sugar was white; Sugar sat on Norris's finger; Sugar said "Birdie" and, according to Norris, was so tame you could leave her in a room with an open window and she'd never fly away. Jesse would have loved to try that one. If Norris wasn't discussing her bed-ridden Hall of Fame, she was talking about Sugar. As she smoothed Jesse's lap blanket, she'd bend over with her Sen-Sen breath and remark, "Sugar's had a spell of bowel trouble lately; possibly too much millet. Her eyes looked tired this morning."

"Why don't you take her pulse?" Jesse suggested. "Better still, give her an enema. You could empty a tea-bag; it would do nicely."

Norris was hurt by Jesse's sarcasm. She was loyal to her parakeet. In fact, Norris had told Martin at her interview that without her bird, there was no point discussing terms of employment, for she would not go where Sugar was not welcome. Martin—who loathed all small, caged creatures—said that the parakeet could have its own bathroom for all he cared provided Norris kept the bird away from him. Norris took this to mean that Martin was afraid his charm might win the bird over, and thought it delicate of him to refrain from trying to woo her parakeet. From then on, Norris was Martin's, as much as Sugar was Norris's.

Late at night, Jesse could sometimes hear the whir of Sugar's wings as Norris let the bird out for its nightly exercise. The velvet sound made Jesse's scalp prickle and she imagined the bone-white bird flying beneath the ceiling like a feathered bat, swooping to avoid the center light fixture. The bird made little noise but every so often, in a paroxysm of joy, it would let out a series of shrill chirps as piercing as a traffic cop's whistle. Then all was silent, and Jesse imagined Norris soothingly lowering the cage cover. Or perhaps Norris took the bird to bed with her and hugged it to her bony chest.

Always, between discussions of Sugar's Hartz

Mountain diet and the condition of the ensuing movement, Nurse Norris was preoccupied with seeing the bright side of things. "See how much free time you have?" she said as she straightened the mess on Jesse's bedside table. Jesse, who had little tolerance for that sort of philosophy, restrained herself from tipping over the full bedpan by concentrating on the flickering TV screen. She had become addicted to the soap operas. She didn't really follow the plots, for they were too convoluted to understand; but she waited vigilantly for some new disaster to strike the characters on screen. If Denise on the serials got cancer, or Geoffrey was paralyzed in a car accident, and if they miraculously recovered (forty or fifty episodes later), it followed that her condition must be responsive, too. The soap operas gave her hope; they were, at least, her Lourdes.

Kogan visited several times a week, bringing mash notes from fans who wanted to know when she would sing again. Jesse ordered him to return all gifts: the bed jackets, Bibles, inspirational needlepoint ("Life is Only a Side Dish—The Lord Serves the Main Course"), and argyle socks. There were dozens of letters from those similarly afflicted, some enclosing snapshots of themselves in their all-electric, battery-operated chairs like demon auto racers ready for the Monte Carlo rally. Jesse threw these messages away. As for articles about miracle recoveries, cures, quack wonder drugs—she read them voraciously without the smallest hope that she might get well herself. Sometimes recovery wasn't what she wanted, not really; she wanted to be left alone, in peace, to die.

"Do you know how ridiculous you are?" Kogan prodded her one day, after she tossed her latest stack of mail in the garbage. "I shall buy you a tin cup and then you may take your coin-rattling business downtown and earn a living. You enjoy your fund-raising disease and that lovely wheelchair of yours. It's your own portable cross."

She hated him. How dare he say that? "Go to hell," she said, turning on her side, away from the television, away from nubile Marsha who was telling her old mother that her brand-new stepfather had seduced her.

"You tell me to go to hell with great regularity. Shall we set up a charter bus? Not answering, eh? Well, I'll tell you what. We'll go out together instead." He tossed an envelope in front of her. "Tickets to Martin's concert next week. We are going. All of us."

Panic rose in her throat.

"How nice," Norris purred, bringing over a glass of juice. "A night on the town."

"We're doing this with or without your cooperation," Kogan said firmly. "You must get out of the house, and not for your insignificant rolls around the park, either. I mean out with people."

"I'm not well enough." She wouldn't touch the tickets.

"The doctors say you are. Just put on a pretty dress. I'll see to the rest."

"I don't want any juice," she shoved Norris's offering hand away. "Pretty, hah! I look like hell."

"Nonsense," Kogan countered cheerfully. "You look fine. We'll get you a seat on the aisle. You can get out of the chair."

"No, no—I have to have my chair," she said, panicking.

"All right, don't get upset. I'll be right by your

side. It should be very interesting—the prodigy, the Klee girl, is making her New York debut."

"That creature who wrote me the letter? Is she still so precocious? She can't be twelve years old anymore; it seems ages ago."

"She's rather nearer fourteen, but they dress her like a child, petticoats and patent leather shoes, I gather. Perhaps they think it makes her more of an attraction. She is supposed to be rather good, though Martin hasn't said anything as yet."

"What's the little genius going to play?"

"Chopin's Second."

"Oh, Chopin," Jesse sneered.

"They say her touch is wonderful. She did the *Wanderer* in Washington last year, but I gather they don't want her to show her hand all at once up here. Leave them begging for more, and all that."

"My, my," said Norris. "A little girl playing the piano with Mr. Boyd. My, my."

"Shut up, Norris," Jesse said. "Isn't that Sugar? Don't you hear that funny noise?"

Norris paled. "I'll be right back."

Jesse sighed in relief. "Have you met the little monster yet?"

"No, I haven't. I must say I haven't much taste for little girls. No Maurice Chevalier nonsense for me. I'm more inclined to place the blame for one like this on the parents, really. What she does is their responsibility. She does look pretty in the publicity stills—"

"This is all Martin's doing, isn't it? The concert and all," Jesse snapped.

"Of course. We both know he thinks he's the original frustrated child genius. It was inevitable he'd tuck some youngster under his wing—someone he can show off, his alter ego. He still says he'd have been twice as good if he'd started performing when he was eight."

Norris returned, hurt and reproachful. "That was mean. Sugar was fine, just dozing on her perch."

"Pardon," Jesse said. "My error."

"It's all set then," Kogan stood up. "We'll go next week."

"I'm not sure," Jesse replied. "I might wait until Martin gets home tomorrow." She turned back to watch the TV. Marsha had disappeared, replaced by the philandering stepfather, a young actor with a clumsy pepper-and-salt dusting of powder on his black hair. It reminded her of an awful *Trovatore* in which she had once performed as the gypsy woman Azucena. The wardrobe mistress and makeup department was one woman—the director's eighty-year-old mother—and she had been in a tizzy and had lost Jesse's wig. Consequently, Jesse sang the role of Manrico's mother with her own long, dark hair. The audience, vague and unfamiliar with the twists of the plot, took her to be his wife or mistress. Backstage, the local crowd praised her youthful, vital performance. She decided then and there that she was a lousy actress and accepted their praise without a murmur. But the music had always seemed more important to her than the stage business.

"Sugar's stool was real hard," Norris informed her after Kogan had left.

"Indeed?" Jesse said. "Then you might try giving her some prunes for breakfast. She can even borrow my Ex-Lax, if you like. I'm a generous sort."

"One would think you hadn't a real heart," Norris said, insulted.

"Why don't you go to my closet and choose

something for me to wear to the concert next week—if we go," Jesse said. "And while you're at it, select something for yourself. You can alter it and keep it."

"For me, Mrs. Boyd?"

"Why, of course you. Whither I rollest, you do the shoving. I'm sure you can find something suitable for a pusher."

"Oh, yes," said Norris greedily.

"You stupid old bat," Jesse said at her retreating back. She settled against the pillows to watch Cynthia give birth to the baby that was really her ex-fiancé's; but he was in jail and her new husband thought it was his child.

CHAPTER

22

♈

Jesse and I sat in the aisle seats on the left side of the hall. The audience chattered expectantly, in anticipation of the upcoming debut. Audiences love prodigies; they embrace them wholeheartedly until the talent disappoints. When the prodigy ages, abandonment is swift. Few survive their initial exposure— those who last into adulthood are forever haunted by comparisons with their younger selves.

"If Martin had performed as a child I wonder how he would have fared," I said to Jesse, to make conversation. She sat listlessly beside me, her head wrapped in a turban, her eyes concealed by dark glasses. She had swathed her body in a black velvet cape, and the costume, combined with her wheelchair, gave the crowd around her some pause. She was an exotic, wheeled diety.

"If you mean survive to grow up and become infatuated with presenting this child, the answer is no," Jesse said. She glared up at Norris who was bending over and fussing with a lap blanket she had brought along. "Cut that out," Jesse said sharply. "Quit it." Norris drew back, offended, and sat down in her seat behind Jesse. "He's got this Svengali thing going; he talks about educating her sensibilities. If that isn't utterly riduculous, I don't know what is."

"Be patient. It's only one appearance. And she's just a little girl."

"Remember that letter? This is no ordinary child. This is a child in a mask."

"You're watching too much television," Kogan said. "Addles the brain."

"Nicholas, really—he's been coaching her privately."

"It is her debut." Jesse had the oddest notions. Since her illness, her point of view had altered considerably. She watched life flicker by from her wheelchair much as she watched the images on the television screen. "She's just an awful little girl," I reassured her. "I finally did get to meet her—she's a gawky thing with Alice in Wonderland ribbons in her hair. And I don't care if she's a musical genius, she chews bubble gum. And she left a wad in my Baccarat ashtray."

Jesse wasn't listening. She glanced around expectantly as the hall filled, watching the people being led to their seats. As they passed her, their eyes widened at the cape, the turban, and the wheelchair; but they walked on without comment. Jesse collapsed back in her chair, then turned and watched the next group coming down the aise. She was, I realized, waiting for someone to recognize her; and, half-terrified, half-disappointed, she could not believe that no one did. Poor Jesse. She barely resembled the concert star whom an audience would instantly recognize. The hair that poked beneath the turban was lank and lifeless, her face was puffy with the transluscent softness of illness and drugs. She might have taken a seat but she clung to her wheelchair as if it were a rolling fortress, her portable, iron-clad excuse for her appearance. *I'm not myself,* it said. *I'm a sick person.*

Her silly jealousy about the Klee child seemed just another reflection of her changed condition. Of course Jesse was jealous of someone healthy, young, talented; but to settle her bitterness on the skinny shoulders of that child seemed ridiculous. Gabrielle was a callow brat who wore Catholic school uniforms with high socks, her yellow hair falling over her shoulders, and a bubble of nauseating gum at her lips. As she blew her gum-balls, her eyes grew wider and wider until the gum popped, leaving a filmy fringe of pink lace across her eyebrows, nose, and upper lip.

"No," I repeated to Jesse, "this child is nothing more than a passing fancy. I'm sure she has no staying power."

"You shall be proved wrong eventually. I have an instinct for these things," Jesse predicted, still watching the incoming crowd. They continued to walk right by her without a glint of recognition, as if she were completely invisible.

During the first part of the program—Resphighi, not one of my all-time favorites—Jesse shifted uncomfortably about and was finally wheeled out by the ever-vigilant Norris. At the intermission, I scurried back to the lobby and found Jesse sitting in a corner, hungrily watching the large crowd gathered there. I bought her an orange drink and tried to make pleasant conversation. She insisted I go backstage and see to Martin. How hard it must have been for her to be part of an audience, an anonymous guest. But if someone had asked her for her autograph, wouldn't she have fled in terror? I didn't hang around asking myself what I should do or say. I obeyed her orders and went back to Martin's dressing room.

He wasn't there; a stagehand directed me to Gabrielle Klee's room. I knocked; he called "Enter." He was kneeling in front of the child, who was perched on a stool, going over a music score he'd placed across her lap. He was pointing at something, explaining it to her. Her head was bent low, next to his. Her parents were nowhere in sight.

"Kogan, my man. Just sharing a few last minute notions." He smiled broadly at Gabrielle. The girl fidgeted, crossing and recrossing her skinny ankles. She wore little white socks and shoes with straps, in the fashion of small Miss Temple, the tap-dancing prodigy of old. I, for one, never fell victim to Shirley's charms. Gabrielle's lure similarly eluded me. They had her rigged out in a high-waisted dress and a fat, red cummerbund that tied in a sash, with embroidered posies on sleeves and hem. Perfect attire for a grammar school dancing class, but hardly appropriate for a New York concert debut. And the child was almost fourteen.

Martin rose to his feet hurriedly. *"Marrone!"* he snapped his fingers. "Forgot to see about that change in the last movement." He darted out of the dressing room without another word, leaving the two of us alone at last. Little Miss Klee and me. Visions of Clifton Webb and the bowl of oatmeal shot through my head as the prodigy swung her legs back and forth, kicking the bottom rung of the stool in measured beats. She looked me over, then turned her gaze toward the ceiling. What is the fascination that budding young girls are supposed to hold for aging men? Are we to fall in love with their gamboling, kittenish charm?

I asked Gabrielle the whereabouts of her parents.

"With Wurtzberg. He's buying them a drink." Her voice was not childlike—serious and slightly husky.

"They left you alone?"

"Mr. Boyd wanted a private conference. And then there's you," she said.

"Ah yes," I nodded. "The very best of luck to you tonight."

She was so serious—a small, implacable sphinx, utterly without charm or spontaneity. "I am quite well prepared." Did she ever smile or run about?

"Mr. Boyd's wife is here tonight," she remarked.

"Yes, she is. You should be quite flattered."

"She's very sick," Gabrielle said innocently.

"She's been a bit better lately. Still, such an illness is disheartening." Why was I telling this to Gabrielle? Was I using Jesse's condition to try and arouse some pity, to see some reaction in that marble-white face? But what would a child—especially this child—know of illness or suffering or pain?

"I must be getting back," I said finally. "Surely you can manage on your own?"

"You needn't hold my hand," she said in her slow, measured tone. Her legs continued to swing rhythmically and, as I turned to go, I realized that she had been counting beats—perhaps her piano part for that evening—during our whole conversation. Clever little thing. There might be something more to her after all.

My insight was proved correct by her performance. Onstage, she was a fragile figure; only the red sash provided a touch of color. Her curtsy was clumsy and touching, her hair fell forward as she bent her head. When she sat down at the piano, there was an anxious moment as she settled herself onto the bench and stretched her legs toward the pedals. Then she nodded and Martin began the concerto.

Martin's conducting was authoritative and assured, and the child matched him passage for passage. In the first movement she easily shared the spotlight with the orchestra. Her solo passages were played delicately, yet with enough of a flourish to capture us all. The work got trickier—glissandos, trills—but Chopin's deceptively difficult writing emerged clear and controlled. I was stunned by her technical ability. I did not dare look at Jesse.

As the work finished, I realized what a showcase it was for Gabrielle. She gave a sophisticated reading and displayed a remarkable sense of melancholy. She might not have had such leeway in another work.

Before Martin could lower his baton, the audience was roaring madly. But Jesse did not applaud at all.

"If anything, it was too good. Too well-planned, too premeditated."

"She wasn't bad," I said diplomatically.

"No," Jesse said firmly. "Chopin should be played as if the artist is feeling him for the first time. He's a composer who demands virgins, and the very best become virgins once again when they play him. This kid is a hooker."

"Really, Jesse." She was quite ungenerous and not at all subtle. "You may not admire her as a person but you have to admire the talent. Her touch is miraculous." Genius was nothing new to Jesse; it's practically a prerequisite in the music world.

"Too premeditated. I can see right through her."

"You're being unreasonable," I scolded her. She used to be so generous toward other artists. She once gave Eric Oldfield a large sum of money to enable him to fly to an important piano competition in Canada.

Gabrielle continued her bows onstage. She received the bouquets of flowers with a surprised—dare I say humble—delight, which charmed the audience even more. Martin deferred to the girl, smiling, and the orchestra applauded as well. Only Jesse remained unconvinced that night.

She demanded that we go backstage. I looked at Norris and shook my head.

"Why can't we go?" she said petulantly.

"Sugar is waiting for us," Norris said gravely, pushing the chair up the aisle.

"Screw Sugar. I want to go backstage."

I was certain that Jesse would cause an unpleasant scene in her present mood, so I gave Norris an elbow in the ribs. "All those people will tire you out too much," Norris repeated nasally.

We hailed a Checker cab and I lifted Jesse up as Norris folded the wheelchair. She was so light for someone that tall. Had her bones grown hollow with disease? I placed her gently on the seat and before I could withdraw, she grabbed my arm. "Listen, tonight I could hear well for the first time. It's going to happen; I'm going to get better." I stared at her dark glasses, unable to gauge her expression, but glad in a way that I could not see her eyes. I was afraid I might have seen something perverse. She did not read Gabrielle's triumph in the swell of applause and the cheering; she saw her own. The bravos were for the one who would rise from the wheelchair and walk. The piano and orchestra were merely background music, that's all.

CHAPTER

23

༒

During the next few months, Jesse did feel remarkably better. So much better, in fact, that she planned a post-concert supper following one of Martin's performances with Gabrielle—her first at-home party since her illness.

"It's only right to have it that night," she explained. "It's Martin's birthday. Besides, he'd insist I invite the child regardless of when I held the party."

"Very big of you," I said, "considering the fact that you haven't a kind thing to say about her."

"She's been all but adopted into the family," Jesse said airily. "Martin spends more time with her than with me. But I won't go to this concert. I'll have to be here to arrange everything and see the first guests."

Her attitude was sour but reasonable, and so I was quite surprised when Martin came to me with a darker tale to report. "I've been to three doctors," he began.

"Great God, you're not ill too?" Frankly, he'd never looked better. He seemed to flourish as Jesse grew weaker.

"No, no—for Jesse. Three psychiatrists, awful bunch of people. They seem to think I'm the one who's sick simply because I need their advice. Then I tell them my wife has m.s. and I want to know how it affects her *here*." Martin lifted a finger and tapped his forehead. "She has the strangest notions. Do you know, she thinks I'm in love with that little girl?"

"Oh no," I demurred. "Not really."

"Ah, but she does. She's never said anything to you, has she?"

"No," I lied. "Not a thing." Not about love, surely; but nearly everything else. Still, why should I tell tales out of school?

"I think she's laying some kind of trap with this party, to embarrass Gabrielle. I think she's going to confront us with her suspicions. Hideous notion, isn't it."

"You're exaggerating. Jesse wouldn't do a thing like that. She's not unhinged. She's a lady."

"But the vindictiveness, the jealousy—she claims that I ignore her, which is untrue. She says I'm being wooed by my alter ego." He leaned over toward me and put an index finger against my chest, prodding me lightly. "She even accused me of planning a seduction."

"That doesn't sound like Jesse."

"She didn't mean physically. I think she meant as a teacher—something about winning Gabrielle over so I could mold her as a musician, as my protégé. Seduce her talent."

"Well, that's a far cry from the bedroom at least," I remarked, thinking that it really wasn't. Tolstoy's *Kreutzer Sonata*, Clara Wieck—who knew what could happen? "Martin, what are your intentions?"

"Dammit, Kogan." He drew himself up, offended by my question. "Certainly not to seduce a child in knee socks. She's a baby. I'd like to help her musically, of course—that's only natural. But I won't spend my best years molding any pianist, no matter how talented. I have to think of my own work. That's what I told these doctors."

He must have been a real peach on the couch. "What did they tell you?"

"One of them finally admitted that there can be certain mental changes associated with this disease." He sat back, triumphant.

"But you may be imagining that this is happening to Jesse." Was he? I'd noticed changes myself.

"Kogan, if you'd known her as I have for all these years you'd see how different she is."

"But I have known her," I protested weakly, not wanting to press my case any further. I wondered if Martin would have thought my attachment base.

"Would you do me a favor? At this party, just keep an eye on her. Just make sure she doesn't do anything unbalanced. I don't want Gabrielle embarrassed or hurt."

Gabrielle again. What about Jesse? I hated being appointed official watchdog. I am watchdog enough as is. I was afraid that I would fail. Could anyone guarantee control over another person, especially someone like Jesse? Even in a wheelchair, or flat on her back, she was a challenge for anybody. We all adored her but no one ever denied that she was a handful. Difficult, charming, perverse—yes, even impossible—but controllable? By whom?

With these severe doubts in mind, I reluctantly agreed to stand guard and Martin was appeased. "Disturbances in balance, loss of physical control— why not mental changes? How do we know what's going on? I tell you, she's not the girl I married."

"She's an invalid. What do you expect?"

"What about all those people you read about, the ones in wheelchairs who write novels and paint watercolors and run for Congress? Jesse has no ambition."

"What should she do? Sing to Norris's canary?"

"It's a parakeet," he said gloomily. "She's got to bounce back."

By now he had thoroughly exasperated me. "You behave as if you thought she made up the whole disease simply to worry you."

Much to my surprise, Martin had the grace to be ashamed. "I know I've been a bastard. But it's hard for me to face her. I'm performing and she's not. There was a time when I thought she might be greater. I thought I couldn't compete with my own wife."

"Why was competition necessary?"

"I have to prove that I have real talent, not just some drawing-room affectation my father called noisy."

"You want to be taken seriously. We all want to be taken seriously. That's the human condition."

"But Jesse refused. She's the only person I've ever known who laughed at me. And I liked it," he said, still amazed. "I loved it."

"Past tense?" I remarked. I was deeply curious as

to his emotional state and, at the same time, ashamed of my interest. Did I want him to admit he no longer loved her? Then I would go out and declare myself? My egotism was as bad as his. What a pair we were, what a matched set of bookends.

"Of course I still love her," he said defensively. I was sorry, but relieved, to hear this. "I just don't know what to do for her anymore. She twists everything to fit her own distorted version of things. And she believes her imaginings as if she were a witness. What can I do?" His stricken face began to crumple. I had to call an end to our tête à tête. I loathe scenes.

"Enough," I pronounced. "It's not your fault she got sick, much as you might like to flog yourself with your guilt." But I had my own sense of responsibility to contend with. Do people ever grow sick on their own? Do viruses grow in a vacuum? Of course not. We, the witches, cook up the stew in which they breed, fantastic dishes of guilt and punishment to justify the victim's plight. How else can we accept the sickening turn of events? If it isn't booze or religion to help you through, it's guilt. Martin and I were fellow-sufferers.

"I always imagine I'll go out on tour. She'll beg me to stay, and then when I return, she'll be gone."

"Oh, stop it. She may outlive us both," I snapped back. But I doubted that. She had a rotten actuarial table.

Poor Martin sat there, brooding, lost—sitting in his pretty clothes like a heap of unironed laundry. His wife belonged to him, completely, and he could not banish her from his consciousness. I had no doubt that the sound of her wheelchair tires rolled across his brain. She was inescapable, and she was all his. It was too late for any changes.

"I have no answers," I told him sadly.

"I didn't think you would." He raked his hand through his hair. "I'll see you at the party."

"I will try and talk to her," I offered, feeling dreadfully sorry for him. He bled all over my office, and I had not a tissue of reassurance with which to staunch the flow. He had brought me fame, money, and Jesse, and I had given him nothing. Absolutely nothing.

24

℞

The night of the party I could see a bit of a change in Jesse. Her face was less puffy. There was still a suggestion of fullness around her eyes and mouth, but the curve of her cheekbones was visible again, and her makeup, stagy and clever, made her resemble her old self. Almost a mortician's cleverness, I noticed on closer examination, then banished the thought at once.

Her new dress was custom-made, she said, and more expensive than anything she'd ever owned. "But this is my debut, is it not?" she said. It was charcoal gray, filmy, both bodice and sleeves spun with a web of tiny sequins; glamorous, sparkling, and a touch spiderish. Her hair (amplified by a hairpiece, she confided) was twisted into a chignon. She looked very much the dowager queen admitting her court in for an evening of obeisance. Though she might have sat in an armchair, she chose again to remain on wheels. "Mobility, Kogan. I want to be where the right people are," she said fiercely. She directed the placement of all the china and crystal atop the buffet tables and spoke mysteriously of a "big surprise" in store later in the evening. She did not seem as moody as Martin described her; in fact, some of her old flirtatiousness had returned. I kept close to her side as promised, happy to see her excitement and eagerness.

As the guests filed in, she greeted each one in turn. They bent low to kiss her cheek and to exclaim about how well she looked. Many people shouted at her, behaving in an exaggerated, theatrical fashion. I think we are all ashamed of our two good legs (and eyes and ears and whatever else we possess) in the presence of those functioning with less. And we compensate with false joviality, hail fellow well met—we raise our voices and wave our arms in the effort to distract the sufferer from his misery.

"I hope I'm not as patronizing," I said to her as the first wave of guests subsided.

"If you mean drool over my hand and hang over me like the Secret Service, of course not. But it's all right. Their intentions are good and they haven't the foggiest notion of how they look from my point of view. Did kings see it the same way? I'm just like a lazy French king, carried about in one of those boxes. Oh, Kogan, do let's get one of those candybox phone-booth things. You and Martin could each take an end. We'll go everywhere!"

"Don't be macabre. Soon you'll be strutting about. You're off the medication, are you not?"

Her hand flew to her face. "I'm much better; half of my problems came from that poison."

I saw Martin enter the foyer, shrugging out of his

coat, followed by a small party with the Klees and Gabrielle among them. Mr. Klee carried a bouquet wrapped in paper which he handed to Gabrielle after she removed her coat. She was dressed in cherry-red velvet, with the ubiquitous sash and puffed sleeves. She accepted the paper cone and then followed Martin demurely to where Jesse was seated, near the hallway to the living room.

"Dear me," Jesse noticed their approach. "Here comes the little genius now."

Gabrielle stared curiously at Jesse, then she flung out her skirt and presented the flowers. She glanced up at Martin for approval. Jesse murmured her thanks and tore away a bit of paper. The flowers were bright red roses, the same color as Gabrielle's dress.

"No," Jesse gave a strangled cry, and she dropped the bouquet to the floor. She leaned back, gasping and choking, and released the brake on her chair, then spun around and moved quickly toward the bedroom.

Gabrielle stood placidly, staring after her. Then she lifted one leg, like a crane, and idly scratched her ankle. Martin put his arm around her. "Are you all right? What happened?"

"You'd better see to Jesse," I suggested. "She was fine until you came in."

"But we got her flowers," he protested.

"Go," I pointed inside.

He left me alone with the girl and her hovering parents. The husband had his arm protectively around his wife.

"Good evening," I addressed them, introducing myself.

"I'm hungry," Gabrielle whined.

"I'll go, dear," Mr. Klee said. He wore a dark suit which hung badly on him. His wife was dressed in a watery blue dress with a bunch of wilting tea roses pinned to her bodice. She had a chalk white face with two pink splotches on each cheek. She made no effort at conversation, simply watched her daughter circle the large foyer. Gabrielle made a tour of the room, examining a small upholstered bench with claw feet, peering at a vase of leaves on a corner table, lifting up an enamelled box, turning it over, and placing it down again.

"How was the performance?" I asked. Gabrielle ignored me.

"My, yes, it was wonderful. Gaby did beautifully," Mrs. Klee said.

Gabrielle gave her mother an angry stare.

"She hates parties," Mrs. Klee inclined her head toward her daughter, who leaned against the wall and scraped one foot on the parquet floor. "Don't do that, sweetheart."

"I want to eat," Gabrielle said.

"Gaby is a little cross. She doesn't have her supper before a performance."

"Could I get you something to drink?" I offered, hoping to escape.

"Oh, no; we were taken out. Mr. Boyd arranged our dinner in a nice place. It was Russian. We had little pancakes and red soup. Gaby would like it, too. Red is her favorite color."

Mr. Klee shuffled in bearing two plates of food and a small glass of what looked like ginger ale. One plate was filled with canapés, an offering of each variety, chosen carefully to tempt an appetite. The other plate held a selection of the hot dishes from the buffet table. Gabrielle examined the contents of both plates, selected caviar on toast, daintily consumed it, then shook her head at the rest.

Mr. Klee, sad-faced with disappointment, offered

one plate to his wife. She sighed, took it, and began to consume the food with a lack of appetite and a weariness that spoke of waste not, want not.

When Martin returned, he waved me toward the living room. "I've talked her into coming back. Why don't you go sit with her?" Then he moved to the group in the foyer. "Are you all right?" I heard him ask Gabrielle. "Come along, I'll introduce you all around." Gabrielle gave him a big smile. I felt sorry for the Klees, who hung back and wolfed down the remainder of the food that Mr. Klee had chosen.

The party guests greeted Martin with visible excitement. They crowded around him and Gabrielle, congratulating them both on the performance. I moved back to Jesse's side. She sipped a glass of liquor, its undiluted color a match for her glossy dark hair.

Before I could say something innocuous, Jesse brought up the incident with the flowers. "He should have remembered," she said. "Red roses all over the dressing room floor, dozens of red roses."

So that was why she had cried out—she'd broken that vase of flowers. Poor thing, everything seemed part of some huge, dark plot to her.

"He should have known. He told me I was acting like a baby. He doesn't understand."

"You're fine," I consoled her. "Remarkably brave."

"He gives me no credit. He saves it all for her." She took a good, stiff swallow of her drink.

"She seems very attached to him."

"And vice versa. The little girl he never had," she said bitterly.

"Have you seen the Steiners yet?" I tried to skirt that dangerous subject. "They're anxious to talk with you."

"He's in love with her," Jesse said.

"Don't be silly. He's over thirty and look at her in those white socks—a mere baby. You can't possibly believe that!" But Martin's stories of her erratic behavior rose up accusingly. "You stop that talk right now. I insist." I would not listen to her. I wanted her just as sane and funny and reasonable as she'd always been. It was one thing to accept physical impairment, but personality changes? "I forbid it," I told her. "You'll not get away with that nonsense around me."

"There is evidence," she hissed. "Listen to me."

"Put down that drink. Stop it. You mustn't let Martin see, don't let him hear you. Don't say anything rash."

"You don't believe me either. You think I'm crazy. Oh God, I'm surrounded by people who want to save me from myself! Why won't you believe me?" She began to get hysterical and I quietly took away her drink, walked behind her chair, and pushed her from the room. She held her head in her hands. Few people noticed our departure and those who did averted their eyes at once. She was far too vivid a reminder of weakness, failing bodies, and death. No one could bear to look at her for too long.

I took her into the bedroom and pushed her over to the window. She always loved to watch the view. I raised the shade and we stayed there, in the dark, as she spoke quietly to me. "I hear him on the telephone. She yells at him, I'm sure of it. He doesn't like to be pushed; he gets very quiet and a funny tone comes into his voice. Then he'll argue back. He'll tell her he didn't play this or that movement too quickly, or that the finale was not too loud. She ties him in knots. He can barely talk when she's through with him. She isn't really a child—that business with the white socks is just an act. She's the one who arranges everything. You saw those parents. What could they possibly do on their own?"

"But I thought it was Wurtzberg," I protested.

"Idiot, she hasn't signed with him. She wants you."

It didn't make any sense. The girl's behavior did not correlate with what Jesse was telling me. "Why me?"

"Because you manage Martin. Because she wants Martin."

Now she sounded crazy. I was flooded with grief. "Jesse, my dearest, you know how I care for you. But all this is so far-fetched. First of all, the child barely acknowledges my existence. And second, you're mistaking Martin's interest. She is simply the career he never had, the chance he was denied. She isn't threatening to him as real competition because she is a child. She's safe."

"On the contrary, Nicholas. She is his nemesis. I'm afraid for my husband."

"I don't think you should repeat this, any of this, to another soul."

"Because she sees me in a wheelchair she thinks she has nothing to fear. She knows I see through her. But I shall fight her and believe me, she won't have an easy time of it."

"Hush," I said, stroking her hair as we looked down at the transfixing nighttime view of the park, the stripped-down strees interspersed with the small lights which illuminated only a small halo of air around them. The ground was as dark and bottomless as the sea. "No one shall ever hurt you," I soothed as if she were a sick child. I knew nothing of children but the words and gestures came automatically to me and I was grateful. *Oh Jesse, I wanted to say, forget the rest; it was all always you*—but I settled instead for Kogan the implacable, Kogan the unflappable, Kogan the neuter. How it hurts to care, I saw as she knotted a handkerchief in her hands. The rubies in her bracelet gleamed as rich and red as blood. They were like a bad luck charm, an omen of terrible things to come, and I wished she would never wear the bracelet again.

"Come, let's go back," she offered finally. "You'll miss my surprise." And when I pushed her into the dining room, there it was—a giant cake in the shape of a grand piano, with thirty-two candles lit for Martin's birthday. And he, quite proudly, allowed Gabrielle to blow them out.

CHAPTER
25
ॐ

"I know I shall die but there's something I must tell you—"

Jesse clicked off the television set. Lately the plot lines had come too close to her own situation. She flung herself back against the pillows and twisted her legs around the sheets. She felt so much better. The sensation of tingling and weakness had been lifting as if she were rising from a canopy of fog. Now, if she could walk by herself, she would be completely well. And sing? Perhaps that, too.

The doctors were smirky with satisfaction. *See? We told you,* they said, and they brandished their ball-point pens and wrote entries in her thick record file. She had learned to read upside down, in order to decipher their notations. But surprisingly, most of them wrote down exactly what they told her. They tapped her, poked her, prodded her, and recorded their findings. But her chart was no Rosetta Stone. She would have to search elsewhere.

The soap operas, a sort of continuing passion play during the worst of her long winter, no longer held her interest. At first, when the characters seemed fresh and new, she would record significant snatches of dialogue in a notebook. *Dagmar:* "I've seen it all before. Men can't bear suffering." *Arthur:* "You're wrong. He's doing all he can." *Dagmar:* "Why doesn't he take it like a man?" *Arthur:* "You expect too much."

For quite a while, Jesse toyed with the notion of using that last line on her tombstone: *She Expected Too Much.* But it did not read well; it was ungracious, unsonorous. She preferred something more melodic, something from the lieder she used to sing. She hadn't yet chosen an appropriate line (too many seemed appropriate), but while she was in the hospital, during her third stay, she had planned her funeral. It was during one of the bad times, when her condition regressed so swiftly she could hardly believe she was awakening as the same person who had gone to sleep the night before. Her systems failed her one by one, until she was reduced to relying on different people with different machines to take over each function. There was her kidney person, her blood person, her breathing person, and her stomach person; all different, as if they were children in a school play portraying parts of the human body. She had been cast in one such pageant in the third grade. "I am your liver," she had announced to the audience. A liver; how ironic. "I am your die-er," she tried instead. "I am going to die." One of the nurses heard her saying those words again and again, her incantation against death in the early hours of the morning. The nurse had come to her bedside and stood there silently for a long time. Then she raised Jesse's wrist and took her pulse. The touch of a well person made Jesse feel she had been visited by the Angel of Life, and the bad night passed into memory.

She found it strange that she should contract so horrible a disease. She had always been so healthy. As a child, when she had been sick with a cold or fever, which was rare, she still maintained a look of glowing health. She was the sort of sturdy, farm-girl type that her part of the country bred as automatically as cows, and she had ripened without incident. No broken bones, no tonsillectomy, nothing.

She wanted a complete recovery. The doctors said "partial remission," but she had heard hopeful stories of people living long periods of disease-free time when machines and chairs were forgotten. She knew her chances for a long remission were slim after so many severe attacks. But medical statistics left room for hope. There was always an extra category that defied classification. It never occurred to her that some of the uncategorized might be dead from secondary causes—pneumonia, for example. She envisioned the leftovers all basking in the sun on a Florida beach, beneath a spreading fringe of palm leaves, laughing about their escape from death, gathered together like a club—the Veterans of Foreign Diseases, or some such. They would all wear paper party hats and laugh themselves silly as they feasted on vast banquets of Miami hotel food. She saw herself graciously heaping plate after plate from the buffet, then sitting down to dine with wine and perhaps a cigarette in a long holder, as she said, "Darling, do tell. Wasn't it the most absurd experience? To have had such a ghastly disease!"

Whenever she saw another person in a wheelchair she turned away. She could not bear to meet their eyes, was afraid that the other person was resigned to a life of bouncing over curbs and being yanked across thresholds like a recalcitrant shopping basket. She looked away and pretended she did not see them, just as she saw other people in the street glance away and ignore her. But the distant ones were better than the over-curious. There was always some sweet, sentimental slob who melted at the sight of Jesse, whose eyes filled with tears and whose purse-mouthed sympathy drifted across a theater lobby or through a crowded elevator, along with murmurs of, "What a shame, so young, look at that, how sad, it really makes you stop and think." Jesse clenched her teeth to avoid screaming. Was that pity, though? Or disguised relief. She had always liked people who nursed abandoned birds back to health with eye-droppers of warm milk, and were these not the same folk who clucked over her, with her broken wings? She felt her personality warping, changing to fit the mold of the wheelchair, just as her posture had adjusted to its curve. She felt neither pity nor sympathy for anyone; it gave her pleasure to swear at Norris. Ordinarily, Jesse would never have allowed herself to show her true feelings. She would have been the lady, and allowed Norris to pass along quietly. Now, stuck in with her for days on end, she cursed her, and told her to shut up, and that she hoped her parakeet would die; and she felt much better afterwards. *I am becoming mean,* she knew, and she took some pleasure in the change.

The worst part of the illness was being alone—not physically alone, for Norris was always around, forever in obnoxious attendance, but emotionally stranded as if she had been washed ashore in a foreign country where she did not speak the language and the customs were frightening and strange. Her illness became her companion, a second spirit, her double. Even its name took on significance. Jesse once asked if she could get license plates for her wheelchair. *MS/JS.* Her own personal disease. The doctor she asked, a neurologist on the hospital staff, did not think her idea was funny. He proceeded to lecture her about how sick his patients were, how none of them would ever really recover in the sense of being disease-free. "So you have the vegetable stand," Jesse said. And he gave her a fierce look as he manipulated her left leg with his puffy, chemical-stained fingers. "Why choose something so hopeless to do? Why not broken bones? Or babies?" she asked. He shook his head and replied, "Someone has to do it." And she thought his answer was stupid and noble. It made her think of a movie Martin had taken her to see a long time ago, a Charlie Chaplin film. She had never seen Chaplin before. In the movie, he played a scruffy soul who took different jobs, one of which was street-cleaner. Pushing his broom down a wide boulevard, he reached the end of the street and, as he did, a parade of elephants tramped into sight. He stood stock-still, and the audience screamed with laughter at the sight of those elephants, and all they implied, confronting the little man with the broom. Jesse thought of the doctor and his hopeless cases and she saw him in his white coat, watching his charges as pathetically as Chaplin did the elephants.

"I seem to have lost my sense of humor," Jesse said one day. And Norris answered, "Have you, indeed?" For once Jesse was grateful that another person was present. Norris sat quietly sewing buttons on an old raincoat Jesse had bought in London. "Norris," Jesse turned toward her and propped herself up on one elbow, "I was once very funny. I did funny things. I went out on the street in costume once, to have lunch with Martin. We went to a coffee shop. It was, it was called—" she hesitated. Why couldn't she remember; she could see it so clearly. Sometimes she had trouble with names. It was hard to have them right there when you needed them. She tried to remember the front of the place, where the name might be hanging over the door. "The waitress was not very friendly. Something like you, Norris."

"Humph," Norris said. "And what was the name of this place?"

"Oh, God," said Jesse. "I don't know."

Norris had been waiting for the admission and she swooped down like a vulture. "Now don't get yourself all excited. Here, I'll bring you a glass of fruit juice and you can just lie back and rest. You're supposed to rest every day. Doctor says it's not good for you to worry too much."

Can I take a course in my life? Could I study everything that has happened to me, all the names and faces and places I have been? I am like a senile old woman at death whose mind washes clean and there is nothing before, only after. Death is everything after. But I'm not ready to die, not yet. If I cannot remember, though, I am coming closer. Panic eddied around her in small tidepools that caught her limbs, and she twisted awkwardly, fighting back. She couldn't remember the name of the restaurant. Norris brought her a glass of apple juice. As she caught sight of Jesse flinging herself across the bed, she called out "Mr. Boyd!" Then she carefully set down the juice glass.

Martin rushed into the room, clad in his favorite

at-home outfit, an old silk robe. Modest Norris gasped and averted her eyes as it pulled open. Martin bent over his wife. "Jess, Jess, can you hear me? What's happening? Is she having a fit? A convulsion? Call the doctor."

Jesse choked and tried to speak. "The place," she said, "the place—"

Norris spoke to the doctor on the phone. "A sedative, yes, right away."

"Jesse, please sit up and try and take a deep breath," Martin pleaded. She was gasping violently; her chest seemed as fluttery as Norris's parakeet.

"I can't remember," she screamed and then, as if she had been convulsing on the words, she stopped moving. She had admitted her failure before the two people from whom she guarded her darkest defeats, and now there was nothing left to fight against. She closed her eyes.

"Remember what?" Martin asked Norris. Norris said nothing. She held out a pill and the glass of juice.

"Take this, Mrs. Boyd."

"What is it you can't remember?" Martin asked.

"Your pill," Norris said sternly.

"Jesse, don't scare me. Answer. What is it?"

"It's time to sit up and drink your juice," Norris scolded.

"In fifteen minutes I have to go to a rehearsal, then I have to go to Kogan's to meet with Gabrielle."

Jesse felt something stir, a small animal in a bush.

"Gabrielle," she said. And the name returned, simply and quietly. "It was Child's." She opened her eyes.

"Oh, for Christ's sake," Martin said, limp with the passing of fear. "I thought you were having a fit. Don't scare me like that again."

He and Norris exchanged looks of disgust.

Jesse sat up in bed and began to arrange her hair. She felt as if she had just pulled herself from a pool in which she was drowning and now, looking back, it seemed as if the struggle were nothing more than good exercise. All of that effort for a word, a simple name, but how good the return of that word made her feel. It was of such small triumphs that her days were composed. She moved haltingly from one to another, as if from rock to rock across a small stream, balancing precariously, always searching for the next stone. And all the while the water rushed on, bearing with it the complexities that looked like so many idle leaves to everyone else but which were, to Jesse, as threatening and vast as the timbers of a giant edifice swept away by flood.

THREE

CHAPTER

26

♈

During the next few years, I watched as Martin Boyd became even more famous. I daresay I wasn't surprised at the fame, just shocked at the form it took. The eager fans at the dressing room gave way to unruly hordes swooning *en masse* as the star machinery cranked out artifacts for public consumption. There were t-shirts that read *BOYD AT THE BOWL* (his famous Hollywood concerts). There were Boyd records displayed in fancy pyramids in store windows and Boyd record-autographing sessions with panting lunchtime lines. Boyd hung next to Bogart and Bob Dylan in midtown poster shops. One eager young lady actually snuck into his dressing room during a concert and stripped off her trenchcoat to reveal the words *ALMA MAHLER* painted across her bare chest. Martin's name was in all the columns and his eccentricities were becoming the stuff of legend.

Had he actually fired two horn players in San Francisco for talking during rehearsal? (No). Did the tympanist of a great European orchestra threaten to punch him out? (Yes). Magazines with his picture on the cover sold thousands more than usual. There was talk of a great appointment in the works, a fabulous position with a top-flight orchestra.

I have in my possession one of the famous Boyd publicity stills distributed during those maddening years—Martin dressed all in black, his hands raised in passionate supplication, the lock of hair falling over his eyes. The members of the orchestra were just a blur in the background. It was Martin's favorite photograph, and Gabrielle's, as well. In *Look* magazine, she was pictured curled up on her schoolgirl's bed surrounded by her collection of international stuffed animals, casting an adorable and adoring smile at The Photo, framed and propped up on her nightstand.

Nowhere was Jesse mentioned. Her disease was too unglamorous to discuss; dying did not have the chic it has acquired today. Everyone says the public has a short memory but I say it has no memory at all. We play with stars like rabbits in a shooting gallery. They scoot along before us as we take potshots and if one gets away, no matter; there are an endless number to follow. The rabbit-producing celebrity machinery is hyperactive—a star a minute. If one disappears, what of it?

As I mulled over my crowded roster, deciding I'd had my fill of stars and star headaches, Martin called me to request that I take on Gabrielle Klee. It was a repeat performance of his maneuverings with Jesse so many years before. But this time, I was determined that he not seduce me again.

"She has a manager. Wurtzberg is a great name. He can sell her on the strength of his reputation alone for the rest of her career."

"She'll outlive him by decades," Martin shot back.

Gabrielle wanted me the way a child wants a kewpie doll prize. *That one,* she pointed, and Martin obeyed. She wanted what she did not have. "I'm not buying it, my boy. No." I had said that before, too.

"We're going to tour together, even Europe," he pointed out. "She isn't comfortable with Wurtzberg."

"Comfortable? This isn't an easy chair. What does she know? She'll throw away her career on a whim," I growled, trying to sound tough.

"You're not implying that you're a bad manager, are you? Come, come. She simply wants the best."

"Such flattery. Dear boy, we both know that his imprimatur is far more weighty than mine. But she is a special case. As she grows out of her child prodigy stage she'll have to be handled very delicately. She's getting a little old for that title anyway. Isn't she near sixteen? I'm not up to the kind of manipulation necessary to book an overgrown adolescent. Suppose she has only a few good years left?"

"I'll guarantee the girl will be great. I'll see to it she isn't exploited."

"So you want to be her manager, Martin. And I should lend my name, be the beard for your enterprise."

"No need to be nasty, Nicholas. I thought I could ask this of you."

"I am opposed and would urge you to consider the details again. Perhaps you're overlooking several things in your haste."

"Perhaps you're being pig-headed," he charged.

"Tell Jesse I'll be calling her tonight. How's she doing?"

"A bit better, I suppose, but she still has her moments."

"Yes, they do get labile," he said professionally.

"They get what?"

"The specialist warned me. Mood swings, up and down." He spoke melodramatically. His wife was his own private soap opera.

"Why tour so much, then??" I said, a fool for interfering.

"What kind of manager are you? Have you seen the reviews?"

"Yes, I know you're the next Toscanini. But if you believe everything you read in the papers we have a problem. Do try and keep your hat size down. And come back home for a bit. You haven't been around for weeks. She's rotting away in that apartment."

"Don't say that."

"I am telling you."

"You're taking sides. How dare you?"

"There are no sides. She is your wife."

"Don't mention any of these plans to her. I'll tell her myself. Adieu," he said curtly.

Martin, Brahmin though he was, had the manners of a pool shark. Should you ever sell your soul to the devil, make sure he has a bit more class.

Taking sides. Did I take sides? I ought to have remained completely neutral, like Switzerland; but I decided that if I planned a short American tour for Boyd and Klee, just a little one, then perhaps Martin would be satisfied and shut up about the change in managers. I telephoned Wurtzberg with my proposal and he agreed, asking only that his name be first in all the advertising. I gladly settled for the role of co-presenter, hoping to knock out all those dreadful little birds with one David-like heave of a stone. A short fall tour, period. No change in status for the Klee girl. I did not want to manage her, for aside from my normal aversion to beings female (save Jesse), there was something about Gabrielle that made me want to keep a safe distance. She played as if possessed by demons, and it worried me that when she stopped performing, the demons had to go somewhere. It was only logical that they took up residence in her soul.

CHAPTER

27

ℛ

Gabrielle sulked at pool-side and tried to distract Martin from the score of the Bruckner symphony he was studying. His eyes scanned the lines and his hands twitched unconsciously. Gabrielle pulled at the top of her bathing suit and tried to expose an inch more of her small bosom. She thought it indecent that at sixteen she should have no chest. She hated being called a child but understood that it had served her well. If only she could shed that skin at concert's end. She sighed dramatically and turned onto her stomach. That made her breasts hang down and seem a bit fuller. She looked at Martin to see if he noticed. He did not. She whined like a puppy.

"You seem to take it personally that the weather is so infernally hot," he remarked, not lifting his eyes from the score.

"Cleveland," she said with a groan.

"A great music town."

"It's a shit-hole," she said.

He looked up. "Where did you pick up that language? Don't let your mother hear you. Where is she?" They were alone beside the over-chlorinated hotel pool, lying on towels in the September sun. The Midwest was suffering a drought, and their last tour booking, in Chicago, had been torture when the air-conditioning in the hall failed.

"I sent her shopping," Gabrielle said, snapping the elastic on her bathing suit top. She grinned. "Wasn't that smart?"

"Poor lady, you ride her like a train."

"I told you we'd get this tour," Gabrielle said. "I never had any doubts."

"Don't remind me. Kogan still doesn't approve."

"He's such a prissy old lady. Has he ever had a girlfriend?"

"My child, that is not your business."

"I think he's queer," she said in a peculiar tone of voice.

"Then why are you begging to switch managers?"

"I want your manager. I don't like mine. He treats me like a baby."

"Don't be so eager to grow up," Martin cautioned. "You'll lose your meal ticket."

"Boyd, I'm good and you know I'm good. I'll make it."

"Not if you don't take off time to study. You've been performing too much. People are going to want to see you branch out and try new things. They'll expect change all of a sudden, when you least expect it. And then you've got to be prepared. Learning new pieces isn't enough. There has to be development.

They'll want to sense that you've been through the fire."

"I'm sixteen," she pouted.

"Sixteen is nothing."

"You'll teach me," she said, moving closer to him.

He turned onto his side and propped up the score. "Gaby, I've taught you everything I can. When this tour is finished, I'll expect to hear that you are going to study with one of the masters."

"So much for you," she said, and she stood up and dived into the pool, neatly and cleanly, with barely a splash.

Martin, who romped like a polar bear when he swam, wondered if there was anything she had not mastered. She knew several languages, she knew art—in fact, she had steered him through the Art Institute when they were in Chicago. She had begun to show him that she had a life away from the keyboard, as if to celebrate a coming of age. His insistence that she take up a period of study was partly professional and partly personal. He was alarmed by this sudden change and did not want to be left alone with her. He did not know what to expect next.

In the beginning it had been easy. She needed direction. She looked up to him and he was happy to oblige, to see that she had the chances he had missed. There was great pleasure in helping her, especially when Jesse had been so ill. It was a relief to feel of use to someone. And Gabrielle had seemed so unloved, so withdrawn. He knew that her parents adored her, but that did not seem to matter. Only when she began to respond to him, to lash out, did he feel that he had touched a nerve. After their second concert, she had accused him of obscuring her part with flashy theatrics. She had raged and yelled, kicking like a child; then collapsed, weeping, in his arms. She had cried and told him she was sorry. He had held her a long time, smoothing her hair, noticing her tiny ears, and how separate each strand of hair seemed, so fine, like silk thread. That was the night of the party—the night he had slipped up and bought the red roses. He had forgotten because he was infatuated with Gabrielle. But Jesse had accused him of worse, darker things, and he had done nothing, nothing. He had comforted a little girl.

Gabrielle dived beneath the water and then emerged, paddling happily. Only a child could be happy in such oppressive heat. Martin watched her from the corner of his eye. She could be every bit the spoiled brat if she wanted attention. But he enjoyed her presence, her clean, unlined face, her lithe motion. She was innocent, charmingly so—the last innocent person he knew. But when they were in the museum in Chicago, he was aware of something more in her touch as she grabbed his hand; an adult's touch, expressing a need of consolation on a deeper level. He was confused. He didn't know what she wanted. He wished she were back in her knee socks and pretty dresses, still clearly a little girl. A woman in the room with the giant Seurat had stared at them with open suspicion. Did she think they were a couple? The woman had frowned at them, disapproval clearly written on her pinched face. Gabrielle had mocked the woman because of her unfashionable clothes, then pranced about the gallery, and the woman had frowned more deeply and left in a huff.

Why was everything in life so confusing except when he stood before an orchestra? He wheedled and pushed and prodded his musicians into shape, driving them toward the perfect sound he demanded and they, resentful, made him the enemy. If he faltered, no orchestra would ever obey him again. Only when he studied his music in private did he feel comforted. Out on the podium, he was engaged in a struggle that ripped great chunks of energy from him and left him feeling old. How did the grand old men keep up the pace? Toscanini, Stokowski, Furtwangler, Klemperer—how had they done it? Younger men than he were pulling up behind him, ready to take his place. And always, behind it all, was the spectre of his wife lying helplessly at home, accusing him of injustices and grave wrongs. What did they all want of him? If only one of them would make his desires plain, then he could act.

Gabrielle climbed gracefully from the pool and padded over to him, sprinkling drops of water on his back. "Come for a swim," she demanded.

"Is that what you want?" he said.

She stared down at him and he, shading his eyes from the sun's glare, caught her gaze and held it. "Yes," she said.

So he threw down his score and tossed her into the pool.

In Buffalo, Gabrielle kept at Martin, insisting that he call Kogan and make arrangements for her to change managers. At first he refused, but as she persisted, he struck a bargain with her. He would ask Kogan again if she would agree to enter a period of study following the tour—no performing, simply study with one of Leora Davis's recommended teachers.

"Davis is a very old lady. The teacher is probably ninety-five, all curled up like a leaf," Gabrielle complained.

"What have you got against old age?" Martin asked as he watched her eat a cheeseburger with ladylike precision.

"Why?" she said. "Think you're getting on?"

"Yes. You're absolutely right," he admitted. Sometimes her perceptiveness staggered him, and he wondered if she were really sixteen.

"Then it's all arranged. You'll call." Gabrielle blotted her mouth daintily, getting lipstick on her napkin.

"Where's your mother," he said suddenly.

"Buying me some necessities. Want to know what?"

"Not clinically I don't."

"You're as much of a prude as old Kogan."

"Will you stop calling everyone old?" Martin signalled for the check.

"But I'm dying to be old. I want to be twenty."

"Whatever for?"

"So I can stop travelling with my mother. She snores. And I hate the way her teeth clack when she chews. All that noise disrupts my concentration. Clackety-clack. I can't hear anything. Across the room, when she's having breakfast, I can hear her."

"I'm glad I'm not your mother. Sometimes I wonder what I do that offends your delicate sensibility." He threw down a few bills and steered Gabrielle out of the restaurant.

She took his arm. "Nothing. You're absolutely perfect." Then, with the sweetest smile, she added, "As long as you don't rush my solos."

Martin called Kogan that night, having assumed the responsibility for Gabrielle's career choices. As long as she was represented by Wurtzberg, he had no say. Kogan, being his friend, would listen to him. Kogan refused once more, but Martin hung up convinced that his manager would reconsider. How could anyone turn down a gold mine?

The telephone woke Martin in the middle of the night. He cursed and knocked the phone to the floor. Bending over, he grabbed the receiver. "Who is it?" he demanded.

"It's me," a husky voice said, and for an instant he thought it was Jesse. Then he realized it was Gabrielle. She sounded frightened.

"What's wrong? Are you sick?"

"I have something to tell you. I'm coming down."

"It's almost three in the morning. Can't it wait?"

"No," she said.

"You can't come to my room—wait a minute," he began, but she had hung up.

He groped for his bathrobe and turned on the bedside lamp, then pulled the covers up over the bed and combed his hair with his fingers. *Jesus, I need a haircut,* he noticed in the elaborately framed mirror that hung over the hotel bureau.

The door handle turned and Gabrielle rushed in, her hair hanging loose, flowing over a printed, sheer robe that covered a matching nightgown. Her feet were bare.

"What are you doing, running around in the corridors like this?" he demanded sternly.

"No one saw me," she said excitedly.

"I want to know what couldn't wait until morning." He folded his arms, trying to behave as paternally as possible.

"I love you," she said.

He said the first thing he could think of. "I am thirty-five years old."

"I do—I want to," she went on.

Martin had not thought of love for a long time. He loved music, he loved applause, he loved fame. Did he love Gabrielle? Did he believe what she was saying?

"Go back to bed, go to sleep. You need your rest. Everything will be fine in the morning."

"You have to hear it. I've been planning to tell you for a long time. Even though I know you can be awful, I don't care. I love you."

Awful? She thinks I'm awful? "You don't really know me," he said, fumbling with the tie on his robe. "You think that because we perform together there is a need for something more. But it's really the music you love."

"Fool," she said. "It's you."

"I don't know why." He was sixteen again, fumbling and awkward, desperately wanting approval but not knowing where to seek it, happy only with his music. It had always been easier to pour it all out through the keyboard than face to face.

"Do there have to be reasons?" she demanded. "Is that how you think when you're thirty-five?"

"You're just a child, just infatuated."

"No. Infatuation is a kind of blindness. I see you. I've seen you be hard, I've seen you unreasonable. This hasn't exactly been a courtship, you know."

"Go to bed," he said, suddenly exhausted. He was all confused. She was standing before him offering herself, and he could not bring himself to take her up or throw her out. She had all the answers. "Please, Gaby. Please go."

"Promise me you'll think about what I told you."

"How can I help it? I'm not very good at this sort of thing—I've never been much with women."

"That's quite funny. I see them throw themselves

at you every night. You don't do badly. You can be very charming, you know."

"Are you sure you're only sixteen?"

"Of course. But maybe I'm not. How strange this is—it's just like music. I can see it all so clearly, as if it were written out. The notes aren't forced; they come naturally. All I have to do is repeat them." She moved over, close to him. She was tall; even in her bare feet, her head reached almost to his shoulders. Before he could step back, she pressed her head against his chest and wrapped her arms around him. Her hair was just as he remembered, soft, lightly scented. He made no move to embrace her. He was afraid she could hear his heart beating, racing wildly. Gently, he removed her arms and placed his hands on her shoulders. Stepping backward, he shook her lightly, saying, "Just go quietly back upstairs. Don't let anyone see you. Tomorrow we go on as usual."

"Martin," she said, and she reached up and kissed him on the mouth. Her lips were warm and firm. All of his thoughts fled in confusion and he kissed her without thinking of anything. He grabbed her and pressed her against him, hard; and suddenly she broke away, running lightly to the door and out, without a glance behind her.

He stood where she had left him, shock and surprise mixed with terror, loneliness, and a sad feeling of advancing age. Tomorrow he would return to his invalid wife, the proper fate for a man so confused that he could be seduced by a child.

CHAPTER

28

♈

"Now the tour is over," Gabrielle said as the plane headed to New York. "Do you remember Rochester's wife, locked in her room? There had to be a great holocaust before he was free for Jane."

"Are they still reading Brontë?" said Martin, ignoring the thrust of her remarks.

"I read the synopsis. Cliff's Notes."

"Shame, child."

"I'd rather read Sagan. My tutor thinks it's a waste of time, but it's not. It's very educational." She glanced over at her mother, who occupied the seat across the aisle. Mrs. Klee had her head thrown back, taking a nap. "Martin, I know you don't want to talk about what happened."

"Nothing happened," he said sharply.

"I just want you to know that what I'm about to say has nothing to do with the way that I feel about you. Well, it does in the sense that I want you to be as great as you could possibly be, with nothing to hold you back. And I think you should know the answer, too. You should leave your wife."

"Gabrielle, that is not your affair."

"Don't be angry. Listen to me, listen to what I have to say. Don't you see how tortured you are? How little you let yourself enjoy anything? You have no freedom anymore, no control over what happens to you."

"I'm damn free. I can do whatever I choose."

"That's a fallacy. Why not ask yourself what would be best for her? You can't tell me you haven't thought of leaving her already. You can't tell me that you love her."

It stung, but it was true. Martin no longer understood his wife. "It would prove nothing," he said angrily. "There is no way I can walk out on her. She's an invalid."

"Don't you want children?" Gabrielle asked point-blank.

He stared at her in wide-eyed misery, feeling much like a dumb, lowing animal about to receive the final blow prior to butchering.

"Open yourself up," she pleaded. "Allow people to love you. The public will change; they'll give you as much as you allow them to give. It will be even greater—it's bottomless, like the ocean. Martin, you have to live. Don't you want to?"

"You're my bad genie," he said. "I rubbed the lamp and you appeared, telling me all the wrong things, granting the wrong wishes."

"The marriage isn't fair to her. You can't let her go on believing you love her if you don't. You can

still pay for her nurses and doctors. I'll make you
even richer. We'll keep performing together—we sell
out every house! I want you strong. You promised
we'd go to Europe; I want you to take me around the
world."

"You're such a child." But she spoke like a
woman and he was caught up in her excitement. How
could he fight her when she was only repeating everything in his own head?

"We'll go to Japan. Have you been to Japan?
They're the best audiences—there's never a sound in
the house. You can feel the concentration. You'll love
it."

Scenes flashed through his head—Venice, Rome,
Paris, London—seeing all of it again, walking through
the streets with Gabrielle, unencumbered, free to go
wherever he chose. She made it sound so easy.

But if Gabrielle knew exactly how he felt, it followed that Jesse might know or might find out. How
could he face her then? He had tried to appease her
with flowers and gifts, daily phone calls; but she was
distant and unforgiving. But forgive him what? He
had not done anything to forgive, at least not yet.

"If you think you're the first man who's wanted
to leave a wife who was ill, you're crazy," Gabrielle
said impatiently. "And were you ever really happy?
What was it like when she was well? How was it
then?"

"It was fine," he said. But what had it been like?
Had he loved her? She had been so strong, so
passionate and so charming; she had overwhelmed
him. Shouldn't he love her even more, now that she
was reduced to some essence of self, the raw Jesse?
He could not think of love. She made him think of

death. He knew that if he did not leave the marriage he risked becoming old before his time—old, used-up and drained of life.

"It isn't for me," Gabrielle said, "it's for you. I want you strong."

She and her mother left him at the airport and climbed into a taxicab with their suitcases, Gabrielle waving brightly, smiling, as if they had just had the most pleasant of conversations. He stared at a family waiting to board another flight—a handsome family, two children neatly dressed, standing quietly. Would that scene of order and serenity ever be his? He knew that he would always blame himself for his wife's illness, always regard her sickness as a reproach. He doubted that he could ever leave her and start anew. The ties he had with Jesse were too strong; they were written in blood. And though he might rail against the bonds, they could hardly be broken at a mere suggestion. He would have to continue as best he could.

But he was unprepared for what awaited him at the apartment. As he unlocked the door, he heard music—an opera record, *Nozze di Figaro*. Singing along, in a parody of her once-lovely voice, was Jesse. Jesse on the record sang Cherubino's love song as Jesse in the apartment strained to match the notes. When he shut the door, she stopped the record and he heard the sound of the tires move across the floor. She appeared in the hallway, her face lit in welcome. "I'm glad you're home," she said, and he knew he would say nothing about the future, nothing at all.

"I'm working on my comeback," she reported as he bent over to kiss her. Her face was less swollen; in fact, without the puffiness it looked ravaged and ill—her cheeks were sunken, marked with deep lines.

But she was more eager and excited than she had been in months. He hoped this was not one of her mood swings.

"I have all the clippings from your tour. Kogan brought the out-of-town papers here. All those new works! You must have put in twenty hour days. You look exhausted. But see me? Don't I look well?" She spun her wheelchair around. "I made Norris see that I was up and dressed by nine every day, then out for our walk and back to work by ten thirty or eleven. Soon I'll call my coach and we'll plan the first recital. See what I've done? I had all the rugs taken up, so I could move around more easily."

Martin's footsteps echoed on the bare floors as he followed her into the living room. The furniture sat dumbly, marooned on a sea of parquet. Some of his favorite antique pieces had been shoved aside and covered with sheets. "I didn't want to leave anything valuable in my way," Jesse indicated with a frantic hand. "I'm still so clumsy at navigating myself about. Norris is no longer allowed to push me inside." She lowered her voice and glanced about suspiciously. "I'm just about ready to ditch Norris. All of this is preparation for the last stand. She's made herself mighty comfortable here; I think she's got a supply of cuttlebone to last that bird the next decade. But she's got to go. I no more need a companion than you do. Kogan thinks my improvement has been remarkable. Don't you?" Her eyes were very shiny, as if she'd just put in drops. Martin tried not to stare too hard at her skinny face. She had tied back her hair in a severe knot and her ears, which he had never much liked, stuck out, looking larger than usual. He disliked her in hairstyles which exposed them.

She pulled out a loose leaf notebook and opened

it to a page of writing. "This is my progress book. Each day, I write down what I'm studying, so as to remember exactly." She reached over toward a small table and grabbed her glasses. Placing them clumsily over her ears, hooking the eyepieces crookedly, she indicated to Martin with one finger where she had written down the hours of practice and which songs and arias she had relearned. The rakish glasses made her look like a foolish old woman. Martin turned away from her and stared out at the park through uncurtained windows. The leaves were ready to fall.

"Where are the drapes?" he asked.

"They absorb too much sound. I had them taken down."

"Oh." The room felt chilly. "And did you stop the heat, too?"

"I had it turned off in the front of the apartment. The dryness made my throat constrict. I want conditions to be absolutely perfect. I'm working toward my greatest recital of all." She flipped through the notebook and drew out a piece of cardboard with fancy lettering on it. It looked like a restaurant menu. "This is my program—subject to change, of course."

She had chosen some of the most difficult works in the repertory, and the second half of the program was the entire *Kindertotenlieder*, which she had never sung before. "Don't you think this is rather ambitious for your return?" Martin asked politely.

"Nonsense," she said, and she snatched the cardboard away, placing it tenderly back between the pages of the notebook. "Did Horowitz shy away from anything when he returned to Carnegie? No. He sat down and played that Bach-Busoni bear right off."

"He hit some clinkers too."

"He left them all on the record. He wants everyone to see him as he is. He came back from a terrible thing. And I will too."

"Singing clinkers is a different story," Martin observed.

"I knew you'd be against me. I knew you'd say I couldn't do it." She jerked at the brake and shoved herself to a far corner of the room, bumping clumsily into the couch and then crashing a corner of her footrest into the wall. Cursing, she maneuvered badly as she tried to work the chair backwards. "Goddamn this mechanical monster," she cried, and then she turned and faced him, "and damn you to hell for not believing in me."

"I believe in you, Jesse," he tried to reason. "But I don't want you to set unreasonable goals for yourself."

"Unreasonable," she shouted. "I'm not being unreasonable. You are. You don't want a wife who performs, who might steal some of your precious acclaim."

Her manic energy had soured, and her face, pinched and accusatory, seemed to grow puffy once again, like an adder filled with venom. *She hates my guts,* Martin realized, and then he knew that she was not a sane person.

"Everything will be just fine," he soothed. "Norris?" he called. He would get Jesse a sedative.

"Don't you call that witch. You stay and listen to me, listen to what I have to say. You're never here. I'm completely alone, and I have to force myself to do the things that must be done. Do you know what it's like for me to try and accomplish the simplest things on my own? The easiest things that any normal person can do without thinking? Do you know how disgusting I am to myself?"

"Jesse," he pleaded.

"You don't know. You have no idea! And you walk in here like a king, ready to throw down your final judgment before you've even heard me sing a note. The only person you listen to is yourself—Martin Boyd, the great conductor. Would you be able to bear it if your wife turned out to be greater?"

He was overcome by the most terrible sense of pity he had ever experienced in his life. She was such a pathetic figure, crumpled in her wheelchair, that he did not know whether he should try and comfort her or flee to his music study and break down. The stripped-down, bare living room with its shamble of furniture and bric-a-brac was the true picture of his life. He felt, at that moment, that to be home was unbearable.

Jesse rolled her wheelchair across the floor, back and forth, in a relentless, rubber-tired parody of pacing. "I wasn't going to say anything about your situation, not a word. I promised myself I would limit my remarks to the two of us. I told myself that this was our marriage; I had chosen to live with you, and if I had to confront you I would not drag in any outside issues." She brought the chair to a halt and stared up at him, her eyes glittering behind her glasses. "I'm breaking my promise. Otherwise you'll think I'm a lunatic, but I've never been saner in my life. Look at me, Martin—will you just keep your eyes turned in my direction? Do you know it's been years since you've kept your head turned toward me throughout one complete sentence? Am I that terrible to see?"

He forced himself to watch her.

"That's it. It's not so difficult." She resumed her rolling prowl. "How long have you been sleeping with that child?"

His mouth twitched into an involuntary smile.

"Don't leer at me, tell me the truth. How long?" Her hands jerked the chair to a stop. He noticed that they trembled convulsively. Was she having a fit?

"You'd better calm down. The doctor said you can make yourself worse if you get upset."

"Oh, I'm upset. Now I asked you the simplest question I could think of. Have I ever challenged you on anything so simple before? Do I bother you with anything truly complicated, like whether I shall walk again, or maybe even die? Be a big boy, Martin. Tell me the truth." Her voice was hoarse from the shouting. He realized that she had never allowed herself the luxury of misusing her voice. Perhaps she wasn't serious about resuming her career. But how could she be? It was sad that there was no real hope. He wasn't worried about her accusation; he believed it was just a hallucination brought on by one of her medications. And besides, it wasn't true.

"Tell me," she shouted, twisting in her chair, trying to throw herself out of the seat.

"For God's sake, Jesse, there's nothing to tell!" He grabbed her and forced her back against the leather support. Her body was tight and unyielding as if constricted by a spasm. But although she was rigid with tension, she had no strength; when he pushed her back she fell gently, unable to resist.

"I knew you wouldn't tell me," she sobbed.

"Hush. There's nothing to say."

"I know you're sleeping with her."

"She is sixteen years old. She travels with her mother."

"When has anyone's mother ever stopped you?" Her crying was messy and unbecoming, tears dribbling off her lips, her nose running, her eyes swollen.

He handed her his handkerchief.

He knelt down beside the wheelchair. How he hated it, the metal parts cold and surgical, reminding him of hospital wards and nurses treading ugly halls on squishy-soled shoes. It was an ugly reminder, bad as an oxygen tank—a chrome and leather announcement of crippled limbs, and death. At least with cancer, there's no way to tell. Why can't she sit in real chairs, covered with pretty embroidered lap blankets?

"Why do you give in to your worst imaginings?" he said gently, trying to sound as reasonable as possible. He felt as if he were trying to converse with a creature who understood only tone of voice, not words.

Still she sobbed broken-heartedly.

"Where is all that energy you had, planning your concert? Why waste it concocting miserable, untrue stories?"

"Martin, I'm not making it up," she said through her full nose. "I know what's going on. I know the truth without anyone having to tell me." She sniffed.

"Oh God, Jesse, this is really terrible. Is someone feeding you lies?"

She laughed, an ugly half-snort. "Me? They're all on your side." She blew her nose noisily into his handkerchief. He was disgusted by the sound and turned his eyes away as she wiped and blew again. Everything associated with her was so messy, so ugly. Where had all her attractiveness fled, leaving her so lacking in grace and charm?

"No one tells me anything," she said. "No one calls me anymore. They don't recognize me on the street. Even the doorman has trouble with my name. Look at me! You couldn't possibly miss me—I'm as

big as a tank in this thing, and everyone behaves as if
I'm invisible. You have no idea what I go through."

Martin loosened his tie nervously and wished he
had a drink. He wanted her to finish her tantrum and
tears so they could return to the semblance of nor-
malcy they had maintained on most of his stays at
home. Even her usual sarcasm was preferable to this
wild sobbing and carrying on. She could end up hos-
pitalized if she wasn't careful. He was quite lucky he
hadn't listened to Gabrielle's advice. How could he
possibly end the marriage? It would kill her. As long
as he could persuade her that nothing had changed,
he could go on with his career and his touring and
not have to worry about Jesse.

"There," he patted her hand. "Feel better? Here,
hand me that handkerchief." He lifted it up with two
delicate fingers. "I'll get rid of the thing. And then I'll
get you a glass of sherry and tell you all about Cleveland, which was marvelous, and Chicago, which was
a sweatbox; and you can tell me about Norris and her
infernal bird."

Jesse nodded uncertainly. "And don't forget Klee.
Tell me about her, too."

He tried a laugh. "Oh, she's just an infatuated
kid. She thinks she's grown up, bats her eyes at you,
twitches her little butt. Of course there isn't much
there, and it's very funny. Like watching a little colt."

"I saw her photographs," Jesse said quietly.
"She's gotten quite tall. And she's really very lovely.
Very mature-looking."

"Do you think so? All I see when I look at her is
knee socks."

"That's funny," Jesse said. "I don't see the child
anymore. Only the mask."

"Mask? What's that?"

"Just something I once said to Kogan about her."

"Kogan, Christ—I've got to call him right away."
He put down his sherry glass. "I may be touring in
Europe next spring," he said casually.

"Maybe I'll be well enough to go," Jesse said,
pushing her chair up behind him. The sherry in her
glass, which she held in one hand, slopped over onto
her dress.

"Careful," Martin warned. "You're making a
mess."

"Hello, Nicholas? Yes, fine, fine. You are? Wonderful. He did? I can't believe it—I've never heard of
such a thing. Yes, at seven. I'll be there. Of course,
and we'll talk. She's fine. I will. Yes. Goodbye."

"You won't believe this," Martin said excitedly.
"This is fantastic, but he's changed his mind. I don't
know why, but he's signed Gabrielle Klee. He'll make
a bloody fortune. He had a great to-do with
Wurtzberg over it, but it's all settled now and
Wurtzberg won't stand in his way. I'm sure he'd
never dreamed he'd have the top artists right out of
Wurtzberg's hands. There will be more defections to
follow, no doubt."

"And you had nothing to do with this switch?"
Jesse said. "I thought Kogan was dead-set against it."

"Think of it! Quite a coup," Martin exulted.

"How very convenient," Jesse remarked, "to
have the blessing of your manager as well." She
picked up her glass of sherry and threw it at his head.
He ducked, and the glass shattered against the wall.

"You really are insane, aren't you," Martin said.

"No." She shoved her chair toward the door.
"But I just broke my contract. With both of you. Tell

Kogan I'm finished. He's no longer my manager. He can consider himself fired. As for you—you may just get what you want after all."

CHAPTER

29

ၛၟ

Jesse realized that she had not been outside by herself for almost four years. Four years of Norris's curbside *whees* and *bumpety-umps*, four years of rolling somnolence, the sensation of being shoved unwillingly through a nightmare. People on the street stared, then averted their eyes and ignored her; small children pointed, and apartment-crazy dogs yipped and barked.

Angrily she shoved her chair forward over the threshold of the lobby door. The insolent doorman sat on a parked car, chatting with a dark-skinned delivery boy. Neither looked up as she struggled to get her wheelchair through the door, clutching the small suitcase on her lap.

As she moved hesitantly toward the street, the doorman lazily untangled his legs and stood up. He approached her nervously, as if afraid that she might ask him to carry her, chair and all. "Help, ma'am?" he said.

"I want a taxi," she said firmly. "Get a Checker."

Naturally he hailed the first available cab, the wrong sort, its back door too narrow to admit her chair. She repeated her instructions as the cabbie waited for his fare. As he glanced at her, he too looked afraid. What did they all think? That she wanted to be borne aloft, a paralyzed Amneris in the second act elephant parade? She looked at the driver as coldly as she could, and he frowned and drove away. The Checker driver was kinder. Perhaps he was accustomed to hauling the halt and lame around Manhattan. At least he was polite and clumsily helpful. She was able to move a bit and could assist in the transfer from the chair to the back seat. Then the folded chair was shoved in the other door, and her case placed on the front seat.

"Where to?" the driver said as he settled in behind the wheel.

Jesse had no idea. She fumbled in her handbag and checked her wallet. She had fifty dollars. She had forgotten to take her checkbook, but she had a credit card, something issued by the bank. "I'm going to a hotel," she said, "but I have no reservation. Can we go downtown and check a few? If you'll let the meter run, we can try and find one that will take me."

The hotel doorman leaped for the door but the cab driver waved him off and kindly offered to check at the front desk for her. In a daze of excitement, Jesse sat in the cab and watched the people pass by—free, unencumbered people going about their life's business, walking alone, casually swinging their arms. The air about them glowed with their independence and well-being. She recalled feeling much the

same toward people on the street when she went to
the dentist, years ago, suffering with the pain of an
infected tooth and thinking all the while that the
people she passed possessed mouths full of perfect,
healthy molars. Once again she felt that she had been
singled out for punishment, that her body had betrayed her. How often she had lain helpless in bed,
pounding her unresponsive legs with her fists. A
muscle in her calf twitched as if in reply. She was re-
gaining some strength in her legs; perhaps she would
have a remission after all. She must call the doctor.

The anxious cab driver returned. "They've got a
room for you."

"Where are we?" she asked in confusion; then
she recognized the hotel as one of the places where
she and Martin had stayed during their first years of
marriage, one of their rendezvous spots between air-
ports and out of town bookings. How like her luck to
end up pressed like a flower in a memory book. The
driver removed her chair and helped her into it, then
shoved her up a side ramp and through the glass
doors into the lobby. He placed her bag down beside
her and stood by expectantly.

She handed him ten dollars. "Keep the change,"
she said, and he hesitated. She wondered if he might
not say something—about how he hadn't helped her
for the money, perhaps—but he only paused to pull a
pencil from behind his ear and mark his destination
on a clipboard. "Sure, lady," he said, pocketing the
bill as if handsome tips were all in a day's work.

She thought the lobby staff stared at her with
some distaste, but she ignored their glances as she
moved over to the reception desk. A man in a dark
suit behind the counter peered down at her over the
top of his glasses, then instantly pinged the brass bell
at his elbow.

I am reduced to the status of rolling baggage, she realized as she signed the register. "Cash or credit card," the man said with a sniff, and she handed hers over to him. He stared at it, then said, "This is no good. It's a bank card for cashing checks—courtesy cards, they're called."

"It is? I thought it was a credit card. I must have picked up the wrong one. Wait, I can call someone and have them arrange credit for me. I'm Jesse Sondergard, the mezzo-soprano." The man stared at her as if she was a lunatic. "Call Mr. Wurtzberg, the impresario, or Rudolph Steiner, or—"

"I'm terribly sorry," he said. Then, sweeping his eyes down over her wheelchair, he extended that 'sorry' to include the entire world of the afflicted.

"I'll bet the hell you are," she said, straining forward as far as she could and snatching her card from his hand. What would she do without a checkbook, or credit card?

"Can we get you a taxicab?"

"No, no. Just show me where the pay phones are."

"You might need some assistance. They're up a short flight of stairs, that way," he pointed with his pen. He pinged the bell again, then placed his hand over it as if to cancel out the last ring. "Here, why don't you come around this way, through that little door to the left, and use the office phone. You'll be far more comfortable."

"I don't want to be any trouble."

"No, no," he said jovially, no doubt happy that she was not staying at his hotel. "This way."

She pushed into a small back office and was shown the phone. "Thank you," she said and lifted the receiver. "Dial 9 for an outside line," he explained helpfully, and she pretended to dial a number as he politely backed toward the door. She had no idea whom she would call. She was completely alone. She had forty dollars, period. Her situation was hopeless. How could someone in a wheelchair ever pretend to be independent? Do paraplegics get divorces? Can they travel anywhere unassisted? She had flown hundreds of thousands of miles and could recall only one or two little old ladies riding in wheelchairs, and even they could walk—the airline officials were only being extra cautious. But a sick person? A diseased person like herself?

The phone made gurgling, choking noises of protest as her fake call clogged up the line. She depressed the black buttons and dialed 9 again. She had no gainful employment and no friends. She could go back to Wisconsin and look up Meierus or Donnelly, but since she had been ill she had not heard from either one. Meierus was probably dead for all she knew. She had stopped reading obituaries a long time ago.

I could sit in the street in front of Saks and sing "Granada" for quarters, with my fur hat in my lap. All the smart lady shoppers will reach into their alligator bags and spare me some change because I'm so pitiful. She slammed down the receiver and, in protest, the phone made a "jang" sound; a small red light flashed on.

• She was running away with several day's fresh underwear, her medications for sleeping and nerves, and three opera scores (all Mozart: *Nozze di Figaro, Zauberflöte* and *Don Giovanni).* Where could anyone go on three opera scores and a bottle of Valium? *What an absurd girl you are,* she scolded herself. *To think you have a life of your own.*

The manager returned, looking pleased with his

generous gesture. "All set?" he said, clasping his hands prissily.

"Right," Jesse answered. "Mind giving me a shove? Gets me going, you know. Better on the short haul than in the stretch. *Hi-ho, Silver,*" she called as he began to push.

"Kennedy Airport," she told the manager as they went down the ramp, and he called over his doorman. One of the cabs on the airport line eased up and Jesse was helped in. It was one of the older Checkers, with the round, tiny jump seats still covered with the original cracked leather. The driver, proud of his ancient vehicle, had mended and patched every corner of the cab. It was immaculately clean, everything except those small jump seats. They were folded, forlorn, and ignored.

"Doesn't anyone ever ride on those seats anymore?" Jesse asked proprietarily.

"Ah, a kid or two; but lotsa the women, they think it's not safe no more. I thinka takin' them out but it's not worth the aggravation."

"It's too bad. I'd sit there if I could."

"You gotta bad leg?" he asked plainly.

"Two bad legs," she said. "I gotta bad condition."

"Oh, yeah," he replied. "I gotta sister-in-law, she has too. Somethin' in the brain. They didda lotta tests. She's got trouble gettin' around. Three kids too. Youngest is one-and-a-half."

"That's terrible," Jesse said.

His shoulders went up, then down.

She stared at his license, peering forward. It was a strange, foreign name—something Balkan, with lots of consonants. She tried to say it, but it was unpronounceable; Cherzew, it seemed to be.

"Life is a funny thing," he said. "We never know how bad we got it. Looka me—thirty years hacking, got no money inna bank, six kids, oldest one's in Germany. He's quartermaster with the Armed Forces. A good future. They pay a pension. Sends me a check every year, Christmas time. Buddy of mine, cabbing, got his throat slit couple of weeks ago. And my brother's wife, with this brain thing. Nice girl like you, ridin' in a wheelchair—I tell myself, if this is what life does, then whadda you worryin' about for? But it's human nature to worry, you see my point? You see what I'm gettin' at? Nobody's happy with what they got. See what I mean? You can't fight city hall. It's all written in the books. You got kids? No? That's too bad. Kids are nice to think about when the Christmas cards come in. Somebody don't forget you. I ride people around all day, for years. Do you think they remember me? Naw. In and out, everybody busy, busy. What's the point? It's all here today and gone tomorrow."

He went on like this for forty-five minutes, in terrible traffic, all the way out to the airport.

"Which airline?" he finally asked, pausing for breath.

"Any one," she said.

"What? Lady, you gotta ticket? Gotta reservation?"

"No."

"But you wanna go somewhere. Where to?"

"I don't know."

"You gotta know. You didn't come out here just to watch the planes take off."

"Yes," she said quickly. "Yes I did. Where can I do that?"

"Well, that building over there, the flat one. It's got a place to watch. You wanna go there?"

"Yes. That will be perfect."

He took her to the departure gate and found the international symbol for the handicapped, the sign with the stick figure in the stick wheelchair. "There," he said. "That's your entrance."

He helped her out of the cab. "A lotta luck to you. I can tell, like my sister-in-law, you gotta lotta guts. Takes guts to get by in this world. It's a crazy thing, come all the way out here to watch planes. But have yourself a good time. Yeah? Okay."

When she returned to Manhattan, to the apartment, every light in every room was turned on and Martin, Kogan, and Norris fell on her hysterically. She told them she had been out shopping, and then she asked Martin to go downstairs and pay the waiting cab driver. She had given most of her forty dollars to Cherzew, pressing it into his hand as he protested. She told Martin to pay the driver handsomely. Norris tried to take her pulse and feel her forehead for fever. Poor Nicholas stood to one side, staring at her in his stoic, stony manner. She turned her head away. They, too, had betrayed her, just as surely as her body had. Without a word, she went to her room to prepare for bed. She was exhausted but she was mentally lifted high above the apartment and the people she no longer trusted; ready to soar with the loud, ugly planes she had watched for hours in the dying light. They were, on the ground, crashing hunks of metal; but once in flight, they were miraculously graceful. And best of all, they were on their own.

CHAPTER

30

You may be wondering why I decided to take on Gabrielle. After all, I protested too much. But in truth, I gave in to the temptation Martin had articulated so well; I would have the top names on my roster. Wurtzberg was slowly withdrawing from the culture scene. He was ill and he spoke often, in public, of retiring. With Gabrielle's name I could attract more of his clients. And frankly, I did not really believe all of Jesse's stories of the child's conniving ways. The girl was a brat, but hadn't Martin been one too? Jesse was so unhinged by her illness that I chose to disregard her fantastic tales about the affair between Martin and the girl. Wurtzberg was still enough of a professional to be stung by Gabrielle's decision to move, and I took it all as a compliment. What fools we managers are!

Jesse was furious with me. She rang up Steiner

and told him how I had betrayed her. She phoned Wurtzberg, and he assured her there would always be a place open with his association. Wurtzberg was very much the gentleman. Perhaps I was not. But we all read some measure of emotional sickness into her behavior. Bratty children do not Mata Haris make.

But after Gabrielle's temporary retirement from the stage (she was studying with Landau in New York, as Martin had suggested), Jesse cooled down considerably and began speaking of a reconciliation. She invited me over to tea one day, and for a nice, friendly chat. Much to my surprise, she was healthier than ever before; strong, and fairly glowing. Though she still sat in her wheelchair, she moved about gracefully and served an elaborate English-style tea with great ease.

"So," she pronounced, as she settled back with a plate of delicate butter cookies, "now you shall manage all three of us."

"You'll have me back then?" I asked, just to be certain.

"I shall have to forgive you. Of all the others, you've stood by the longest. I have grown to depend on you. That's why it was so shocking when you went over to their side with so little protest. But it's your career and I was thinking only of myself. I've always confused business with pleasure, I'm afraid."

"My darling, I did protest," I corrected her. "I fought Martin for a long time. But your husband is quite persistent, and when Wurtzberg himself intervened, I had to consider the matter seriously."

"Does Wurtzberg pimp for you on a regular basis? Oh, don't look so offended. You must be the only person I know who thinks any four-letter word is dirty. *Pimp.* It's not so bad. It's not *fuck.*"

"Stop it," I said sharply. I was quite sure that she was preparing to attack me at length. I didn't want to hear any more and so I tried to change the subject. "How are you and Martin doing lately?"

"The usual truce. Have a cookie. Norris went all the way to 57th Street for these."

"Thank you. Any new plans?"

"I'm thinking of making some recordings. A series of lieder records; possibly also a collection of arias. I want to talk to Eric Oldfield about the lieder. I wouldn't do it without him."

"It's a difficult way to go back."

"We'll see." She glanced at her watch. "I'll have to throw you out soon. My coach is due at four-thirty. I'm going into training."

"Jesse, to see you perform again would be the greatest thing in the world. But don't rush it; don't push yourself too hard."

She smiled, and dunked a cookie into her tea. "I won't be the first to come back from the dead. You'll see." She chewed eagerly and dipped again.

I watched her gravely. What mysterious plans had she cooked up this time? She stirred her tea as if it were a witches brew, then swallowed it in quick gulps. She was spinning her web. According to Martin, she had been feverish with plans since the day she had disappeared. Now I saw that the activity continued. Her movements told me she was working—working every second, without pause. Her hyperactivity was as admirable as it was frightening.

She pushed beside me as I walked to the door. "Where's Martin?" I asked politely.

"He's off teaching his master class. His students adore him, naturally. They bring him flowers and apples, like first-graders. Some of them are quite gifted, and they've scared him into working even harder. The man is a maniac. At least now I have my own work to keep me busy. Soon enough we'll both be traveling again."

"Yes," I lied.

"Well, goodbye, Nicholas. I've decided you're not fired anymore. You may represent me during my resurrection from the dead. Oh, and one other thing— the next time Martin makes plans to go abroad, I'd like to come along, too."

"Do you think that's possible?"

"Surely. They'll take a wheelchair on a plane, if necessary. And I'm so much stronger now." She wagged her fingers at me. "Toodle-oo, Kogan."

The door closed. I stared at it, convinced that the curtain had just fallen on a great stage performance. She was playing a leading role, the heroine who returns, and exacts her revenge. These new career plans were a disguise for some elaborate scheme. But what she had in mind, I did not know. She was singing her song, gently and persuasively, waiting for someone to come crashing up on the rocks. Not me, I prayed with a shiver.

We all played right into her hands. Martin decided to go to Europe for a short spring visit—six concerts, which left plenty of time for sightseeing—and I was forced to tell him what Jesse had asked me to mention. "She intends to go with you."

"Naturally. Gabrielle is going along as a special treat after all these months of study. She'd like to perform, as well. Can we add her to one of the concerts in Venice?"

"Martin, it's Jesse. Jesse wants to go."

"Impossible," he exploded, shoving the folders

and papers off my desk. "What does she think I am, a travelling hospital? I can't be responsible for a sick wife in a foreign country. And the doctors over there—you know what they're like!"

"She says she's not sick. She's working again, training."

"Is that work? You ought to hear her. The coach comes as a favor. She'll never concertize again."

"She mentioned recordings—"

"Who would record her? She's nobody. She's been gone too long."

"It would seem to me, dear boy, that you are a bit anxious to be thrown together with the girl again."

"Now you sound like Jesse. Just another dirty-minded cynic like the rest. Look, I'll never be able to concentrate with Jesse along. There are too many things to worry about, and that nurse of hers buzzes around all the time. Not that I wouldn't like to see her get away—but this trip is still business. I'll be performing, after all."

"You're afraid the child will object."

"Gabrielle? She's very concerned about Jesse."

"Oh, your phony solicitude makes me ill."

"Jesse will listen to you, Kogan. You said she's seeing you again. Be her friend. Explain to her that it's just not the right time. Next time, tell her, please?"

He wanted to please everyone with a minimum of effort. Perhaps that is why, like so many other artists I've known, he performed gloriously while his personal life went to hell. Artists learn to make quick little hops from crisis to crisis, like cities on a tour, all the while conserving their real energy for the music. As soon as Martin got on the plane, he would immediately forget all the lies and promises and concentrate on his scores.

The one person who might have provided the truth at this juncture was Gabrielle. But my little client and I did not speak. We made all of our arrangements through Martin. I was indeed the beard for their enterprise. But I would soon find it was even worse than I had suspected.

As it turned out, I would not have to wait long for my chance to discover the truth. My days as an observer were numbered. I, too, would be called on to act and, having waited so long, I would play my scene like a ham.

CHAPTER
31
☙

In May, Martin, Gabrielle, and Mrs. Klee left on a trip to London, Paris, Rome and Venice. Much to my surprise, Jesse accepted their plans with hardly a murmur. She said she was too preoccupied with her work to bother arguing with her husband. And she didn't confide in me. She said she had no time for visits, or tea.

When my doorman called me up to announce that I had a visitor, that Eric Oldfield was in my lobby, I was positive he had come about Jesse. Ordinarily I do not admit mere mortals to what Jesse liked to call my burrow, for I am fanatically neat and would not want anyone to misinterpret the pristine condition of my apartment as anal compulsiveness or some such rot. Order is simply my nature, the reason I have never considered living with another human being. I have grown far too accustomed to respecting my own needs first.

But when my doorman said "Mr. Oldfield," I feared the worst for Jesse and had him sent up. Not having seen her made me afraid that her condition had worsened. Oldfield was one of the few people who had remained loyal throughout her ordeal. And he was not the sort to make a great fuss over my obsessiveness and then publish the fact.

Eric looked thin and tired, dressed in smart European-styled clothes, his face Van Dycked. "You'd better go to Italy," he said. "Instantly."

"What is it?" I was surprised that the news did not concern Jesse's health.

"Your client is making a fool of himself."

"That is hardly unusual. Would you like a drink?"

He shook his head. "He and that girl are cutting a path across Europe that is leaving everyone talking. Haven't you heard anything?"

"Dear boy, the manager, quite like the husband, is usually the last to know. But what do you mean? They travel with her *duenna*."

"I haven't laid eyes on the mother in days. In Rome, one of the contest sponsors invited me to a formal ball, and Martin brought *her*."

"The child?"

"She's your client, too. Have you seen her? I mean, *really* seen her? She smokes cigarettes. She drinks. She dances with everyone. She wears expensive clothes. And she leads Boyd on as if he had a ring through his nose. She's no child—she's a woman. And she is telling the world they are going to be married."

"Does Jesse know about this?"

"Of course not," he said crossly. "What do you think I am? I called her when I arrived yesterday, and she gave me a story about working on her voice. I didn't know what to say. But she never asked about Martin. She knew I'd been in Rome. I think if she suspected anything, she might have told me, or at least tried to confirm the information."

"She's been trying to tell me about it all along," I said. "She's always known something."

"You'd better get over there and clean up this mess. It will kill Jesse. And it makes your pretty boy look quite bad, even though that child is no child. It will be the ruination of him. He follows her around like a blind man."

"Where is the mother?"

"Rumor has it she's propped up at the bar nightly, drinking herself into oblivion. She pays no attention to her daughter. The pair of them carry on their courtship dance without any notice from that corner. But even if Mama were to notice, that vixen would have her stopped cold. Do you know, Gabrielle said I should make certain to send Jesse her regards? She said I must call and say that I had seen them both and that they were having a marvelous time. She would like to see Jesse put away for life on the strength of the gossip about their affair."

"I really had no idea," I said slowly, trying to absorb the information Oldfield was conveying so anxiously. "I'll do what I can, I'll go see him and try and talk some sense into him. But I have no control over the girl. Do you think she might be play-acting? After all, he's not about to get divorced, is he?"

Oldfield frowned. "I wouldn't be too sure. He's like a man hypnotized, a sleepwalker. Even his work is suffering. You can't tell me they're not having an affair."

"I don't know," I said, trying not to imagine the worst.

"Ah, you're a prude," Oldfield said. "But you'll see."

The trip to Venice was excruciating. The only plane I could book was the Alitalia night flight; the old world grandparents' red-eye, it turned out. They packed the waiting lounge, toting American loot crammed into bulging paper shopping bags. It would be a long flight, I knew, for I could not book a seat in first class.

The cappucino machine on board sprayed loudly throughout the journey. I tried to assemble my thoughts, to arrange a speech that would have conviction. Could I ask them first if the gossip were indeed true? The music world stinks with all of the garbage that floats to the surface. High-class music is no sign of a rarefied atmosphere; things sordid occur just as often. But Martin Boyd was no child-seducer.

The shopping bags toppled as the plane bounced. My seat mates ate their pre-packed dinner—some frightfully smelly salami and hard cheese which they cut with a long knife (one of those Italian stilettos?). They offered me some cheese. I declined, "*Grazie*," and shook my head. The grandmother smiled, showing the spaces where her teeth were missing. She took me for a friend and spent the next hour happily showing me her purchases from America. She had paper bags filled with stainless steel kitchen equipment—can openers, grapefruit knives, cherry pitters, cookie cutters, egg slicers. She demonstrated each item proudly, then lovingly rewrapped it in newspaper and placed it in her sleeping husband's lap. When the stewardess appeared to offer pillows and blankets, she hid her Vega-Matic under her sweater as if she were importing contraband goods.

At the Rome Airport we spent an hour in a drafty

shed, waiting for our baggage. As a result, I nearly missed my connecting flight to Venice. My bag tottered off the luggage ramp last, preceded by a row of cellophane-wrapped stuffed animals—the giant ones that cost a great deal of money—pastel-colored giraffes, bears, lions and elephants, all somewhat the worse for wear. Great "aahs" of concern went up over their condition. Was this the land of Leonardo and Michelangelo? Did they "aah" so heart-rendingly after the great floods that had recently washed away so many national treasures? I grabbed my bag and ran for the Venice connection.

When I reached the Venice airport, my nerves were shattered by lack of sleep and the cumulative effect of the coffee which I had drunk steadily throughout the night. Headed toward the *vaporetto* terminal in a hired car, I no longer cared about the ugly gossip. If I had dreamed of riding to Jesse's rescue, now I was faced with the notion that I was sticking my neck out, meddling where I least belonged. The trip seemed silly. And Venice, that oddball, charming, ugly cowtown on water, held no appeal for me. I was not in the mood. I should have stayed in New York, caught a taxi to Jesse's apartment, held her hand and told her that her husband was a fool. Of course, she already knew as much, did she not?

At the hotel, I registered for a room and asked about Mr. Boyd. "Not disturb," the manager said. "No calls." And the Klee party? "Out," responded the manager with a wave of his hand. Both Mrs. and Miss Klee? "*Sì*," he informed me, consulting some handwritten notes. I gave my bag to a porter and followed him to my room. For such an expensive hotel, marble-lobbied and luxurious, the room seemed an afterthought—damp and dark, one small window overlooking a side canal. Garbage floated in the water, fallen from one of the scows anchored right beneath my room; fruit peels and newspaper lapped idly in the dark water. I stared outside, the Byronic prisoner sentenced forever; and as I watched, the sun came out, changing the entire prospect. The water became transluscent. Two hefty young men appeared and moved the scow away, trailing a pretty little wake which pushed the garbage scraps out to sea. The sun warmed a small stone bridge and lightened the walls across the canal. Suddenly the city was charming and I felt a great surge of energy. I decided to disregard Martin's orders and go straight to his suite. We would have our talk and then I would be free to wander about. Perhaps I would take a boat to the Lido. I had not been to Venice since a trip long ago with my mother, when I followed her from glass factory to glass factory in search of a certain set of crystal.

I washed, shaved, and changed into a clean shirt and a light cashmere jacket. I walked the flight down to Martin's floor. As the manager had indicated, there was a sign on the door. But a room service cart stood nearby, laden with round metal covers and serving platters. Martin must be having his breakfast—a late but luxurious meal, knowing my boy—and I looked forward to the prospect of joining him. A bit of hot chocolate and plain biscuit would do me nicely. I knocked on the door but there was no reply. I knocked again; still no answer. He might be in the shower. As I was about to turn away, I decided to try the knob. It's not like me to pry, but I was not in the mood to eat in my dismal cell or to walk all the way to San Marco Square for a bit of pastry. Martin's suite faced the front of the hotel, overlooking the main canal and a glorious view—surely breakfast there would be a pleasure. The knob turned and I opened the door. "Martin?" I called out.

I heard his voice come from the terrace, then a clinking of china and a high, silvery giggle. My stomach heaved. There was a woman with him. I stepped backwards, quickly, and knocked into a table. An ash tray skittered to the floor. "Hey," Martin called out. "Not yet, you're too early. We haven't finished."

I couldn't speak—it was as if I were being strangled. Surely he would appear in an instant and catch me sneaking out. "*Scusi,*" I said lamely.

"My God," he said. "Nicholas?"

He appeared in the room and, as I walked toward him, I saw the bed, crumpled and torn apart as beds always are in the hotel suites inhabited by Martin. Then I saw past him to the table out on the terrace, the cloth white and bright in the sun, the chairs nestled around, the scene inviting; and Gabrielle seated across from Martin's place, her hair combed out long, her body enveloped in a beautiful silk robe with Martin's initials on it.

All I could think was, so this is what is known as in flagrante delicto. Before, it had always reminded me of a flambé dessert on the gourmet menu of a Carribean resort hotel.

"Hi," Gabrielle said calmly, lighting up a cigarette. "Why don't you join us?"

Martin stared at me as if he had awakened in a nightmare only to find that it was real. He was wearing pajama pants but no shirt. I had never seen him undressed before; he had always worn t-shirts. He was hairless, smooth and boy-chested, soft in the upper arms and with something female about the chest—a suggestion of androgynous, Greek marble.

His skin was very white. "You may as well sit down," he said sullenly.

I simply wanted to drop dead and disappear in a cloud of smoke, as neatly as Margaret Hamilton had done it in *The Wizard of Oz*. I felt like a fool, standing there in my British Isles touring togs; and more of a fool for not believing Oldfield or Jesse when they had tried to tell me the truth. How we had maligned her so. Would she be damaged forever by the power of our disbelief?

I was an interloper on foreign soil, much as those old Italians had been by visiting America. But unlike my happy seat mates on the plane, I would bring home no precious souvenirs. I would simply be haunted by the notion that I had intruded where I least belonged, in someone else's bedroom. How stupid of me not to have kept out. It is not my natural habitat.

CHAPTER

32

ꝙ

For several mornings, Martin had breakfasted
with Gabrielle on the terrace of his suite. Gabrielle
had sent her mother off on guided tours with unctu-
ous bilingual guides who promised to show Mrs. Klee
the *real* Venice. And, of course, the day included lunchtime cocktails at Harry's Bar. After these jaunts,
Mrs. Klee returned to the hotel and slept until eight
o'clock when she awoke to find her daughter gone off
to a party or dinner. She retreated to the hotel bar for
the rest of the evening and slept quite soundly
through the night, unaware that the adjoining bedroom was empty.

Martin did not sleep with Gabrielle until Venice.
He had refrained, politely and fearfully, from any
continuation of the scene that had begun in Buffalo.
He had not lied to his wife about Gabrielle, but he
was aware of what would happen the next time they

were alone. He knew she would lure him into bed. It was all quite out of his control. She was strong and young, and the longer he resisted, the more drained he felt. Sleeping with her came to represent an act of rejuvenation, a recharging of batteries. Had Gabrielle known this, she might not have been so persistent. She wanted to believe it was her charm that worked miracles, not her age.

She was seventeen. She was graceful and theatrical. She reminded Martin of the girls he had known in prep school—rich, jaded girls on the eve of their debuts; vain, self-centered and complete unto themselves. Their vanity was the heart of their charm. To Martin, they were unreachable. He was ill-at-ease, chubby and awkward, unable to express his frustrated longings. He had been a great masturbator at the age of seventeen and, when he wasn't hiding in the bathroom, he was seated at the keyboard, driving his father crazy.

Now a remarkable, genius girl (who played brilliantly—an exceptional admission coming from Martin Boyd) calmly pursued him. She had grown up quickly—smoking, drinking cocktails, dressing in evening clothes, dancing with crowds of hungry men. She made him jealous; he had ordered her to stop. She teased him, ordering him to make her. And so he had. But who had been first? She was pliable, lithe, experienced. She was seventeen years old, in possession of the darkest secrets, a sac of knowledge she swung before him and then lifted away before he could see. Wild with jealousy, he had promised her whatever she asked. All she wanted, she said, was him. He could not believe it. She seemed to have vast, all-consuming desires. She told him that they would become the most famous music couple of all time, more famous than Robert and Clara Schumann. If he believed that, he knew he would believe anything. But he swallowed it whole.

In Venice, he recalled his younger self—there on his honeymoon, callow, raw, unsophisticated, and young. He had been a baby, a little fool, ignorant of manners and style. With Gabrielle it was completely different. He was the guide, the man with the connections. He got them into museum exhibitions after hours; he took her to the finest restaurants; he escorted her to parties and introduced her to the titled royalty that floated ensemble from watering spot to watering spot.

Gabrielle loved every minute of it. She drank and ate a great deal. She spoke Italian fluently and carried on long, private conversations with waiters and shopkeepers, laughing over shared jokes as exotic courses arrived at their table, or tray upon tray of necklaces and rings appeared from curtained back rooms. Gabrielle had a private arrangement with the world; she announced her needs and, one by one, they were satisfied. Martin sometimes wondered if he were not merely the *sorbet*, the palate-replenisher between courses at a giant banquet. As he watched her eat breakfast, he realized that she had her whole life ahead of her. She spread her bread lavishly with preserves and drank cups of chocolate, watching the sun-tipped water with a proprietary air. *When she is thirty, I will be fifty,* he calculated unpleasantly.

"You don't want these?" she asked, reaching for his breakfast rolls.

"No, go ahead."

"What's the matter with you? Look, the sun's coming out again. There are no more clouds. It's going to be a gorgeous day, not as nasty as it was this morning. Where shall we go?"

He shrugged.

"Don't be so grim-faced. It's not all that bad here. Aren't you having a good time?" She licked the jam off her fingers and lifted another piece of roll to her mouth. "I don't like the bread as much as Paris. They don't know how to do it quite right. It looks better than it tastes. It's missing something."

"Salt," Martin said.

"That's right! How'd you know that?" she asked suspiciously.

"When you get to be my age you find yourself full of interesting information."

"My, we are feeling sorry for ourselves today. This is supposed to be a vacation." She said something in Italian.

"What does that mean?"

"It sounds dirty, doesn't it? I just said I wanted a glass of milk."

"You do? I'll ring for room service."

"No, no," she laughed. "I didn't mean it. I just wanted to see if you thought I was saying something nasty. It sounds nasty, doesn't it? Italian is supposed to be such a gorgeous language, but I think French is nicer, don't you?"

"It's all the same to me."

It was her turn to shrug. She picked up her cup of chocolate and faced out toward the sea. "I could live here," she said.

"You'd be bored in six months."

"How do you know? I think it would be divine."

"You sound like that terrible countess we met the other night. *Divine* is all she said the entire evening."

"It's probably all the English she knows. Except curse words. She knows those."

"Indeed?" he said.

"She told the man with her to fuck off. I heard

her. He invited her back to his palazzo for some sixty-nine and she said 'Fuck off.' "

"Little eavesdropper."

"She said it plainly, right out, in English. She wanted me to hear. Everyone tries to shock me." She swung her bare legs over the side of the chair and ate another jam-smeared roll. "I don't know why I'm so hungry this morning. Is it still morning? It must be afternoon already. I think this is the height of elegance. Let's get some more chocolate."

"You'll spoil your lunch."

"You sound like a father."

"Not yet, thank you."

"I've been rethinking my future in that respect. I'm not even positive I'd like to get married. I've never had a chance to do anything on my own. Getting married would be like signing for an extended tour; but there would be no final concert, no end. Finito. It's very depressing."

"You're far too young to sound so bored. Nothing has happened to you yet."

"Ah, but you have. Isn't that something?" She jumped up and wrapped her arms around his neck, leaning forward and stealing a bit of cheese from his plate. She ran to the balcony and leaned over, tossing away bits of silver foil from the cheese as she watched the traffic move through the water, leaving behind swirling tides that lapped against the stone of the buildings. "Do you think it's going to flood again? The water looks terribly high to me."

"It floods all the time."

"No, I mean flood like it did last year, and ruin so many things."

"You sound as if you'd like to see it. That was a terrible event, my love—art treasures ruined. Don't you remember the benefit I did for the art committee?''

''But wouldn't it be exciting to be trapped somewhere and have to watch the water getting higher and higher and there was no escape, no exit—you'd have to watch your death coming slowly at you, inch by inch.'' She sat down and stared at him eagerly.

Martin almost said, *like my wife*, but he caught himself. ''No. I don't agree. One should never have to watch one's own death. It should happen suddenly, with no warning.''

It was then that they heard the ash tray hit the floor, and Martin found Kogan in the bedroom.

''My God,'' Martin said. ''Nicholas?''

Gabrielle seemed amused, almost happy, at being discovered. ''Hi. Why don't you join us?'' she said, gesturing toward a chair.

Kogan looked stunned. Martin, who had always taken Kogan's approval for granted, realized that he had finally crossed Kogan's subtle and arbitrary boundary between gentlemen and louts. How his manager resembled his father! He had never noticed before. The whole act—unforced dismay and disappointment—how familiar it was to Martin.

''Nicholas,'' Martin stammered, ''I'm sorry. I had no idea you were coming. I—'' he broke off and shrugged, wondering why the sun was still shining. Perhaps Gabrielle had been right. Perhaps another holocaust was due.

''If I were to believe every bit of gossip I have been told throughout my twenty-eight years in the music business, I would be forced to swallow tales as unappetizing as a plate full of slugs,'' Kogan said. ''My mother, rest her soul, had the notion that exposure to life in the music business would render me unfit for proper company. She thought no one had any class. She used to remind me, 'Nicky, class tells.' Until this moment I had decided she was, to use an unfortunate phrase, dead wrong. Now I see otherwise. Therefore, I am bowing out. Immediately."

"Nicky," Gabrielle said harshly. "Sit down."

Much to Martin's surprise, Kogan sat, or rather fell into the chair. Gabrielle continued to pull on her cigarette. She offered one to Kogan. They were Gauloises. He refused. She played with the wrapper on the pack. "Martin, would you please order some coffee for Nicky and another pot of chocolate? We should treat our manager decently, offer him breakfast. He must have flown all night to get here so rapidly, so quietly, on little cat feet. Nicky, you do look terrible, really. Haven't you had any sleep?"

"Oh God, Gabrielle, would you shut up?" Martin said fiercely.

"Don't you tell me to shut up! Don't you ever say anything like that to me ever again, do you hear?" She did not move. She sat perfectly still and then continued to speak in a normal voice. "Nicky knows. He's always known. Why else would he have taken me on as his client? He sees the truth. He's very perceptive, Nicky is."

"No," Kogan replied. "You're wrong. I never believed it."

"Well, now you know," Gabrielle said briskly. "It was bound to come out. When this trip is over, we're going back to tell Mrs. Boyd, and then we will announce our engagement."

"Gabrielle!" Martin cried.

"Why? Why? Does it make any difference now? Do you want him to think I'm some kind of slut who led his innocent lamb-boy away from the lady in the wheelchair? Don't you take any responsibility for your life, *maestro?"*

"Nicholas, please go. Come back in a little while," Martin pleaded.

"No," Gabrielle insisted. "He'll stay right here and we'll discuss this together. There's no separating us anymore. Isn't that so, Martin?"

Martin stared helplessly at Kogan, who did not say a word.

"Martin has always had total artistic control," Gabrielle explained calmly. "The complete master of the orchestra. I've never been around a more masterful conductor. But really, he is such a little boy. Sometimes I feel far older than he is. He's never really lived, has he? Going around shut up in his music thing, never having the chance to experience life. I want to have a life and I think Martin wants one, too; only he doesn't know how to ask for it. I'm going to show him how. He'll be even greater then. Can you imagine how it will be for the public, exposed to someone who has suffered and loved and who communicates it all through his music?" Gabrielle threw up her arms joyfully. "We will both, both, be so famous. And you, Nicky, will be the greatest manager ever."

"You're fired," Kogan said. "Both of you."

"Nicholas!" Martin cried, and he rushed over to him. "You can't mean that. Please, what can I say? It isn't what you think."

"He's not serious," Gabrielle said. "He's bluffing."

"No," said Kogan, standing up and pushing his chair away. "This is the end."

A rapid knock came at the door and a voice called out. *"Avanti!"* Gabrielle called back—a bowing porter hurried through the suite and out to the terrace. "Signor Boyd?" Martin raised his hand as if in a class-room, and the man handed him a cable. Martin fumbled at his pajama pants, then realized he had no pockets and thus, no change. "Nicholas?" he said imploringly and Kogan gave the man a tip. Martin tore open the envelope and read the telegram, his face a mixture of pain and astonishment.

"What?" Gabrielle demanded. When he placed the cable down she snatched it up and read it out loud. "Send Kogan back at once. Needed for concert tour. Recording contract to be signed. Remission at last. Jesse?" Gabrielle's voice rose at the end of each sentence and then shot up at the signature. "What's going on? How did she know?"

"She doesn't know a thing," Kogan said, taking the telegram from Gabrielle and glancing at it himself.

"I'm not sure," Gabrielle said. "Who could have told her?"

"I'm not going to argue with you," Kogan said with irritation. "I'm leaving. I'm needed in New York. I'll pass your bookings on to your new manager. Let me know as soon as you have found your man." Kogan glanced at Martin, who stood woodenly in front of the littered table. "Put something on, dear boy. You'll catch your death. The sun's not out anymore."

He walked out.

"She knows," Gabrielle said.

"We've just lost our manager," Martin said in amazement.

"Forget it. That prissy old prude. He can't fire us. We have a contract."

"I never signed a thing. We did everything on the basis of a handshake."

"How stupid," Gabrielle said.

"Did you sign?"

"I suppose Mother did. She'll sign anything you put in front of her."

"What am I to do now?" he said. But he was not really asking her.

"Nothing. Not yet, at least. When we get back to New York, you can tell your wife exactly what we'd planned. It will all be much easier if the cable's true. She'll have her own career, and she's much better. You won't feel so corrupt."

"I can't believe she's well. She was still sick when we left—she had those mood swings. Suppose it isn't true? Suppose she's just the same?"

"All right," Gabrielle said sharply. "I'll tell her."

"You won't dare," Martin threatened.

"Why not? She'll accept it better if it comes from me."

"No. I forbid it."

"I'm not waiting any longer. We agreed that the time has come."

"I won't have you seeing her."

"Now it's your wife you want to protect. And you want Nicholas back again. Don't you see that I want you free from all that nonsense? All those old, babyish nursery-toys you've kept around until they're worn out. They'll hold you back. They'll keep their hooks in and you'll never be free—free to be great. Let me go see her."

"No," he repeated.

"I think I'll order that chocolate now," Gabrielle said brightly. "Here," she said, as she pulled off Martin's robe and tossed it to him. She had nothing on underneath. "I'm going inside to call room service." He watched her walk away, bare skin gleaming, moving gracefully on her long legs, walking coolly over to the telephone. He followed quickly, stepping over and pulling the receiver from her grasp. "Later," he said into the phone, and as he put his hands on her, she laughed.

CHAPTER

33

♈

Jesse Sondergard Boyd stood next to the grand piano in her living room and touched the Baccarat vase of tiger lilies which she had placed atop its lid. The sight of their orange impudence filled her with a sensation of life restored. She, too, lifted her head once again. Jesse attributed her remission entirely and idiotically to her changed mental state. Charts and statistics on her illness would not sway her; she had brought on this state of grace via her own mental powers. And now she gloried in the chance it gave her to sing again.

She had hidden all signs of the change from Martin. Before he left for Europe, she remained bound to her wheelchair. Once he was gone, she put the chair in the hall closet, fired Norris, rehung the drapes, and rolled the carpets back into place. Then she called Eric Oldfield and asked if he would begin to work with her again.

Her voice had changed somewhat. The clarity of her high notes had diminished and she found it difficult to maintain her breath control. Hard work might help those problems. But she thought her voice had a newer, more luxuriant quality. Her voice coach agreed. "You have a nice, relaxed quality there, as if you're not forcing at all."

"I'm just trying to make it through," she replied.

When Eric came to work with her, he made a similar observation. "Maybe the secret is that your new goals are more modest. Anyway, you sound good—rough, but good. They'll write a lot of trash about the old Sondergard and the new Sondergard, but don't listen to a word. No one can really compare with all that time gone by. And you won't want to do the same things anymore."

"No. I want to do the *Kindertotenlieder.*"

"Quite a choice. All right, we'll work on it and see how we do. Want to try some of your old repertory?" He chose some Schubert songs she had loved. She thought of Martin when she sang—of that private performance long ago when he had accompanied her.

Eric was silent when she finished. Then he cleared his throat noisily. "You need a lot of work on the voice, there's no getting around it. The time lapse shows; there's trouble with the breathing, the intonations, the phrasing. But your feeling in these songs is remarkably clear; brilliant, in fact. You sing without pushing, as if you meant every word. I'm impressed."

"Let's work," Jesse said. Later on, when they were sitting on the couch together, going over her old clippings and laughing about how they had travelled to so many disagreeable places, she told him, "It's hard to talk about it, but it was like touching bottom inside me—the place I'd been afraid to go near. I can feel the same space inside me when I sing, but now it's a place I don't mind going. I used to be terrified of it. Now it's familiar."

"We're all scared. We surround ourselves with people, with things. But you had that taken away. You had to face the truth. And you have."

"Making a comeback sounds so awful, like a sports match, or some racehorse."

"But that's what this is. You can dress it up in white tie and velvet, but it's no better than the track. We're all running hard to prove we're still hot. What if you'd continued—would you be anywhere by now? There have been careers that have gone out, *poof*, like a light. People who never became as good as they were once upon a time. The past is a golden era, and nothing is supposedly ever the same as it was once."

"Eric, I honestly believe I don't care. All I want to do is walk on that bottom, feel it under my feet and know that I can't fall any further. Metaphorically, that is."

"You've got the answers now."

"Listen, if I hadn't been sick I'd have stayed the world's great dope. I never made any real decisions; there was always someone else there. I never thought about what I wanted. I made some big mistakes. Remember Carmen? That was wrong for me. But I thought I was a vamp, that I could stick out my chest and make the damn thing work. But you get to see yourself quite well lying in bed a while. I wondered who I sang for, what I was trying to prove. I wanted to do all that lieder and I don't know if I ever put anything of myself into it—maybe once, maybe the night I got sick. But the rest of the time it was as if I were proving I had grown up—opera's for kids, you know, play-acting and costumes and all—and I wanted the weight of the world transferred to my shoulders."

"What do you want now, Jess," Eric asked, reaching over and stroking her hand gently.

"Not to be afraid anymore. To be at peace. To be able to think of music as part of my soul, whatever that is. Maybe it's that place I went, down on the bottom; the place my father spoke of when he played. It's so silly. You study music for years. You see it least when you're young and strong, when you understand so little. It's only when the power slips that the light goes on."

"Sure. It's an old story, except for the lucky few who manage to have those great years when the knowledge and ability click in and hold. There have been some of those."

"Not me, Eric. I'm going to get sick again before I get my chance."

"Don't say that."

"Why not? It's true. It's in the books. It goes up and then it goes down. One day it never goes up again and there you are, headed for the bottom of the mountain."

He watched her closely, with fear in his eyes.

"But not yet," she said. "Let's keep going."

Each week she refilled the vase of tiger lilies because the burnt orange reminded her of her father, of going through fire. She hated the color red (all those roses, and the rubies) and orange seemed a nice contradiction. The flowers said *no*. She practiced saying no herself, preparing for the scene she knew was inevitable. After she sent the cable, she waited calmly, studying her scores, practicing, thinking of the fire in the flowers.

Three days after she sent the telegram, the maid announced a visitor. "Miss Klee."

Eric pushed his chair away from the piano. "I'm getting out."

"You can stay if you like," Jesse offered.

"No thank you. I've seen enough of her. But would you like me here?"

"No," she said. "I don't need help anymore."

He walked back toward the kitchen. "I'll be inside if you need me."

"Show her in," Jesse called, and Gabrielle appeared in the doorway.

She was dressed in a severely-cut suit, far too matronly for her young figure. She walked in with a grand, sophisticated air; but when she caught sight of Jesse standing by the piano, she stopped and gasped for an instant, as a child might.

"You're so tall," Gabrielle said. "I had no idea you were so tall."

"You've never seen me standing, have you?"

"No," Gabrielle said. "Never."

"Do come in and sit down," Jesse offered. She saw how the girl had grown, and how smoothly she moved across the room. Sexual awakening must make a difference, oiling all the joints, removing that hesitancy in the legs and gait which says *child* so plainly. Gabrielle was a girl no longer. But hadn't Jesse known that for some time?

Jesse remained standing. "You have something you wish to see me about?"

"You must know by now," Gabrielle said impatiently, smoothing down her expensive skirt as if the gesture pleased her, then repeating it. Her legs were long and slender, perfectly shaped.

"Then why did you feel compelled to come here, if I already knew?"

"Because your husband is afraid to see you."

Jesse laughed the old, deep laugh that was so attractive and so characteristically hers. "Gabrielle, my husband never does anything he doesn't want to do. And, I gather, neither do you."

"We want to get married," Gabrielle announced.

"You expect me to shriek and cry and put up a fuss?"

"No," the girl parried confidently. "I think you should be informed, that's all."

"But you couldn't come to me before, when I was, how shall I put this delicately, indisposed. Not a nice thing to do, steal a man away from a woman in a wheelchair."

"You sent a cable."

"Yes. I knew exactly where to send it and exactly who would see it."

"You did? You knew then?"

"I have my sources."

"Then you knew for certain Nicholas would be there." Gabrielle looked surprised for a moment, but then she caught herself and changed her expression back to its haughty blandness. "You sent him to us."

"Indirectly."

Gabrielle sat back against the couch cushions and gave Jesse a sharp look. "How clever of you. He's fired us both as a result."

"Yes? Good for him. It's taken him a long time to wake up. But he's come to at long last, bless him."

"He'll have us back."

"I doubt that," Jesse said confidently.

"He needs us. We're quite a drawing-card, or haven't you heard? You've been shut up for so long."

"No need to be nasty, child. You see, you're already Martin's ruination. You don't want to drag all of us down, do you?"

"I beg your pardon," Gabrielle said prettily. "I don't understand."

"Oh, I'm sure you do. You'll have Martin making all of the wrong choices. He's not hard to manipulate. Once he's yours, the game is over. What will you do with him then?"

"I suppose you were wonderful for him," Gabrielle said with a flutter of her thick lashes. She pulled a pack of cigarettes from her snakeskin bag.

"Come now, it's not all that simple, marriage. Especially when there are a few trip-wires built in. I may have been a burden, but I allowed Martin to make all of his own mistakes. Will you? Or will you force him to make all of yours?"

"Why don't you sit down," Gabrielle insisted.

"I don't want to. I've sat down long enough, I daresay."

"You can't give him what he wants."

"And I suppose you can, is that it? I warn you, he'll not take well to competition."

"We won't perform together all the time. Martin is going to do some chamber music."

"Martin? He'll hate it. What a ridiculous notion. No one was less cut out for chamber music than he."

"It's better than opera. That sort of conducting is a waste."

"You don't like opera, I gather."

Gabrielle blew out a long stream of smoke. "I think it's an awful, perverted sort of concert music. Phony theatrics, terrible plots."

"Too bad," Jesse murmured. "You could have learned a great deal. I have a theory about people who abhor opera. Not the ones who've heard only bad opera, because bad opera can make anyone loathe it. But people who reject it outright—knowledgeable people like yourself. It's a kind of blind spot. You can't draw back and follow the line. You see only the small details and you criticize them fiercely. It's like the crowd in a museum that won't step back from a painting. There's no overview."

"No?" Gabrielle stubbed out her cigarette in a crystal candy dish. "Why mention it then?"

"Nothing gets past you, junior, does it? All right, then you shall have it, right between the eyes. I've thought for a long time that you would be the end of Martin Boyd. I fear my sad prophecy will come true. He hasn't got any real friends, you see. I was his best friend. I'd always had it backwards; I thought I depended on him. But one very long, sad day I found that I had resources of my own. It was a real find. I had the self-knowledge I'd never needed before. I knew how bad things could get but I also knew I wasn't finished. Nothing had ended. If you are pushed aside often enough, you either die or you make something of waiting in the wings. You've never sung in the chorus, have you? No, you haven't. Neither has Martin. The two of you lack that special understanding. In any event, good luck. And enjoy being alone together. I guarantee that you will be."

How easy it is to be young, Jesse thought as she watched Gabrielle rise gracefully. Shadows are banished at will. She wished she could see Martin. She wanted to tell him that no matter what happened, she would still be his friend. He wouldn't understand; he would think her a fool. But she wanted him to hear it just once, because she thought of him as someone lost to her forever, and she didn't want him to go away with nothing of her in his pocket. How sad it all was. She did not believe that the future would prove her wrong.

"Go away now, I'm tired," said Jesse as Gabrielle waited by the sofa.

"One more thing. I'd like to make sure you won't interfere with Nicholas."

"Interfere? You mean if he wants to change his mind not talk him out of it? Oh, there's no danger of that. You see, Kogan won't change his mind. Though he is the most loyal man in the world, and he loves Martin a great deal, he has finally done something on his own as well. We've both grown up, Kogan and I. We've been hatched from the same shell. I doubt whether he'll retreat. You'd better find yourselves another manager. If you like, I'll put in a word with Wurtzberg's people. He's quite ill but his successors might prove to be decent."

"No thank you. We don't need your help. Individual managers won't do much good anymore. The business has changed. Martin and I will probably sign on with International quite soon."

"He'll hate that. They don't stand in the wings for you over there."

"Their publicity department is marvelous."

"I must say I don't think the pair of you need publicity. You seem to grind it out on your own quite well."

"I can do a great deal for Martin," Gabrielle said fiercely.

"You think it's all sex, don't you. Let me tell you a secret. There was never any time, throughout my illness, when my husband could not have gone to bed with me. Do you find that revolting? Why? Do you know I might have conceived and borne a child? Other people with my illness have done it. The reason I did not is because your precious Martin ran out of steam. Even before I was sick. And my becoming ill was a grand excuse. Everything he has goes into his work. He's better on the run, in short doses. I was fooled for a long time because that's all we had. Someone of your consuming passion had better know that you'll eventually end up in bed staring at the back of a music score. He's really rather unsexy."

"To you, perhaps," Gabrielle pouted, throwing out her hip and posing like a streetwalker.

"Don't bet on it. Neither all of your charm nor all your desire will make a new man of Martin Boyd. He learned at a very young age that the only safe place to be was buried in his music. He's paying back the world for the miseries it inflicted on him, poor little rich boy. You hold sway over him merely because of your associations with his thwarted childhood career. He satisfies his hungers by putting you on display. Once you've grown up, and I must say you're pressing the issue, you'll lose much of your charm. You'd be better off in pinafores."

"You do hate me," Gabrielle said. "I knew it from the first time I saw you. You and Kogan, the pair of you, conspiring against us."

"Oh, bullshit," Jesse said.

"Martin says Kogan is in love with you."

"Did he say that? Nicholas? What a delightful suggestion. But that is not the issue now."

"I think Nicholas is queer."

"You would, wouldn't you. What a baby you are. In his way, Nicholas Kogan has a capacity for more passion and love than Martin Boyd could ever hope to experience. You're a foolish little girl. Now get out of here. You and my idiot husband deserve each other."

"You look so different," Gabrielle wondered aloud as she left the room, turning back to stare at Jesse one more time. "Quite different," she repeated.

The apartment door slammed. Jesse felt quite light-headed. She knew Gabrielle was afraid, and would run to Martin and try to prevent him from seeing her. At last, she was a threat to someone! She laughed dizzily, then clutched her head as she lost her balance and the blackness descended.

Eric found her lying on the floor by the piano. "Jess girl, no, not again," he called out to her miserably. And he lifted her to him and kissed her face.

The doctor came immediately and told Eric Oldfield he was afraid the remission might be ending. Within a few weeks, Jesse was back in her wheelchair and Gabrielle Klee had nothing to fear.

CHAPTER

34

ჶ

Martin stared at Jesse through the glass window of the control booth. She did not see him; her wheelchair faced in the other direction. She waited for her recording cue. A score lay open beside her but she did not consult it.

"I can't explain," Martin said to Kogan. He was almost sobbing. "She's like a queen to me. So regal, so beautiful."

"You've given her up," Kogan said bluntly. He was embarrassed to see Martin at the studio. Martin stumbled like a lost man. He aroused great pity in Kogan. But there was no going back. Jesse's remission had ended, the marriage was over; Martin Boyd and Gabrielle Klee were clients of the International Agency.

"I want to see her again," Martin said, swallowing hard. The sight of his wife was too much for him to bear. How could he have left her?

"Take a good look," Kogan said. "Because she won't see you, dear boy."

"I'm not crazy about International," Martin replied hopefully.

"It's a good shop," said Kogan. "I understand you've booked some appearances as a soloist again."

"Helps pay the bills," he explained. "Some chamber music, too. We've gotten together a rather fine trio."

"Bully," Kogan said.

At a signal from the control booth, Jesse and Eric Oldfield began the next song. A half-dozen technicians busied themselves with their dials and meters as her voice poured out, languid, lush and so beautiful that Martin thought his heart would break. She had never sung so well, not in all the years when she had her health and was on her way to becoming a real star. Now, when it was all but over, when her health had failed her, she had complete command over her voice.

"My God," Martin breathed deeply.

"She is quite a woman," Kogan said, and they listened together as the dials on the meters registered the sound while the softly whirring machines recorded the *Kindertotenlieder*.

"Break for lunch," the producer announced when the song ended. Kogan and Martin watched as Eric walked over to her. Eric was clearly pleased with her performance. Jesse shrugged expressively.

"I'll go to her," Martin said.

"This is very selfish of you." Kogan put a restraining hand on Martin's arm. "Why confuse the issues? Why upset her? There's no need for it."

"I want her to know something," Martin insisted.

"It's too late."

"She's my wife!" he cried out.

"No," Kogan reminded him. "She is like me. We are a pair of ex-Boyds."

Martin pushed through the back door of the booth and ran through the corridor to the studio doors. He collided with Eric Oldfield, who was carrying two empty coffee mugs.

"Greetings," Martin said.

"What are you doing here," Eric said sullenly.

"Paying my respects. You're doing a great job."

"How is Gabrielle?" Eric asked with a cruel smile.

"Look, I know you can't stand the sight of me—I guess everyone around here is on her side. But I think I have a right to see her if I want to."

"Why don't you allow her the choice?" Eric said. "After all, she can't walk out on you." He pushed open the doors and called out to Jesse. "Look who's here. Shall I throw him out?"

Jesse turned her chair around. When she saw Martin, her face changed rapidly from a mixture of pain and sadness to a quiet delight. "Oh, Eric, do let him come in. I've been meaning to call, Martin, really."

"See?" Martin murmured. And Eric, with a look of disapproval, allowed Martin to pass.

"You have quite a palace guard," Martin said evenly. But he was dismayed at the sight of her face, gaunt and tired. Was she beginning to get puffy again from the drugs? The bad part was starting all over again. How many times would it go up and back, he wondered. The doctors never seemed to know. Hers was the most arbitrary of diseases.

"Martin, why haven't you come before?"

"I was afraid, Jess. I've acted the ass for so long."

"I'm glad you said it." She smiled her long,

sweet smile, and he wished that instead she might miraculously rise from her chair and give him a stinging slap across the face.

"Remember when you hit me?" he asked. "After the concert?"

"You deserved it. Pompous ass even then."

"Yes." He accepted her remark as if it were the most loving of endearments.

"You said I did Verdi in a tearoom. See my new tearoom?" She gestured at the studio. "It's my only chance to do anything. I don't think concert-goers are prepared to watch a singer in a wheelchair. My vanity won't allow that either. The album will cover up all those flaws, however."

"But your voice is wonderful."

"Recordings are bloodless, actually. But it's something to leave behind."

"Don't say that," he broke in.

"Why not? Isn't it about time that someone among us accepts the truth?" She smiled again, her eyes moving up and down him warmly as if drinking him in. "I was always afraid you would think of me as the enemy."

"Jess—"

"Let me finish. You mustn't go away believing I would ever hold you back from something that would make you happy. You suffered a great deal with all that's happened."

"Don't say anymore."

"Martin, please. Before the drugs make me crazy again, I want to see everything settled. Remember those moods I had? They'll come back again. I'm not myself when I'm in the grip of that fear. Listen, now, while I can still make some sense."

"I want to help you. What can I do?"

"There's nothing. Just listen to me."

"I am listening. Has your lawyer told you about the money? You're going to receive a percentage of everything I earn, all my concerts, recordings—everything I have done or will do."

"That isn't necessary, really."

"I want to help you. I want to watch over you."

"Look." Jesse pointed behind him, toward the control room booth. Martin turned around and saw Kogan standing in there, hovering in the shadows, watching them. "He can't hear us," Jesse said. "But see how he looks after me? There is no one more faithful."

"He loves you," Martin said.

"I know." She smiled.

"I do too."

She nodded.

"But you won't have me back?"

"No," she said. "Absolutely not. Neither will he. It's odd to see yourself reflected in another person, like a living mirror. There is Kogan, finally learning to stand by himself, making choices and accepting the results, just as I have done."

"You didn't choose to be ill."

"Of course not. But I've decided to be alone now, and I want it. I crave it, in fact. There will be no public martyrdom for me. I shall exit very much the lady, quietly and with dignity." She inclined her head toward Kogan again. "Look at him, foolish old watchdog. He finally learned to care about someone. Now he doesn't want to let me go. I have to sneak about, otherwise he's right behind me. He doesn't know what to do for me next." She sighed. "So late in life to find one's soul. But I guess that's how these things are written. It's so perverse. You've found your way, though, and I hope you stick to it. Keep your convictions, Martin. Don't let go of yourself, please."

"What will you do?" He raked his fingers through his hair with a nervous gesture.

"I shall finish my Mahler record, and then I'll go on to my collection of arias. I so want to sing Cherubino again, and this seems the only way. They haven't got the confidence in my health to wait until they can assemble a cast for a new record. So I'll incorporate *Nozze* into some kind of 'great arias' thing. It's sort of nonsense, I suppose, like the LPs they offer with the world's most beloved classical hits. But I want to do it very badly. You never did see my Cherubino, did you?"

"No, Jess." He made a choking noise.

She stared at him sharply. "You're not getting all weepy, are you? For a grown man you seem to cry without much provocation. Well, you must pull yourself together. You'll have quite a time ahead of you with your new wife."

"She's not my wife yet. Legally, you're still my wife."

Jesse waved her hand dismissively. "Oh, pooh. She's staked out her turf. The Lord help those who trespass against her. You'd better be very good to her. I gather her standards are quite high. Do you think she has a real future?"

"I didn't come to discuss Gabrielle."

"But we are discussing her, are we not? Isn't she the presence that lingers behind the words? You ought to be grateful that at least something has been resolved for someone. You are, at long last, making your move. Tell me," she said kindly, "don't you think that I did the same thing for you? We women shift the gears and take you out of neutral. It's what you find so attractive in a person with direction."

"It's not the same with Gaby."

"I daresay not," Jesse said. "But you'll make a new start, and you can consider having a family."

"Hush," he said. "Stop it."

"You don't have to want me any more, Martin. It's all right not to want a person you've once lived with. Really. You don't need a papal dispensation to fall out of love."

"Please take me back."

"You don't mean that. And I don't want to be pitied. To be perfectly honest, I much prefer being alone. No husband, no Norris, no parakeet, no television. I threw mine away. Not even Kogan dares to intrude on my inner sanctum. If I can live with myself, surely you can manage to learn to live with that very attractive young woman. Only please, think for yourself and try to refrain from giving her everything at once. You don't want to satisfy her too quickly. It will spoil all the fun."

Martin knelt by her legs and pressed his head into her lap.

"Get up," Jesse hissed. "People are watching you."

"I don't care," he said.

"Do you think this is Verdi? That you killed my father and possibly an elder brother or two, and now you want me to take you back to my bosom—forgive you, and sing one last aria before I die? Forget it, Martin. It won't do." She backed her wheelchair away and pushed over to the doors. "Remember your art. Remember what you are most fine at accomplishing. Remember me. There won't be many who will. But please go. You're only making it worse for both of us."

He got to his feet and brushed off his suit. "I have to know something."

"Will you go then?"

"Did Gabrielle—did she, when she visited you—did she do anything which made your condition worse?" He moved anxiously, his legs doing a jittery dance, as he spoke.

"No," Jesse said emphatically. "She was a lady. Whatever happened was no fault of hers. I hope you don't think she's that cruel."

"Maybe I'm doing the same thing," he said miserably.

"Martin, we've got to learn to live with what we've got. That's especially hard for the gifted. But it's true. Goodbye."

He walked to her, bent over, lifted her hand and kissed it. She felt the dampness of his cheeks and turned her head away.

"Goodbye, Jesse Sondergard."

"Work hard," she called after him.

The doors swung shut. Jesse looked over and saw Kogan behind the glass, watching steadily as if they had enacted a silent movie for his private viewing. She waved as gaily as she could, but he stood perfectly still, her sentinel, her private watchdog. He was guarding her against pain and death. She would have to teach him to look after himself as well. She sighed and picked up her music score. There was far too much work left to do.

CHAPTER
35

꙰

"Ah, Kogan," Jesse said to me after she sent Martin away. "You don't know what all this has cost me."

Jesse my love, I wanted to reply, *I do.* Should I have told her? I am haunted by my failings in that respect. I was raised to feel exquisitely inadequate. I wonder what it would have lent to Jesse's life had I been different. As it was, she saved me. I carry inside me the picture of Jesse behind the glass wall of the studio, sending away the man she foolishly loved.

I heard everything they said through the studio microphones. I did not dare breathe, for fear of having them discover that I could hear as well as see. But Jesse knew she was being watched; she knew I was her guardian angel. And what a show she put on! She gathered up whatever strength she could muster and performed gallantly. It was a wonderful final curtain, a great role for a prima donna.

Why do I say final curtain? It was final because the *Kindertotenlieder* was her last record. Her Mahler is now considered among the finest ever produced. Critics say the interpretation is moving—whether it is the voice or the qualities of phrasing and line, they do not know. They, like me, are moved beyond words when they realize that the artist and the woman were finally melded. The songs express such grief and such understanding all at once that the knowledge is almost unbearable.

She got much sicker when she finished the record, as if finally allowing her body to let go. As the days passed, she struggled with bouts of stuporous helplessness. At first, she went to a hospital. But when I came to see her there, she expressed such rage and dismay at being kept in an institution that I tried to have her sent home. The doctors were obstinate at first, insisting that she needed full-time care and monitoring.

"But will it keep her alive?" I pressed. "If she stays here, as opposed to going home—with full-time nursing care, of course—will she get well?"

"She will never be a well person," one of them said plainly. "And she'll be more comfortable here."

"She loathes it. She wants to be in her own room, with her music scores and records, and her view of the park. I'm certain that will help her improve."

The doctors shrugged. "It's really not that critical," one pointed out.

"Not that critical?" I pressed hopefully. "She does have time left?"

"It's impossible to say. She could get pneumonia, her kidneys could fail—any number of things."

"You mean, it's a choice of how she'll suffer, not

if she'll suffer." I could not bring myself to say the word *die*.

One of the doctors looked directly at me. "Are you her closest relative?"

"In a manner of speaking, yes."

"Then you may decide what to do. With good at-home care, she might do nicely. Speak to the floor nurse, she might suggest some good private nurses who'll go home with the patient."

So I did do something for Jesse after all. I got her out of the hospital. We went home in an ambulance and I held her hand as she stared up at me and smiled her wonderful smile. "Thank you," she said when we arrived at her door, as politely as if I had brought her home in a taxi after an evening out.

We hired a nurse who was silent and efficient, and who understood how to operate the stereo and tape recorder. Suddenly, as if reversing her former preoccupation with things visual, Jesse refused to look at television. She wanted to hear music. I thought it was becoming, and suitable, that she should want to be surrounded by her favorite music. Later on one of the doctors told me she was suffering from double vision again, but that she didn't want me to know.

For a while, she was a bit better at home. She even listened to some of Martin's recordings, though she avoided operas and song recitals of any sort. She favored Mozart, Schubert symphonies, and Beethoven piano sonatas. One day, she had me sit and listen to the Cesar Franck Violin Sonata—Jascha Heifetz, she told me, a wonderful recording. When it had ended, she was crying a little, and she told me that her father used to play that sonata with his closest friend—a violinist, the man who had discovered her voice.

"My father thought another instrument was appropriate, so he had me take up the violin. I didn't much like it, and when I played, I would kind of sing along with the music. Meierus made me stop playing and keep singing. He'd show me music and I'd sing it. He said I had perfect pitch. He talked to my father, and my father sent me to a voice teacher. That's when it all began. After my father died, they held a musical tribute to him at the school. Meierus and another instructor played the Franck sonata."

"It's a lovely piece of music," was all I could think of saying.

"I couldn't listen to it for many years. Now it seems. . . " She searched for the right word. "Fitting," she finally said.

I don't want anyone to think that her days were all so romantic, that it was anything like Camille (or Violetta, perhaps more appropriately), languid, pale days propped up by pillows. She suffered a great deal. She had no muscle control from time to time, and she would occasionally be contorted by spasms. There were even times when I thought she was almost in a coma. I gave up much of my work to be with her. For several weeks, I was there night and day. I slept on a cot in her music room. It was as close as I have ever come to living with another soul.

One afternoon, when the nurse had gone out on an errand, I sat with Jesse as she slept restlessly. I tried to read, but mainly I watched her. She wasn't very pretty then, all those days of being bed-ridden and affected by the disease; but she was still so much Jesse, with the loveliness of being just herself, that I thought I couldn't stand another minute. She opened her eyes and looked at me, and in that quiet moment I tried to tell her that I had never lived with anyone before, that she was as close to me as anyone ever was.

"Hush, Kogan," she said firmly. "I don't want to

hear anything more. Some things are better left unsaid. They're more valuable."

I never violated her wishes. There were no sickbed confessionals from me. And she, I imagine, was grateful. It's not what she wanted.

Sometimes she was well enough to laugh again, and make jokes. She would tell me about various mishaps that occurred while she was performing. Once, during a long duet, a famous baritone stopped singing and began munching a piece of fruit from the bowl provided as a stage prop. She had to finish singing alone, and when she did, he tossed the core over his shoulder and told her, "Boy, was I hungry." A tenor who thought practical jokes were funny once handed her a letter that she was supposed to read in the course of the action. When she opened it up, she discovered several pornographic cartoons pasted inside, and she could barely stop laughing long enough to sing. "And as if that wasn't enough, Kogan, I was once in a *Nozze di Figaro* staged in some college gymnasium. When Cherubino does his flying leap out the window into the garden, I dove through the window frame and landed on what the stage manager thought was the ideal fall-breaker, a trampoline. Of course I bounced right back up, and everyone in the audience was treated to several more views of my ass."

I laughed with her; she so enjoyed it all. "You'll perform again," I promised her.

"Probably not," she said without any self-pity. "But you know, they can use it all in my life story when they make the film. There's one good thing about having this ludicrous disease—it's good script material. It's even good opera material. Did you ever see *Interrupted Melody* with Eleanor Parker? She played that opera star who got polio—what was her name? I forget. Anyway, there's this incredible scene at the end when she finally goes back to work—sitting down, naturally—and she's doing Tristan, and at this orgasmic high point in the music of the *Liebestod*, she rises up to hit her note and she stands, for God's sake; and Glenn Ford is watching from the wings, and the music crests and she hits her note. Incredible. But I don't think my movie will have such a terrific ending."

"Why not?" I said, afraid of her answer.

"Silly," she said. "You know I never could sing Wagner."

How we had laughed then. But the good days were fewer and further apart, and I grew afraid. I would call Martin regularly to tell him how she was, and he would telephone her a great deal; but I don't know if he came to see her. She didn't want to see him, of that I'm sure. In fact, she said specifically that she didn't want to see anyone. Once she even said she knew she'd reach a point when she didn't want to see me.

"You can't keep me away," I said.

"Yes I can. I can by asking. You have such awfully good manners, such a refined sense of taste and propriety. And I can count on that, even if I can't count on sentimental old you to fill the bill. I don't want any scenes. I'm too tired for that. Those soap operas I used to watch taught me a lot about maudlin sentimentality. It doesn't ring true. It looks great when it's followed by a commercial for ring around the collar, but it doesn't wash in real life. And besides, there's nothing I'll want to say. All of my secrets go with me." And then she smiled, deliciously.

How I wish that one of her secrets was that she loved me! Yes, I'll admit it. Kogan in love—what a fatal error I'd thought it would be. And yet, if there were ever a woman to love. . . But I can't start on that again.

She died alone, completely alone, in a hospital room overlooking the river in the middle of the night. I believe it is exactly what she wanted. No scenes, no confessions, no hovering friends, no one to admonish her for taking herself away. I came when they called me, but it was too late and I stood outside the door for fifteen minutes before I decided not to go in. She wouldn't have wanted me there. It was over and there was nothing more I could do.

But I did love her. How my mother might have laughed at that final joke, learning one's destiny right outside a hospital room with the door closed forever. But Jesse wouldn't have laughed. She never made light of me. Who knows if she was the one person I might have cared for? Who cares? Knowing her was enough. She was the classiest person I ever met. And believe me, class tells.

EPILOGUE

I have not retired from life; on the contrary, I am aware of everything that goes on. What's more, I am more active than ever. My roster has grown large and fat and I get great pleasure out of my younger artists. I don't expect to find another Jesse, but I think of her often when I listen to rich, young voices. She is as much their inspiration as she is mine.

I see that Martin still conducts, though he is no longer the *wunderkind*. Some of the sexual appeal has evaporated and, artistically, he never became truly great. He is workmanlike—durable, steady. He had turned away from opera some years ago, but I see that lately he is back at it. He received poor reviews for his work in the chamber group. He never should have attempted it; artistically, he is dead wrong for any such delicate collaborative effort.

Gabrielle married him. Her career is far less substantial now. Her reviews have a sad, looking-backward quality, often injected with comments on the prodigy manqué. She has never been as good as she was as a child. I wonder what Jesse would have made of that piece of information.

I find the irony of it all insults my intelligence. No, that isn't quite what I mean. Perhaps it's just that the fates are sometimes too cruel to be borne. I want to believe that talent will win out. The destruction of talent, its wasting, its deterioration, saddens me. I had thought that Martin was a genius. Perhaps he ought to have stuck to the piano. As for Gabrielle, I remember with what revulsion I watched her bare legs swinging over the arm of her chair on that balcony in Venice. Her careless sexuality already seemed a squandering, a waste. But what good has it done me to preserve all of my precious energies and drives? I am no musical genius. There isn't much one can say about a successful life of managing musicians.

Except one thing. Jesse permitted me to see that it was reasonable to care. It may seem a small difference to you in light of all the larger consequences. And what's the good?, you ask—the girl's dead anyway. You'd never have married her, you old bat, you fuss-budget.

See if I care.